ROME'S EVOLUTION

(Rome's Revolution: Book 3)

BY
MICHAEL BRACHMAN

ROME'S EVOLUTION

Also by Michael Brachman

The Rome's Revolution Series
Rome's Revolution 3455 AD
The Ark Lords
Rome's Evolution

The Rome's Revolution Saga
Rebirth: The Rome's Revolution Saga – Book 1
Rebellion: The Rome's Revolution Saga – Book 2
Redemption: The Rome's Revolution Saga – Book 3

The Vuduri Knights Series
The Milk Run
Rome's Devolution 3465 AD

The Vuduri Universe Series
The Vuduri Companion
Tales of the Vuduri: Year One
Tales of the Vuduri: Year Two
Tales of the Vuduri: Year Three
Tales of the Vuduri: Year Four
Tales of the Vuduri: Year Five

Dedication

First and foremost, I have to thank my brother Bruce. Not only is he my editor and artist and the inspiration behind MINIMCOM, but he is also fiercely protective of the Vuduri culture and characters. Bruce creates the amazing covers, the book trailers and makes my writing so much better. Bruce, I could not have done it without you.

Thank you to all my readers. All of you helped to make this what it is.

And finally, yet again, thank you to Rome and Rei. They kept telling me their story wasn't over and they were right.

Guide to the Vuduri Universe of the 35th Century

Vuduri: 24-chromosome mind-connected humans of the future. Their collective consciousness is called The Overmind. They are the ruling class on Earth. They have a small contingent on the planet of Deucado and a larger one on the planet Helome.

Essessoni: Humans from the 21st century. The name Garecei Ti Essessoni means The Killer Generation. The Vuduri hold them responsible for the near extinction of the human race. Over nine billion people died in the late 21st century. The event is referred to as The Great Dying.

Mandasurte: The word means mind-deaf in Vuduri. Typically, a mandasurte has a genetic complement of only 23 chromosomes. They are excluded from most of the Vuduri affairs and have flocked to Deucado since its liberation.

Erklirte: The word means Ark Lords. These were colonists from the Ark V (original target: Chara) who returned to Earth nearly 600 years after launch. They were very cruel. They reintroduced slavery and tried to take over the Earth.

Ibbrassati: The word means oppressed in Vuduri. Many mandasurte scientists and other important members of their society were kidnapped and transported to the prison world of Deucado. They were placed there to die in an asteroid strike but were spared when Deucado was liberated.

Deucadons: Descendants of the Ark III (original target: 82 G. Eridani) who crash-landed on Deucado five hundred years before the story takes place. They had to take refuge underground to avoid the meteors and asteroids that were constantly striking the planet. In some ways, their society is more technologically advanced than the Vuduri.

Mosdurece: This is the Vuduri word for half-blood. A full-blooded Vuduri would have a diploid complement of the 24th chromosome. A mosdurece has a single pair. They have all the capabilities and

4

characteristics of a full-blooded Vuduri however there is a social stigma attached to being only a half-blood.

Onsiras: Living robots. When MASAL introduced the 24th chromosome which created the Vuduri, he also designed it so that eventually humans would be born with dark eyes and a brain that was more of an organic computer. The Onsiras have their own Overmind which was MASAL when he was still alive.

The Grays (Darwin): Approximately 20% of the people who came to Deucado aboard the Ark II were part of a secret project, code-named Darwin. They were encased in special gray sarcophagi. Led by Captain Keller, they were dedicated to someday returning to the Earth and conquering it. After defeating them, Rei banished most of Darwin members to the planet Helome in the Alpha Centauri system to help the Vuduri inhabitants in rebuilding their gene pool.

Dramatis Personae

Rei Bierak: An engineer and one of the frozen passengers aboard the Ark II, launched from Earth in 2067AD (original target: Tau Ceti). The Ark II went off course and was not discovered for nearly 1400 years. Rei was the first human awakened and responsible for eventually getting the Ark II to its original destination, Tau Ceti, now called Deucado by the Vuduri. Rei is a Caucasian male, a little over six feet tall with broad, swimmer's shoulders. He has boyish good looks and sandy brown hair, never properly combed, to go with his piercing blue eyes. He favors wearing brown shirts and khaki or brown pants.

Rome: A half-blood (mosdurece) Vuduri woman from the 35th century who fell in love with Rei and eventually married him. Originally connected to the Overmind, she was cast out (Cesdiud) when she consorted with Rei. Rome is a stunning Vuduri female with olive-tinted skin and an athletic build, bordering on the spectacular. She is short, barely five feet tall, with shoulder-length brown hair, flecked with strands of gold. Her eyes are very dark and because she is Vuduri, they appear to glow even in the dimmest of light. She favors wearing a traditional Vuduri white jumpsuit.

Aason Bierak: Rei and Rome's four-year-old son. He is very precocious.

MINIMCOM: Originally an autopilot computer that was fused into the airframe of a Vuduri space tug. Circumstances and experience caused him to become self-aware. Now a starship, MINIMCOM can fly as fast as 15,000c using what is called the null-fold stardrive.

Junior: MINIMCOM's son although technically Junior is a clone. The first starship "born" not built. He has all the abilities (null-fold stardrive, stealth shield) of his father.

OMCOM: Originally a standard computer installed on Skyler Base within the Tabit System. Eventually he transferred his consciousness into a mass much larger than a planet.

Fridone: Rome's father, a 23-chromosome mandasurte (mind-deaf) oceanographic scientist. Rome calls him Beo which is the Vuduri word for father.

Binoda: Rome's mother, a full-blooded 24-chromosome Vuduri. Binoda is an animal husbandry expert. Rome calls her Mea which is the Vuduri word for mother.

Pegus: Leader of the Vuduri contingent on the planet of Deucado.

The Overmind: Group consciousness created by the mind-connected Vuduri.

Maury Keller: Captain of the Ark II and de facto leader of the colonists from old Earth. He was banished to the planet Helome along with the rest of the Darwin members.

Nick Greer: One of Captain Keller's soldiers, also banished to Helome. He lost his right hand in the final gun-battle at Darwin Base.

Bukky: Leader of the Deucadons, descendants of the Ark III which crash landed on Deucado 500 years before the story begins and lived underground for most of those years.

Ursay: A Vuduri commander, currently living in retirement on Earth. Ursay was Rome's original commander when she was deployed in the Tabit system.

Hanry Ta Jihn: A legendary hero and martyr from the past, responsible for organizing the resistance that eventually defeated the Ark Lords, called Erklirte in Vuduri.

MASAL: A supercomputer that designed the 24th chromosome which was responsible for the rise of the Vuduri. His plan was to engineer the humanity out of mankind. He was destroyed by Rei and Rome.

Sussen: An Onsira spy sent to Deucado by MASAL when it was still a prison planet. Her mission was to ensure that the mandasurte remained imprisoned there until the planet was destroyed by an asteroid. When she saw things unraveling, she escaped in attempt to return to Earth to warn MASAL. Rei, Rome and MINIMCOM beat her there and had already destroyed MASAL before she ever arrived.

Virga: Leader of the Vuduri contingent on the planet of Helome. She had captured Rei hoping to mate with him. She released him on his word that he would send mandasurte to help her rebuild the gene pool. Rei came through on his promise.

Bonnie Mullen: A female member of the Darwin group. She was also the colony's historian. She was banished along with the rest of the Darwin group to Helome. She was pregnant at the time with Edgar Mullen's child. She stands five foot six, has wavy dark hair and is a little bit older than Rome.

Preface

This story takes place a little over two years after The Ark Lords.

Chapter 1

Year 3460 AD (1379 PR)
Second Planet (Deucado), Tau Ceti System
(11.9 Light Years from Earth)

REI BIERAK BENT HIS HEAD AND DUCKED HIS SIX-FOOT PLUS FRAME down as he trotted through the trellis leading up to his home. One close call with a 'falling blanket' last year and even Rome had to admit having one in front of their home was prudent. She had dressed it up with some plants imported from Earth but Rei scarcely took the time to breathe in the sweet honeysuckle aroma that permeated the area. He bounded up the three steps and flung open the all-white front door, hoping to make a dramatic entrance.

"Daddy's home!" he said with a flourish. But his performance played to an empty theater. There was no one about. He shouted out, "Rome? Aason?" There was no reply. He closed his eyes and used his sonar vision to sweep the house, listening for signs of life. The only sound he heard was a strange tick-tack-tick noise coming from the kitchen. Other than that, it was deathly still.

He opened his eyes again, activated the 'cell-phone' in his head and called out, *"Rome? Where are you? Where's Aason?"*

"I'm at the library," his adoring wife replied after a moment. *"Aason is here with me."*

"What's going on?" Rei asked. *"It's getting kind of late."*

"I'm so sorry, mau emir," Rome answered. *"We may have had an incident occur and we're trying to sort it out."*

Rei looked around then set his shoulder bag down on the dining room table and headed toward the kitchen. *"What kind of incident?"* he asked as he was walking.

"Nothing major," Rome responded. *"The interns were away for the celebration of Tamas and when they returned, they found some items missing."*

"What kind of items?" Rei asked, sauntering into the kitchen.

"As far as we can tell, the only things missing are one of the Deucadon's invisibility cloaks and Hanry Ta Jihn's handgun."

"That's an odd set of things," Rei remarked. *"Do you think somebody took them?"*

"We don't know yet," Rome replied. *"The girls are trying to contact the remaining interns to see if one of them borrowed the items."*

"OK," Rei said. *"Are you going to be a long time?"*

"No. The girls will figure it out. I'll come back here tomorrow. Let me gather up Aason and we'll come home."

"Don't worry about it," Rei said. *"Take your time. I'll get dinner started."*

"All right, mau emir. I will see you shortly." With that, Rome cut the connection.

Rei looked around the kitchen. Something smelled funny. It was faint but had an acrid, almost electrical odor to it. Remembering the odd ticking sound he heard when he first entered the house, Rei closed his eyes and performed an aural sweep again. He determined that the sound was coming from under the sink. He stooped down, opened the cabinet and found a large black box sitting there, with elaborate electrical circuitry and wires hanging from it. Mounted on the side was a digital timer that was counting down: 007, 006, 005. Rei leaped up and raced for the front door. He barely made it out when a tremendous explosion tore the front of their house apart. Rei was lifted from his feet and flung through the air like a rag doll. Something heavy hit his back then his head then everything went black.

***

Pain has its own chronology. The simplest and easiest to remember is visceral pain, the kind that goes down in the gut and radiates from there. Like the pain Rei felt the first time he ran the marathon or the pain he felt when they froze him alive. Rei also remembered the pain when the auto-defibrillators incorrectly concluded his heart did not start and shocked him an extra time upon being reanimated. The misguided life-saving gesture almost killed him.

Next in line was the pain Rei remembered when he almost asphyxiated in the Vuduri airlock, a result of Estar trying to kill him. He also remembered the pain in his back from 1400 years of degeneration that OMCOM cured with his magic pill.

As Rei's consciousness bubbled up and he became more aware, he remembered emotional pain, like the pain of leaving his parents behind as he traveled to the stars. Like the pain Rei felt when Sally Reynolds told him she was not going to accompany him on that trip. However, the worst heartache Rei ever felt was when Rome was integrated into the Overmind on Deucado and he thought he had lost her forever.

All of this aside, none of it compared to the pain he felt now.

Maybe pain was not the right word. Bone-deep soul-sucking piercing, throbbing ache might better describe it. His head ached. His neck ached. His shoulders ached. His arms ached, especially his right arm. His chest ached. The only thing that did not ache was his legs. His ears were ringing and at the same time felt like they were stuffed full of cotton. His eyes were closed but his head was flat so he couldn't activate his super-hearing to figure out his surroundings.

And that was baffling because he had absolutely no idea where he was. As hard as he tried, his eyes wouldn't open. He racked his brain trying to recall something, anything that might give him a clue. He started with what he did know. He knew his name was Rei Bierak. Recalling the sequence of pain helped him remember being frozen and sent to the stars. He remembered being so cold when they first thawed him out. He remembered that two beings, dressed all in white, were attending him. At first, he thought they were monsters or aliens who resurrected him. Luckily for him, one of those monsters was Rome. Wait, Rome! That was the answer. His amazing, loving wife. He could picture her stunning face so clearly. He thought he caught a whiff of her wonderful smell, like vanilla surgical scrub. He missed her so much. Where was she?

Rei was now more determined than ever to figure out where he was. It took a heroic effort but he managed to get one eye partially open. The bright lights of the room were dazzling. It made Rei blink rapidly. Everything was white. Well everything except for the large black figure, complete with cape, standing with his back to Rei, arms akimbo, set firmly on his hips. Rei looked out the corner of his eye and saw his beautiful Rome dozing off in a chair in what looked like a very uncomfortable position.

"Rome?" he croaked, barely able to speak.

Rome's eyes jolted open. "Rei!" she shouted, jumping up. "You're awake!" Her smile spread from ear to ear as she raced to his bedside and put her arms around him.

"Ouch," he said as she squeezed his shoulders. "Take it easy," he murmured.

"I am sorry, mau emir," Rome said, releasing him then kissing him tenderly. "I was so worried."

Rei was finally able to force his other eye open. He tried looking about the room. "Where am I?" he asked.

The large black figure at the base of his bed turned around. It was MINIMCOM's livetar, his mouth slit curled upward in the largest smile Rei had ever seen on the animated shell.

"You are in a hospital in Vuduri City," Rome said, caressing his forehead gently.

"What happened?"

"There was an explosion, at our house," Rome said sadly. "That you survived…"

"An explosion?" Rei interrupted her, confused, "What…"

Rome pressed her finger gently to his lips. "Just rest," she said. "I'll tell you everything in due time." She turned her head. "MINIMCOM, will you fetch the doctors, please?"

"`Of course,`" replied the livetar and the large black figure strode out of the room.

Rei tried to take a deep breath but a sharp pain in his rib cage cancelled that notion. His shoulders slumped and he closed his eyes again. Just their brief conversation had exhausted him. Then he realized he didn't have to speak out loud to talk to Rome.

"*Is Aason OK?*" Rei asked mentally.

"*Yes,*" Rome replied. "*He is fine. He's with my parents back at New Ark City. Junior is there as well.*"

"*That's good,*" Rei noted with relief. "*How long have I been out?*"

"*Almost two weeks,*" Rome said. "*I kept calling to you. You didn't answer. I was afraid that I lost you.*"

Even though it was difficult, Rei opened his eyes and tried to smile. "*I would never leave you, Romey, you know that.*"

Having said that, Rei started closing his eyes again but his peace was interrupted by the bustling noise of two men, one tall, one short entering the room. They were followed by MINIMCOM's livetar. The shorter man was dressed in a standard white Vuduri jumpsuit. The taller one was wearing Essessoni clothes covered by a white lab jacket. He came around to the side of the bed, opposite Rome, while the shorter man, obviously Vuduri, remained at the foot of the bed, staring at Rei intently.

"Hello, Rei," the man to Rei's right said. "Do you remember me?"

Rei turned his head slightly to look at the man. "Sure, Russell," Rei answered. Russell Montrell was the colony's physician.

"How're you doing?" Russell asked him while withdrawing a penlight from his pocket. He moved the tubes connected to Rei's body aside and waved the penlight back and forth, shining the light into Rei's pupils, observing their reaction.

"I hurt everywhere," Rei answered in a scratchy voice, considering his own words. He scrunched up his face. "Except my legs. They don't hurt. It's weird."

Russell withdrew the penlight and replaced it in his pocket. He took a deep breath. "You were severely injured. You have a cracked skull. In fact you lost a piece of it. I find it strange to say but you're actually lucky. You had significant brain swelling and the hole in your head actually allowed the pressure to stay manageable. We only sealed it enough to keep in the cerebrospinal fluid."

Rei closed his eyes and focused on the back of his skull. It burned and he could feel the wad of bandages piled up behind his head pressed against the pillow.

Rei opened his eyes again as Russell continued. "As far as the rest of you, your eardrums were ruptured and you have a broken arm." Russell tapped on the cast surrounding Rei's right arm. At least that explained why it felt like there was cotton in his ears. And why his right arm ached more than his left. But there was something in Russell's tone that made Rei look more intently at the doctor's face. It wasn't what Russell was telling him. It was what he wasn't telling him. Rei looked down at his feet. He tried moving them. Nothing happened.

"What about my legs?" Rei asked. "What's wrong with my legs? How come they don't hurt?"

Russell's shoulders sagged. "The lumbar section of your spine was smashed. The L3, L4 and L5 vertebrae were crushed. I'm afraid they've pinched off your spinal cord."

"What!?" Rei exclaimed, trying to sit up. "What are you saying?" He looked down at his feet trying once again to move them.

"I'm saying your legs no longer function. You're paralyzed from the waist down."

Rei was stunned. He had trouble coming to terms with the concept. "You mean, like permanently? You're saying there is no way I'll get better?" he whispered.

"We'll put a plate in your skull. Your bones will knit. Your eardrums are almost healed. But there's nothing we can do about your spine."

"No!" Rei exclaimed. He tried with all his might to move his legs. Nothing happened. He turned to face Rome with a panicked look on his face. "Romey, no…"

Rome put her hand up to his cheek. "It will be OK, Rei. We'll deal with it."

"No!" Rei said angrily. "I'm no good to you this way." He stared at the Vuduri man standing at the foot of the bed. "You," he called out. "Are you a doctor?"

"Yes," answered the man in a rusty voice. "I have been trained in the medical arts and on this equipment."

"So can you fix me?" Rei asked. "You people have all sorts of super-advanced technology."

"I am afraid that we do not have the ability to perform a microsurgery in the manner you require."

"So I'm stuck this way forever?" Rei lashed out angrily. The Vuduri doctor shrugged. Rei turned to look at Russell but only saw disappointment in his face.

"I'm sorry, Rei," he said. "There's nothing that can be done."

"Not necessarily," MINIMCOM interjected.

All eyes turned to him. "What do you mean?" Rome asked.

"OMCOM sent along the complete capabilities of Rei's genetic enhancements when he delivered our Library OMCOM clone. It is well within Rei's capabilities to heal himself."

"I'd like to hear this," Russell said stepping toward the end of the bed. "How is that remotely possible?"

The livetar held up his hand and the air shimmered in front of him. The palms of his hands morphed into holo-projectors. The image displayed was a three-dimensional projection of a portion of the human spine.

`"OMCOM gave Rei a pill five years ago. It contained an extra chromosome which gives Rei some rather unique capabilities. Among other things, it was specifically designed to enhance and restore his spine."`

MINIMCOM twitched his hand and separated the 3D image into two sections. `"All I would need to do would be to reform his crushed vertebrae back to their original structures and open up the central canal."`

A section of the simulated spinal cord glowed red. Individual long, thin threads of axons and dendrites glowed with a downward wave connecting the upper section to the lower section. MINIMCOM added an animation of sparkles which presumably represented neural impulses.

`"Once his spinal cord has been freed, Rei's natural, or perhaps unnatural, recuperative powers will do the rest of the work. His brain will re-energize or even re-wire the spinal cord as needed. Within a month or so, his spine would be completely and totally healed."`

Rei shook his head slowly. "I know you can do just about anything but this? Are you going to cut me open?"

`"That will not be necessary."`

"Then how are you going to see in there? How will you know what to fix?"

`"I will not be able to see directly,"` MINIMCOM replied. He smiled slightly. `"However there are some ladies who I am certain would be willing to help."`

"What?!" Rome cried out, fear creeping into her voice. "You would inject Rei with VIRUS units?"

`"Constructors, yes,"` MINIMCOM said calmly.

"You're going to inject me with VIRUS units?" Rei said, restating the obvious. "How do you know they won't just eat me up from the inside?" he asked worriedly.

`"You yourself have dealt with them before. They will do exactly what we ask and no more. When they are done, they will shut down and your body will eventually absorb them."`

Rome's eyes narrowed. "MINIMCOM, have you ever performed this type of procedure before?"

"No," answered the livetar. "And I do agree there is a difference between theory and practice, I propose that I try this technique to heal Rei's broken skull first. I will rebuild the missing section in layers by using a miniature null-fold and transport some dura mater, bone, muscle and so forth then some scalp. The VIRUS units will assemble them in the proper form. That should be enough to fine-tune the methodology. If I cannot do that, then I will reject the technique as unworkable."

Russell Montrell shook his head and turned back to Rei. "I've heard some incredible things about your ship but this? It sounds impossible to me."

Rei looked up at him. "If MINIMCOM says he can do it, that's good enough for me. That explosion was caused by a bomb. I saw it. Somebody tried to kill me. And whoever did this is still out there. How am I going to protect my wife and child from a wheelchair? No, I'm in." Rei turned to the livetar. "I'm all yours, buddy."

"Very well," MINIMCOM said. "However, to guarantee the best chance for success, I would like to do this while you are weightless. I need to reduce the stress on your spine as much as possible. Which means we must go into space."

Rei turned back to his wife. "What'ya say we go for a ride?"

Rome smiled bravely and nodded.

Chapter 2

WITHIN MINIMCOM'S CARGO CHAMBER, THE HYBRID computer/spaceship had set up a modest surgical suite complete with white drapes along his outer hull walls. Rather than take a chance on jarring Rei any further, MINIMCOM had transported Rei and his hospital bed directly into the cargo hold. He also brought Rome and Russell Montrell along. The Vuduri doctor had declined to participate. He wasn't of much use, anyway.

MINIMCOM, the starship, used his EG lifters to gently arise in the air until he was high over Deucado. He fired his plasma thrusters on their lowest setting, accelerating as minimally as possible, until they achieved a circular orbit around Deucado 200 kilometers up.

`"I will be shutting off the artificial gravity shortly,"` MINIMCOM announced from a grille in the wall. `"Rome and you, Dr. Martell, if you go into the side airlock, you can put on a pair of magnetic boots. That will allow you to remain in one place as I perform the procedure."`

"OK," Rome said. She pointed then walked forward through the main corridor, followed by Dr. Montrell. She showed Russell the side airlock and when they returned, they were using the balky gait required to break the magnetic connection on the under-soles, one step at a time.

After they were back in the cargo bay, Rome said, "We're ready." She and Russell took up positions, standing by Rei's bedside.

`"Very well,"` MINIMCOM said. `"I am shutting down the EG lifters now."`

In the background, Rome could hear the sound of the magnetic shields rotating in place. As they were turning, Rome and Russell could feel all the weight draining from their bodies. Rei started rising up very slowly, held in place only by two loose fitting straps that had been secured around him before they took off. Rome had to fight off the urge to grab him and push him back down. She had to have confidence that MINIMCOM knew what he was doing.

With a whoosh and a pop, MINIMCOM's livetar appeared in the cargo hold. He was holding a syringe in his hand filled with a grayish liquid.

Rei turned his head to look at it. "This is really going to work, right?" he asked.

"`To the best of my knowledge,`" replied the livetar. "`You still have time to change your mind.`"

"No, just do it," Rei said. "I trust you."

"`Very well,`" MINIMCOM said. He set the syringe down on Rei's bed and reformed one of his fingers into a very short range PPT thrower. He drew it carefully along the cast encasing Rei's arm. In one smooth motion, the cast split in half and MINIMCOM removed it. The livetar retrieved the syringe and inserted the needle into Rei's bicep. He pressed on the plunger gently and the fluid level decreased slightly.

"`I am going to knit your broken arm first,`" MINIMCOM said. "`This is the simplest test I can think of such that the VIRUS units can learn to work with my miniature null-fold.`"

"Whatever," Rei said. "Get to it."

Two holographic projectors lit up and showed a blood-red field with a milky white rod passing through.

"`I have equipped these constructors with multi-spectral sensors,`" MINIMCOM said. "`I am synthesizing their imagery as we would with the star-probes.`"

The image in the air shifted and a dark gray, jagged line appeared. "`By using infra-red imagery, we can discern structures within the space. I am using false color but that is the actual bone fracture,`" MINIMCOM said. "`I will transport random bone cells from the undamaged portion of your arm to the fracture. The constructors will move them into final position. Watch.`"

Like an army of tiny ants, little grains of white appeared in the dark area. Slowly but surely, the areas of dark became light and soon there was no evidence that a break ever occurred.

"`The bone is set,`" MINIMCOM announced. "`However, there is no actual rigidity yet. You will have to wait several hours for the amalgam to cure. It will take a day or two until the bone returns to its normal state.`"

"Incredible," Russell said. "This is an amazing leap forward in medical science. Nothing we have can even approach this."

"`You ain't seen nuthin' yet,`" MINIMCOM said, trying to amuse. Actually it was fairly funny hearing the former computer speak this way. "`Rei, I must rotate you around your`

`transverse axis to try the next stage and repair your`
`skull."`

"You're going to flip me on my stomach," Rei said. "You could just say that."

`"Technically, you will not be on your stomach,"` MINIMCOM said, `"but yes."` The livetar looked at the two humans. `"Will you assist please? We must be very careful not to flex Rei's torso in any way."`

"Of course," Rome said and she clomped forward. Together, the two humans and one livetar gently flipped Rei over so that he was facing down.

MINIMCOM removed the bandages and packing from the back of Rei's skull. Rome gasped at the size of the wound. The portion of Rei's skull that was missing was a full two inches in diameter. His living brain was exposed, the gray matter pulsing with his heartbeat. Only a thin plastic film covered the area. MINIMCOM removed it and cerebrospinal fluid started gushing out for a moment then the tiny flood stopped. MINIMCOM held it at bay with an outstretched hand and a small null-fold twist.

`"I will place a thin bio-polymer film underneath the` `remaining bone,"` MINIMCOM said. `"I have coated both` `sides with an arteriogenic compound that should cause` `new blood vessels to form. This will help in the healing` `process. The film will also prevent Rei's brain from` `leaking any more fluid."`

Mercifully, the film that MINIMCOM placed over the wound was opaque such that Rei's exposed brain was no longer visible. MINIMCOM retrieved the syringe with the grayish liquid. However, instead of injecting Rei, MINIMCOM merely expelled a few drops of the fluid with enough force that despite the lack of gravity, they spread evenly across the film, held in place by surface tension.

`"First, the dura mater,"` MINIMCOM said. Cells from all over Rei's skull were transported to the film and assembled by the VIRUS units. Soon a visibly thickened layer of tissue was formed.

"Won't removing the tissue from other parts of his head cause damage?" Rome asked, even as she watched the fascinating display.

`"No,"` MINIMCOM said. `"I am taking less than .01% of` `the cells from any given area. Any micro-perforations` `this causes will heal instantaneously. No section will` `even miss them."`

Rei grunted.

"**Am I causing you pain**?" MINIMCOM asked with some concern. "**I can apply an anesthetic if you need it.**"

"No," Rei said. "It's just a little weird being your science experiment. I'm fine. Keep going."

MINIMCOM nodded. Layer by layer, MINIMCOM built up the tissues culminating in a fibrous bony surface covered by muscle. Finally, MINIMCOM took tiny sections of Rei's scalp and knit them together, closing the wound completely. In another age, it would be considered the ultimate in hair-plugs.

"That's amazing," Dr. Martell said, bending over to inspect the repairs. "If I hadn't seen the wound myself, I'd swear it was never there."

Rome reached forward to touch the newly healed area. MINIMCOM jutted his hand out and grabbed Rome's arm before she could make contact.

"**Give it a little while to heal,**" MINIMCOM chided gently. "**These cells have never lived together before. They need a bit of time to get to know each other. It should only be a few hours.**"

Rome pulled her hand back. "Of course," she said. "I just could not believe my eyes. But I will accept your word."

"**Good,**" MINIMCOM said. "**Are we all in agreement that this technique is adequate?**"

The livetar looked at Rome who nodded then to Dr. Martell. "We're way beyond anything I know," the doctor said. "But it certainly appears that way."

MINIMCOM looked down at Rei. "**Are you ready to begin the main event?**" the livetar asked.

"You bet," Rei said facing downward. "The sooner, the better."

MINIMCOM nodded. He removed the bed covers from Rei and opened up his hospital gown so that they could see his naked back. It was clearly evident where whatever had struck Rei made its indentation. The bruised flesh was a mottled arrangement of red and purple/blue. Where the blood had pooled, the contusion was brownish with streaks of gray and even a bit of green. MINIMCOM pressed the syringe into the area and injected the final contents into Rei's lumbar area.

For a long while, the livetar just stood there.

"Are you going to start?" Rei asked, finally.

"I have a problem," MINIMCOM said.

"What kind of problem?" Rome asked worriedly.

MINIMCOM activated the holo-projectors and the air lit up with a pink/gray goopy-looking mass of tissue with flecks of red and white all around.

"The bones have been so thoroughly damaged, I do not know if I can reconstruct them exactly correctly. I could use the vertebrae higher up as a model but then mechanically, they would not fit in the precise fashion required. I have access to some anatomical charts but they are only 2D, not three dimensional."

"Use me," Rome said immediately.

Rei turned to look up at his wife. "What are you talking about?"

"MINIMCOM can inject me with VIRUS units. They can give him a picture of an intact spine, vertebrae by vertebrae. He can use me as his model."

"No offense but I'm a lot bigger than you," Rei said. "I don't think I'd do too well with a girl's spine."

"Rome's idea will work," MINIMCOM interjected. "I will compare her L2 vertebrae to yours to get the proper scale factor. Then we will work our way down, vertebrae and disk alike."

Rome smiled and nodded. "What do you want me to do?"

"Remove your magnetic boots," MINIMCOM said. "Doctor, I will need you to hold her in the same horizontal position as Rei while I perform the reconstruction."

"I can do that," Russell said. "Finally, I can contribute something."

Rome slipped off her magnetic boots and immediately began rising up into the air. Dr. Martell reached out and Rome gripped his arms so that Russell could steady her. Soon she was floating in the air perfectly horizontally. She rested her head on her arm so she could see Rei's face and not think about what was going to happen. MINIMCOM produced a new syringe then came over and injected Rome's lumbar spine. The livetar looked off into the distance.

"Yes," the all-black animated shell responded, "this will do fine." MINIMCOM turned back to Rei and put his hands over Rei's lower back almost like a faith healer. He froze for a moment while integrating the data streams. At last, he was ready.

"**Now we begin,**" said MINIMCOM and he commenced with the reconstruction project.

As he was concentrating on the procedure, MINIMCOM did not bother with the holographic display. Rome and Dr. Montrell could only stand by helplessly as the livetar performed his magic. MINIMCOM did take a moment here and there to announce the next step but mostly he concentrated on his work. He segregated all the bone fragments and gently coaxed them into a shape nearly identical to how they appeared, pre-injury. He reconstructed the vertebral disks, inside and out. He straightened out the dura mater. MINIMCOM was very careful to never move the spinal nerve fibers but rather built around them.

It took about two hours but finally MINIMCOM announced that he was done. He used a pulsed application of the microscopic null-fold field to ensure that the cerebrospinal fluid was flowing properly. Satisfied, he gently rotated Rei around along his transverse axis so that he was facing upward.

"**The VIRUS units are shut down. Their carcasses will serve as a matrix to give your spine some rigidity until it is fully healed. How do you feel?**" MINIMCOM asked.

"The same," Rei said, disappointed. "I still can't feel my legs. I can't move them."

"**The nerves have been severely shocked,**" MINIMCOM intoned. "**There will be a progression of return of functionality. The first neurons to activate should be the nocioceptors.**"

"What are those?" Rome asked as Russell lowered her back to the deck. Rome pressed her feet back into her magnetic boots so she could stand.

MINIMCOM reformed one of his fingers into a sharp point. He stuck it into Rei's left sole.

"Ouch!" Rei exclaimed then he laughed. Rome was confused but then she smiled too. "Pain receptors. I get it," she said.

"**Yes,**" MINIMCOM said. "**Proprioceptors next, then motor neurons, then the full complement of efferents and afferents.**"

"What can we do to help?" Russell asked anxiously.

"There is nothing to do," MINIMCOM replied. "The only thing any of us can do now is wait."

Chapter 3

TWELVE HOURS LATER, MINIMCOM MADE A SLIGHT BUZZING NOISE through the grille in the cockpit.

"**Rome. Dr. Martell,**" MINIMCOM whispered. "**It is time to check our patient.**"

Rome shook her head, trying to clear it. She had been dozing off while strapped into the pilot's seat. Russell was stirring too, in the co-pilot's seat.

"OK, MINIMCOM," she said as she unbuckled the X-harness. Her magnetic boots locked on the floor of the cockpit immediately. She never stopped to think how MINIMCOM was able to coax the constructors making up his airframe into a magnetic alignment. There were so many things about MINIMCOM that she didn't understand, she had given up trying.

Russell followed her through the archway which also served as an auxiliary airlock and down the corridor until they entered the cargo bay. Rei was sleeping soundly, floating gently above the hospital bed. The sounds of the magnetic boots clomping awakened him.

He smiled and reached out with his hand. Rome came over to take it. With a whoosh and a pop, MINIMCOM's livetar reappeared. The tall black entity put his hand under Rei's back, touching it gently.

"**Your spine has set very well,**" MINIMCOM said. "**Let us perform a few tests but please try and keep your back as still as possible.**"

"Sure thing," Rei said.

MINIMCOM uncovered Rei's bare feet.

"**Can you wiggle your toes?**" MINIMCOM asked. Rei did so vigorously which made him laugh. MINIMCOM lifted Rei's right leg and bent it back at the knee. "**Can you straighten your leg?**"

Rei was able to straighten it easily and with no pain. They repeated the procedure with the other leg.

"**Can you push harder?**" MINIMCOM asked. Although he had lost a little bit of strength, Rei was able to generate a surprising amount of force which made MINIMCOM nod.

MINIMCOM said, "**I am satisfied. Doctor?**"

Russell came over and tickled the bottom of Rei's feet. Rei laughed again. Dr. Martell tested Rei's ankle, calf and thigh muscle tone. After he exhausted every diagnostic he could think of, he stepped back.

"This is absolutely beyond incredible," he said in wonder. "There is no way any human surgeon or any medical procedure we have ever developed that could come close to this. This is a flat-out miracle."

Rome bent over and kissed Rei's forehead. She looked up the doctor. "Not a miracle," she said. "It is MINIMCOM. He never ceases to amaze us."

The livetar smiled. `"I do aim to please,"` replied MINIMCOM, shrugging in a very human-like manner. Then the expression on his bullet-shaped head became more serious. `"However, now we must see if Rei can stand."`

The livetar unbuckled Rei and carefully maneuvered him around so that he was perfectly vertical. The livetar pressed down on Rei's shoulders ever so gently until Rei's feet were flush against the floor of the cargo compartment. MINIMCOM waved to Rome and Russell. They came over and each put one hand on Rei's shoulders to keep him in place. Rome pressed her hand against Rei's chest. Dr. Martell pressed his hand gently against Rei's upper back so that he stayed in one position vertically.

`"I will now begin to engage the artificial gravity,"` MINIMCOM announced. `"We will increase it in small increments and see how Rei tolerates it. Rei, are you ready?"`

"Absolutely," Rei said. He lifted his arms and placed one across Rome's shoulders and the other across Russell's shoulders. "Let's do it."

`"Very well,"` MINIMCOM said. `"One-tenth g."` In the background, they could hear the gentle whirring of the magnetic shields drawing back and the superconducting magnets coming up to speed.

Rome could feel her body pressing ever so gently into her boots. She looked at Rei's face as he stared down at his own feet. They flattened slightly. Rei looked up and nodded. "More," he said.

`"Very well,"` MINIMCOM said. `"One third g."`

This time, the increase in gravity was noticeable. Rei's knees bent slightly but then he straightened up again.

"**Any pain?**" MINIMCOM asked.

"None," Rei said. "I'm ready for the full load." He waved his hand in a circular motion trying to encourage the livetar.

"Rei, we should take our time," Rome cautioned. "There is no need to hurry."

Rei sighed. "You're right," he said. "No sense in taking chances. OK, MINIMCOM, just bump it to one-half g."

"**Very well,**" MINIMCOM replied. As the gravity increased, Rome could really feel Rei's arm across her shoulders now. Rei's knees did not change at all.

Rei nodded. "More," he said. This time it wasn't a question.

"**Three-quarters g,**" MINIMCOM announced. As soon as the gravity increased, Rei's knees began to buckle.

"Back it down," Rome shouted with alarm in her voice.

"No," Rei said. "I'm OK. I just have to figure out how much force to exert. Look."

He straightened up again. He bent his knees and then stood upright to demonstrate he had full control. "I got this," he said.

"**Please try and flex your back as little as possible,**" MINIMCOM cautioned. "**The mixture of bone and constructors is set and it is true that with each passing minute, it will become more solid. But I would like to keep the stress to a minimum.**"

"Well, if I'm going to go back to the planet, I have to be able to take full gravity. Let me try a few steps."

"Rei, are you sure?" Rome asked.

"Yeah," Rei said. Rei removed his arms from both of his two helpers' shoulders and simply placed one hand on each. Satisfied, he pushed each of them away, reaching down only to hold Rome's hand. Carefully, he lifted his left foot and took one step forward. His knee seemed to give out slightly but Rei was able to recover quickly. He took a step with his right foot and there were no noticeable effects.

"OK, guys," he said, letting go of Rome's hand. "Here we go."

Like a little boy trying on new shoes, Rei took small careful steps, walking from one end of the cargo bay to the other. As he walked, his confidence grew greater and greater until he was walking in what looked like a completely normal gait. Russell Montrell whistled his approval. Rei bowed his head slightly then came back to stand by Rome and he took her hand again.

"OK, buddy," he said to MINIMCOM. "One full g. Time to get this show…"

"On the road," Rome chimed in. "All right, MINIMCOM, full gravity."

"`As you wish,`" replied the livetar.

The change from three quarter to full gravity actually seemed less noticeable than the prior increments. Rei tested his ability to walk again and did quite well. In fact, on his last lap, he actually jogged a bit.

"I know I should be overwhelmed," Rei said, walking over to MINIMCOM. "But you've always been there for us, buddy. I guess I never had any doubts."

"`Thank you,`" MINIMCOM said. "`However, your recovery is far from complete. Your spine is still very delicate.`" The livetar turned away then turned back with a contraption built of two black plates held together by leather-like thongs. The front plate was sculpted in the form of a human chest. The back plate was smoother. About 18 inches from the top were four straps attached to the frame on both sides.

What is that?" Rome asked, coming over to see.

"`This is a portable, miniature self-sustaining PPT tunnel,`" MINIMCOM said.

"What's it for?" Rei asked.

"`Allow me to attach it and I will explain,`" MINIMCOM replied. The livetar lifted the two plates up and lowered the assembly over Rei's head. Once the upper thongs were resting on Rei's shoulders, MINIMCOM cinched the lower straps along the sides until they were snug around Rei's waist. After checking the fit, MINIMCOM waved his hands over the front and suddenly, Rei's chest, in fact his entire torso, disappeared. It looked like his head, arms and legs were completely separated from each other.

"What the hell?" Rei exclaimed as he tried to wrap his head around what he was seeing or in this case, not seeing. "Why do I need this thing?" he asked.

"`Your spine is solid and clearly you can stand the strain of being vertical. However, the mixture of bones and constructors do not have as much reinforcement against lateral sheer. This vest will prevent anything from coming in contact with your spine until you are fully healed.`"

To demonstrate, MINIMCOM pushed one of his hands through the region where Rei's stomach would have been. The arm emerged from behind Rei's back as if he were not there.

Rei reached around to poke his own hand in the tunnel but MINIMCOM grabbed his arm and pulled it away.

"`You must be very careful with this,`" MINIMCOM cautioned. "`As you know, the edges of a PPT tunnel are sharper than any blade in the universe. Nothing must come in contact with those edges.`" MINIMCOM squeezed Rei's wrist. "`For example, if something were to be inserted within the tunnel and you turned suddenly, whatever it was would be severed immediately. And that includes limbs.`" MINIMCOM shook Rei's arm to emphasize his point.

"I get it," Rei said, pulling his arm away from MINIMCOM's grasp. "I'll be careful." He looked down at his chest or at least the region of where his chest should have been. "But, like this is really weird. I understand why I need it but how am I supposed to walk around with no chest? It'll scare Aason. It'll scare everybody."

MINIMCOM held his hand out and a long brown shirt appeared, somewhat reminiscent of Rei's normal attire. "`Put this on,`" the livetar said, shaking the garment.

Rome helped Rei put on the shirt. Once all the buttons were fastened, it completely covered up Rei's invisible chest. "Hmm," Rei grunted. "Weird but that'll work."

"`Yes,`" MINIMCOM said. "`It is coated on the inside with an electrostatic material. It acts as an inflating agent. I have tailored the fabric so that your torso will appear normal to the outside world until you no longer need the vest.`"

"So how long do I have to wear it?" Rei asked, running his hands down his chest carefully. Knowing what was under there was really bizarre.

"`You will need to wear it about a month,`" MINIMCOM said. "`You may take it off to shower and to sleep. But that is all. After a month, your spine should be completely and totally healed and you will no longer require this protection.`"

Rei looked over at Rome and raised one eyebrow. "Are you going to be able to handle this?" he asked.

Rome winked at him. "We'll be fine," she said, laughing. "It will remind us every day of what a wonderful friend our MINIMCOM has been."

"This is beyond friendship," Russell said. "This is an incredible advancement in medicine. You must share this with the world at large. Think of the good you can do."

MINIMCOM's eye slits narrowed a bit. `"I do not know if I am ready to reveal this just yet. I have only recently shared my secret of the continuous PPT drive with the next generation of fastships. I have been heavily involved in their training. It is very time-consuming."`

"There's no comparison," Russell said insistently. "This is far too important to keep to yourself. Rei, can't you make him share it? He's your ship."

"No," Rei said. "He's not my ship. MINIMCOM was emancipated a long time ago. He is his own entity. He's not a thing. He's family. He chooses when and where he goes and what he does. You'll just have to trust him to do what is right and in his own time."

`"Thank you, Rei,"` MINIMCOM said. `"Dr. Martell, as Rei said, you will just have to trust me to do what is right. All I can promise you is that I will get around to it eventually."`

"An emancipated ship," Russell muttered to himself.

"And a loving father," Rome threw in. "He has a child of his own."

Russell lowered his eyes to the ground. "I guess there are just some things I'll never get used to."

***

For their return trip, Rome helped Rei buckle into the pilot's chair and she took her place in the co-pilot's chair. Russell kneeled down and held on to Rome's chair for dear life as MINIMCOM performed a traditional aero-braking reentry. Once he was fully within the atmosphere, MINIMCOM made a bee-line toward Vuduri City where they dropped off Russell Montrell. Following that, MINIMCOM returned Rei and Rome to New Ark City, to Binoda and Fridone's home.

"Daddy!" Aason cried out when he saw his father entering the door. He raced over and tried to leap into his father's arms. Luckily, Rome was able to catch him in mid-air and absorbed his momentum. Gently, she handed their little boy to Rei.

"Hey, buddy," Rei said, kissing his son on the forehead. "I missed you so much."

"I missed you too, Daddy," Aason said, snuggling his head against his father's neck. Even though his back had been fully reconstructed, Rei's muscles had still atrophied slightly while he was in the coma. Aason was large for a four-year-old and weighed well over 40 pounds. Rei felt his arms sagging so he handed Aason back to Rome before he dropped him.

Binoda and Fridone came over to stand by Rei. Binoda took Rei's shoulders and turned him around slowly. She gently ran her hand over the back of Rei's scalp and shook her head.

"How is this possible?" Binoda asked her daughter. "He was so damaged but now he looks perfectly fine."

"You can thank Doctor MINIMCOM," Rei interjected. "He kind of rebuilt me."

"He can rebuild people?" Fridone asked.

"I was there," Rome said. "It is as Rei says. MINIMCOM uses technology beyond anything that the Vuduri and Essessoni have. We must be careful, though." Rome patted Rei's shoulder gently. "Even though he looks alright, Rei is not fully healed."

"Yeah," Rei said. "In fact, I think I need to sit down for a bit."

"Come into the living area and tell us all about it," Binoda said, leading the way.

For the next hour or so, Rei and Rome took turns explaining all that had transpired since Binoda and Fridone had seen Rei last. After the story had been recounted, Rome and her parents were chatting when Rei decided to interrupt.

"All this is well and good," he said, "but everyone here is forgetting one thing."

"What is that?" Fridone asked.

"Somebody tried to kill me. In fact, that bomb was set to kill all of us. If Rome and Aason hadn't been delayed at the library, they might be dead too."

"Who would try and kill any of you?" Binoda asked, horrified. "You have done nothing but good ever since you arrived at this planet."

"We discussed this very fact and we can only come up with one explanation," Rome said.

Rei nodded. "It had to be one of the Darwin people. When we rounded them up and sent them off to Helome, there's no way we got them all. There has to be a couple of them left, running around crazy."

"Even so, why would they want to kill you?" Binoda asked with a furrowed brow.

"You don't know these people like I do," Rei said. "They were none too happy when we shipped them off-world. It doesn't have to be a very complex reason. I don't think we need to look beyond simple revenge."

"If that is all it is," Fridone said, "then they will find out eventually they did not kill you. What is to prevent them from trying again?"

"Nothing," Rei said. "Our only hope is to figure out who it was and track them down. That's the only way to stop them before they try again."

"They could be anywhere on this planet," Fridone said with increasing frustration. "We must be ever vigilant."

"There is no we, Beo" Rome said. Rome touched her finger to her temple. With a whoosh and pop, both MINIMCOM's all-black livetar and Junior's smaller one appeared in the room. Junior's livetar had darkened significantly and was much larger as compared to when he was originally 'born'. The current version stood well over a meter and half tall and his skin was now a deep slate gray. Every day, he looked more and more like his father.

"Hello, Auntie Rome," Junior said. "Onclare Rei. I'm glad you're out of the hospital. Dad filled me in on what he did."

"Thanks, Junior," Rei said. He turned carefully back to face his in-laws. "Rome and I talked about it. We don't want you or Aason around until we've caught the assassins."

"Where would you have us go?" Fridone asked skeptically. "You do not know where they are. Nowhere on this planet could be safe."

"You are right, Beo," Rome interjected. "Not on this planet. Junior has agreed to take you to Earth."

"Earth?" Binoda exclaimed. "We were banished from there, just as you were. We are not allowed."

Rome stood up. "Junior will take you to Commander Ursay. He will hide you on his farm until it is safe to return. Junior has all of his father's stealth ability. He will get you there unseen."

"Cowering like children out on a farm," Fridone scoffed. Then he realized Aason really was a child. "I understand," he said reluctantly.

"Mommy, Daddy," Aason said, jumping up. "I don't want to go." He ran over and grabbed his mother, wrapping his arms around Rome's legs.

Rome stooped down and cupped her son's chin. Tears were starting to overflow her eyes and run down her cheeks.

"We have to do this, my baby. It's not safe here. We can't allow anything to happen to you. Grandmea and Grandbeo will take good care of you. Daddy and I will come and get you as soon as it is safe to come home."

Aason hugged his mother around her neck. "Mommy, I'll miss you so much."

"And I will miss you, my love. But I would die if anything happened to you. Daddy and I can't take that chance."

Aason pulled back. He was crying too but he made a brave face. "I understand, Mommy. Whoever those bad men are, I hope you catch them and kill them back."

"No," Rome said. "We don't kill anybody. But we will stop them. Then we can all be together again."

Rome looked up at her mother. Binoda nodded.

"Come, Fridone," she said. "We must pack some clothing. This might be a while."

***

After a prolonged and tearful goodbye, Aason and his grandparents left in Junior for Earth. As soon as they were gone, Rei, Rome and MINIMCOM reconvened around Binoda's dining table to make their plans.

"Rome, MINIMCOM," Rei said. "I know we have a tall task in front of us. But I need you both to understand my super-hearing is kind of busted right now. Plus I had a pretty hard knock to the head. I don't know if you can tell or not but I'm still pretty fuzzy."

"You had a severe concussion," Rome said. "You don't need to excuse it."

"That's not what I'm getting at," Rei said. "What I'm trying to say is I might not be able to think clearly enough or act fast enough to get us out of this mess cleanly."

Rei leaned forward to take Rome's hand. "Sweetheart, you have to be the one in charge. If I say something that doesn't sit right, you have to overrule me."

Rome nodded slowly. "I understand. But I'm not worried. Let us get to the business at hand. As my father pointed out, these persons unknown could be anywhere on the planet. On top of that, we don't know how many of them there are and we don't know who they are. Where do we start?"

Rei stood up carefully and left the room only to return with a piece of paper and several of Aason's crayons. He picked up the blue crayon and drew a long rectangle. He took a red crayon and stroked lines across the rectangle in a dense pattern.

"Say this is the Ark," he said, circling the rectangle. "We know that the Darwin people were shipped out here to Deucado in the special gray sarcophagi."

Rei grabbed a black crayon and blocked off the front of the crudely drawn ship. "Rome, do you remember the cages in the front?"

Rome nodded.

"I think the first thing we do is go back to the Ark and calculate how many of them there could be."

"You were there when they started pulling them out, wouldn't you know?" his wife asked.

"I didn't pay enough attention," Rei said. "I think we need to go back and actually count." Rei turned to MINIMCOM. "How many of the Darwin people did you and Junior cart off to Virga on Helome?"

"84 the first trip. 20 the second," MINIMCOM answered. "104 total."

"There," Rei said. "So all we need to do is figure out how many we started with, subtract out 104 and what's left is how many we're looking for."

Rome smiled. "I do not think your ability to think has been much impaired. However, you forgot one person."

"Who?" Rei asked.

"Captain Keller. No matter what the theoretical number, you must add one since he was one of the original 84 sent to Virga on Helome."

Rei sighed. "Yeah," he said. "I don't know if this helps or not but I know that some of the sarcophagi were damaged. I remember seeing them in the cave behind The Cathedral."

"Were they white or gray?" Rome asked.

Rei put his hand up to his head and rubbed his forehead. "I don't remember," he said. "Dammit."

"It's OK, Rei, we will check it out," Rome said. She turned to MINIMCOM. "Would you mind taking us to Rei's Ark and then to The Cathedral?" she asked. "We need to do our survey."

"Your safety and well being is my first and only concern at the moment," answered the livetar. "I am at your service until this matter has been resolved."

"Then let us begin," Rome said, rising.

Together, the group left the house. What they did not see was that after they were gone, the front door opened, apparently all by itself, and then closed again.

Chapter 4

REI'S ARK HAD CRASH-LANDED ON A RIDGE PART WAY UP THE SLOPE of the northern mountains over four years earlier. In the two years since Rei and Rome had been here last, the Ark II had continued to rust, some parts of it completely rusted out. The outer hull, what was left of it, was orange-colored with streaks of brown and black. This was due to the fact that the upper two-thirds of the gigantic, cylindrical spaceship was made out of pig iron and Deucado presented enough moisture and oxygen to cause portions of the roof to collapse. Some of the pieces were fairly large.

The lower third of the Ark was made of martensite, a kind of stainless steel so it was in much better shape. While the upper portion of the Ark was softer and more malleable, the lower third had to be more rugged because when the Arks came in for a landing, they had no wheels or landing gear. They glided in then just belly-flopped their way down to the ground at a rather sizeable velocity. The martensite was not just a heat shield and a potential building material, it was also the world's biggest landing strut. At least, that was the way it was planned. The way the Ark II actually arrived on Deucado was beyond anything the mission planners could have imagined.

Rei and Rome held hands as they carefully made their way up the entrance ramp into the long-abandoned crew compartment. Once they reached the top of the ramp, Rei tried to pull his hand free but Rome would not let go.

"I'm OK," Rei said. "I can walk by myself."

"No," Rome said forcefully. "I don't want to take a chance of you slipping on one of the pieces that have fallen from the ceiling."

"But…" Rei protested.

"You said I was in charge," Rome said proudly. "This is a command decision. You hold my hand."

Rei smiled. "Yes, dear," he said submissively.

Carefully, they worked their way toward the front of the ship. Well up ahead were the special cages made to hold the gray sarcophagi. A cracking noise emitted from the ceiling overhead. Rome's eyes widened as she saw a rather large chunk of the ceiling bend down. Calmly but with great firmness, she pulled Rei back and put him behind her.

The piece of ceiling broke loose and fell to the floor with a bang. Dust and dirt spread everywhere. Rome put her arm up to block her eyes. Rei did the same.

After the dust had settled, Rome inspected the way in front of her. The metal mesh walkway was now blocked by the huge chunk of rusty ceiling.

"Should we get MINIMCOM in here to move that?" Rei asked, pointing to the obstruction. Rome looked around.

"Not necessary," Rome said. She walked over to the nearest rack. She shimmied up on one of the middle row of shelves that had held the white sarcophagi, rotated around and gently lowered herself to the floor on the other side, neatly bypassing the shrapnel that was blocking their way. She brushed off the dust on the front of her jumpsuit then patted the shelf.

"Be very careful," Rome said. "You do what I did but do not twist your back."

"Yes, dear," Rei said. He knew this was a phrase he was going to be uttering a lot in the upcoming days. Cautiously, he executed a maneuver matching Rome's who, in turn, guided him as he lowered himself on the other side. Now past the obstruction, they were able to make their way to the front where there was a pair of large metal cages encasing another two sets of shelves, one on the left, one on the right. The shelves within the cage were far more substantial than the flimsy ones in the rear. Rome reached up and took a hold of the metal mesh fencing and shook it with her hand. There was no more give to it now than there was two years ago.

Rei stooped down, making sure he did not bend at the waist, and mentally counted the stanchions that were used to hold the sarcophagi in place.

"Three on the bottom, middle and top," Rei said out loud. He turned and pointed. "Another nine on that side so that makes eighteen per row."

He gingerly made his way to the front, stopping short of the edge where a portion of the Ark had been torn away when it hit the asteroid. The lead edges were ragged with shredded sheet metal curled and bound by the inner seal. Even though much of it had dulled with time and rust, many of the metal shards still had razor sharp edges that splayed outward. Rei shivered just thinking about them. He turned to the matter at hand.

"I count six rows," Rei said. "So if my math is correct, that makes for 108 of the Grays."

"109 counting Captain Keller," Rome corrected him.

"Right," Rei said. "So that's our upper limit. MINIMCOM said he transported 104 of the Darwin people to Helome so worst case, we're looking for five people."

Rome nodded. "This is an excellent first step but to have that many running loose on Deucado is a little bit dismaying."

"I know I saw some cracked sarcophagi back at The Cathedral but I don't remember if they were gray or white," Rei said. "We'll need to go there to confirm. That may cut down the number."

"Agreed," Rome said. She put her finger to her temple. "MINIMCOM says he will just transport us back to his cargo bay. I don't want to take any more chances with your back than we need to."

"Yes, dear," Rei sighed.

***

MINIMCOM lifted off and flew them north until they approached the canyon where Trabunel and the rest of the rebel Ibbrassati had taken up residence. The starship floated over the cane-tree woods until he was hovering over the gorge leading to the Ibbrassati secret enclave. The gorge was narrow but there were definitely some sections that were wide enough to hold his bulk. MINIMCOM located one such a section, as near as possible to the hidden cave where Rei and Rome were taken when they first arrived on Deucado. The starship rotated so that his cargo section was pointing in the direction they had to go then cautiously began lowering himself to the floor of the gorge. He had to bend his wings up a bit but was able to land safely.

As such, it was only a short hike from where MINIMCOM set down to the opening in the rocks signifying the entrance to the secret Ibbrassati enclave. When they first came here, the opening was covered with rocks and cane-tree trunks as camouflage. After the Ibbrassati had abandoned it, it had remained untouched until the

Darwin group kidnapped Aason and Binoda and held them captive here two years ago. For Rei and Rome, it had been four years since they set foot in the area.

This time, the entrance was unblocked. MINIMCOM sent his livetar along to help Rei and Rome as they picked their way through the opening. After passing through some tunnels, they came to a sizeable cave with what remained of the racks the Ibbrassati had used for storage. MINIMCOM lit up his shoulder lamps partially to help them see. The racks themselves were made of cane-tree wood. On them rested a few ratty blankets and some other paraphernalia. The room smelled dusty and dirty and still contained a hint of smoke and sweat. Off to the side was a little pile of rocks. Rome smiled to herself. When Aason was kidnapped, even though his life was in mortal danger, all he could think about was how he only had rocks to play with. Thank goodness he would soon be safe on Earth with Rome's parents and Junior to protect them.

They entered a tunnel on the far side and continued on a downward slope, deeper and deeper into the mountain. The temperature dropped noticeably as did the remaining shards of sunlight from the cave's opening.

At last they arrived in the large cave that the Ibbrassati had called The Cathedral. MINIMCOM lit up his shoulder lamps even brighter so they could see their surroundings clearly. Rome looked all around, thinking back to her time here. She shivered. When they first arrived, she was suffering from severe polyhydramnios and had difficulty walking or even breathing. It was here that she and Rei had spent their first night on Deucado, huddled by a fire. She had been in too much pain to spend much time looking around. This time, however, she did. She looked straight up and cocked her head.

"MINIMCOM, can you make your shoulder lights brighter?"

"**Of course,**" replied the livetar.

Rome inspected the ceiling very carefully. "Rei," she said. "Look up."

Rei complied. "What do you see?" he asked.

"Don't you think the ceiling of this cave is too rounded to be natural? It reminds me of the cave we discovered on our way to encountering MASAL."

Rei stared at it for a long time. Finally, he spoke. "I agree it is pretty smooth but your father's people wouldn't have had the wherewithal to round it out. And why would they?"

"I don't know," Rome said. "You've never been to the Deucadon's underground city but their caves were the same way. It was almost like they were carved out."

"Maybe it's just how erosion works on this planet," Rei said. "Why would anybody dig them out?"

"I don't know," Rome answered. She turned to MINIMCOM. "When you excavated the storage chamber for the Library OMCOM's memrons, you mentioned there were already a number of small caves beneath the library. Were their ceilings as smooth as this one?"

"Now that you mention it, yes," MINIMCOM replied. "However, at the time, I was preoccupied with the excavation process. I did not think it was important enough to document or measure."

"Hmm," Rome said, "I must think about this." She shrugged. "It will have to wait for later. Let us continue on our search."

"Sure thing," Rei said and he turned to walk away.

Rome just stood there for a moment then shouted, "Wait!"

"Now what?" Rei asked, turning back to her.

"There," Rome said, pointing to a small alcove off to the side. "Come with me," she commanded as she strode over to it. "MINIMCOM, you come too."

The little alcove had a small fire pit, long unused off to the side and a dilapidated cot. Rome stood at the entrance and smiled broadly. Both Rei and MINIMCOM came up to join her.

"This is the room where Trabunel performed our Cesa ceremony," Rome said to MINIMCOM.

"Very nice," MINIMCOM observed. "Very picturesque."

Rome breathed a short laugh. She reached up and stroked the side of Rei's face. "Rei, do you remember?"

"How could I forget," Rei said, putting his hand on hers. He looked around. "It's a lot smaller than I remember though. And kind of dirty. I guess time has a way of sweetening the memories, not the reality."

"Nevertheless, this is a very special place." Rome cocked her head. "You know that I love you and I would have married you anytime, anywhere. But looking back, given how my life was in danger, what made you decide to do it in this place, at that time?"

Rei sighed. "When you're in love, your brain doesn't always work logically," he said. "Now that you mention it, logically, I guess it could have waited. I guess we didn't really have to get married at all."

Rome scowled and pulled her hand down from his face. "Are you saying you are no longer in love with me?"

"God, no," Rei said. "I love you more than anything." Gently, he put his arms around her and drew her close. Not too close, though. He didn't want Rome to sink into his non-existent chest. "It's just that I agree, I wasn't thinking too clearly. The stress of almost being killed when we first got here. The fact that you were suffering. They said you could die. I just wanted to be bound to you forever before things got any worse." Rei struggled with the words. "I'm just saying that hindsight is always 20/20."

"What does that mean?" Rome asked.

"It means that after all the facts are sorted out, anybody can figure out what you *should* have done. And after all we've been through, I can see now that we could have done it later. But back then, it was all that I could think about."

Rome smiled. "I think I am kidding you," she said. "It was very romantic and I wouldn't have done it any other way." She stood up on her toes and kissed Rei on his cheek. "We should get going, though. It was just a nice memory that I wanted to relive."

Rei nodded. Rome pushed past MINIMCOM and Rei and walked to the back of The Cathedral to a tunnel leading even deeper into the cavern. She waited until MINIMCOM caught up to her and passed her, leading the way into the darkness. Rome held out her hand which Rei took and they continued on.

They came upon another gigantic cave that dwarfed The Cathedral. This was the cavern that the Ibbrassati had used to build the equipment that was going to start their rebellion. They also used it as the staging area when they first brought the crew back from the Ark II still frozen in their sarcophagi. Captain Keller's red-striped sarcophagus was sitting near the front, just off to the side. Farther back to the far left were stacks and stacks of the white coffin-like chambers and to the right were the gray. The fact that they were segregated was probably a byproduct of the order in which they were retrieved from the crew compartment of the Ark.

Rei pulled his hand free of Rome and walked over to the stacks of gray sarcophagi. He started counting. Finally he spoke.

"105," he said. "I've counted them three times. Not enough. We're still short three."

"Where do you think they put the others?" Rome asked.

Rei turned in place and pointed off to the far right. "I remember seeing at least one cracked sarcophagus over there. Those catacombs were where Captain Keller set up shop."

Rei started to lead the others across the length of the cave when he stopped suddenly.

"What is it?" Rome asked.

Rei whirled in place. "There's something wrong," he said. He looked back at the stacks and stacks of sarcophagi and stared at them intently. He returned to the nearest one and stooped down low, being very careful to bend only his knees and not his back. He cocked his head.

"They're all missing their power rods," he said after a bit. He pointed at the twin circular holes in the base of each of the sarcophagi.

"Is that important?" Rome asked, coming over to him.

"Only that they are radioactive," Rei said. He straightened up. "I wonder what they did with them."

Rome looked at them and then back across the cave. "Is it germane to our search right now?" she asked.

"No," Rei said, shaking it off. "It's just odd," he said. "Let's see if we can track down the missing chambers. We're still missing three."

The three beings walked across the length of the cave to the entrance to the catacombs. Off to the side, standing upright, were five sarcophagi; three gray and two white. Rei approached the closest gray one. The nameplate said, "Stanton, G." Rei peered into the faceplate. The remains of the occupant were still in there. A sizeable crack had caused the rehydration fluid to sublimate out and the vacuum of space had mummified the person inside. It was just a pile of skin, bones and jerky, barely revealing the fact that the remains were once human.

Rei pulled back and turned to Rome and MINIMCOM. "That does it," he said. "Not including Keller's, we've seen all 108 of the grays. And we know that 105 of that group survived plus Keller for a total of 106 alive."

"And MINIMCOM and Junior transported 104. So we are only looking for two people?" Rome asked with a smile. Somehow, that number seemed much more manageable.

"As far as I can tell," Rei said. "MINIMCOM, let's start a list of people who we know the bombers couldn't be."

"There's Captain Keller and Bonnie," Rome offered.

"Yeah, sure," Rei said. "Plus Stanton here and Pierre and Wright over there." Rei pointed to the other cracked sarcophagi. He held up his hand and counted on his fingers. "And we know Ionelli and Greer went. I can probably rattle off about ten or twenty more but…" His shoulders slumped.

"But what?" Rome asked.

"Even though we know how many we're looking for, there's still going to be a huge gap on who else to eliminate." Suddenly, he snapped his fingers. "MINIMCOM, between you and Junior, do you think you could identify who you transported."

`"I would be able to tell you the ones I carried. I suspect Junior would be able to do so as well. But you sent him to Earth, remember?"`

"Oh, yeah," Rei said. "So we're back to square one."

"Not completely," Rome said. "If we can get our hands on a crew manifest, we can get MINIMCOM to at least eliminate the ones he transported beyond the people you have already named. And that is a substantial number."

"You're right," Rei said brightening a bit. He looked toward the entrance to the catacombs. "I seriously doubt there is anything like that in there but let's do a quick check."

Slowly, carefully, they made their way through the catacombs. They found nothing but cots and blankets. The only unusual room was the one that Keller had set up as a temporary office where he made his plans to storm the Vuduri compound. Rei and Rome carefully inspected the room but the only things they found were some maps and charts spread over the crude desk. As they were getting ready to leave, across the room, a white bottle caught Rei's attention. He went over and retrieved it.

"What is that?" Rome asked.

Rei brought it over to her. "This is the bottle of pills that OMCOM gave me to fix the crew's backs, remember?"

"Oh, yes," Rome said.

Rei shook the bottle. It seemed too full. He screwed off the lid and held the bottle up so that MININCOM's shoulder lights illuminated the interior.

"I guess not everybody took one," he said.

"How do you know that?" Rome asked.

"Besides the two yellow pills that you and I took, OMCOM told me he made 600 doses. The bottle is almost half full. I guess some people refused."

"Does that mean anything?" Rome asked.

"Just that some of them were stupid," Rei answered. "I bet they wish they had them now."

He screwed the lid back on the bottle. He looked around the room one last time.

"There's nothing here," he said. "I didn't think we'd find anything but we had to look."

Rome snapped her fingers, mimicking her husband. "If a crew manifest exists, I know exactly where it would be," she said proudly.

"Where would that be?" Rei asked.

"Darwin Base."

Rei's eyes widened. You're right," he said. "Let's get going."

Chapter 5

IT DIDN'T TAKE MINIMCOM LONG TO TRAVEL THE 100 KILOMETERS to the west, well north of the giant crater lake, Lake Eprehem. They flew just a few hundred feet over the tree tops of the intervening dense cane-tree forest. Up ahead, Rei could see a large clearing followed by the grouping of Quonset huts huddled on the edge of the tarmac. There was a classic two-story tall old Earth-style control tower attached to the farthest building but it looked like one or two of the windows had broken out.

"Darwin Base," Rome said as they approached. "I don't know how they thought they were going to keep it a secret."

In addition to the buildings Rei had seen the first time he was here, he spotted another long low building set back in the cane-trees with a flat roof. The top of the roof was painted in the yellow/green splotched pattern of the cane-tree vegetation. Obviously, some sort of camouflage.

"They sure tried," he replied. "But clearly they didn't think about much beyond their mission," Rei added with some disgust. He pointed to the taxi portion of the landing area. "Set down anywhere," Rei directed to the grille mounted on MINIMCOM's front console.

An indicator lit up announcing that MINIMCOM's landing gear was fully extended. The starship rotated around so that the cockpit was facing away from the base. They felt the slightest of bumps as MINIMCOM settled on the ground. The former computer now space-plane lowered his cargo ramp, raised the hatch and Rei and Rome exited down the back.

Still parked along one of the buildings were a few of the huge transports they had brought from Earth in their Ark. The rest of the borrowed vehicles were gone. Rei surveyed the area and said, "What if we split up? I can go down to the far end and check out the big hangar. You could start here and work your way toward me. Just holler if you find something."

"No," Rome said. "That is a bad plan."

"Why?" Rei asked.

"Because I am not totally familiar with your culture. I might encounter something important and not know what it is. I think we should stick together." She put her finger to her temple and

MINIMCOM's livetar appeared. "However, we will start with the large hangar as you suggest and work our way back here."

Rei knew better than to argue so they walked across the landing area to the large, aluminum clad building at the far end. There were two oversized hangar doors that were sealed tight. Rei reached his fingers in the tiny crack between them.

"Stop!" Rome shouted. "You must preserve your back." Rei muttered something and stepped back. Rome turned to the livetar. "Do you mind?" she asked.

"**Not at all.**" MINIMCOM's livetar put both hands between the doors and was able to open them easily.

"I'm not too happy with you treating me like a weak old codger," Rei said.

"It's just until your back is healed," Rome said, coming over to him. "Then you can go back to being the big strong man in charge."

Rei laughed. "OK," he said and they entered the hangar together. The bright light of Deucado streamed in illuminating the front section. Rei looked around then went over and flipped on a light switch. Bright overheads glowed with a harsh fluorescent white light all the way to the back of the hangar.

"I guess we know what they did with the power rods," he said matter-of-factly.

In front of them were the skeletons of four airships in various stages of construction. The one closest to them was three-quarters complete. The one in the back to the far right was nothing but a series of circular spars, like the remains of a space whale. They were all of similar design. They looked like a sleek cross between the long-retired space shuttle and a Vuduri space tug, like MINIMCOM before he became, well, whatever he was now.

"Starships," Rei said, whistling. "And really nice ones." He looked at Rome. He wasn't sure if he was proud or horrified. He decided righteous indignation was probably the best road to take. "They really were going to go back and conquer Earth some day."

Rome walked over and looked underneath one. "EG lifters," she huffed. "Where would they have gotten them?"

"You know the Vuduri," Rei said. "They don't care about material possessions. Keller's group probably just asked for them.

The Vuduri wouldn't have even thought to question what they were going to do with them."

"You're right," Rome said with a hint of sadness in her voice. "It's clear that the Vuduri need to develop a sense of suspicion when it comes to dealing with the Essessoni."

"Hey," Rei said. "I'm Essessoni. It was just these jerks you have to worry about. And now they're gone. The rest of us are OK."

Rome nodded. "More than OK," she said, smiling. She continued looking around the rest of the hangar. "I don't think there is anything like we seek here. This building seems fully dedicated to the construction of these starships."

"You're right," Rei said. He pointed to the western wall. "There's a door that leads to the next building. Let's check it out."

With MINIMCOM leading the way, they entered a much smaller building. It was a well-stocked metallurgical lab with the converted particle beam drillers and smelters. There were racks and racks of raw metal planchets and shelving with assorted parts and electronic gear. There was one shelf piled high with what looked like silver ingots. There were a couple of gold bars, too. Rei thought to himself how his people would have to let go of some of their old habits. Of course, things like valuing material wealth would be hard to give up.

On the main floor, there were lathes and saws and drill presses. Pasted on the walls were charts and lists, some of them drooped over. From the lack of footprints, it was clear they were the first visitors since the Darwin group had been exiled.

Rei inspected the equipment and the storage racks. "This is where they were building and machining the parts, I guess for the spaceships next door," Rei offered finally. "Probably nothing here, either."

"I agree," Rome said. Let's try the next building."

The building they were in had no door on the far wall so they had to go out through the front door and enter the next building the same way. This building looked more like a research lab with tubing and vats and burners. There were canisters and barrels with raw materials. The door to this hut had been opened to the outside and the layer of dust and dirt was thicker than in the previous two buildings. There were two desks sitting side by side in the near corner. Rome went over to them and rifled through the papers and equipment lying there. She moved aside a translucent slab, standing upright within a black t-shaped clip. The slab had a thin white border.

"I don't see anything," she said.

"Uh, you know that is a computer in your hands," Rei said, pointing to the slab.

"No, I did not," Rome replied. "Can you turn it on?"

"Sure," Rei said. He came over and brushed the chair off and sat down carefully. He moved the translucent slab front and center and blew on it a couple of times to remove most of the dust. He tapped the upper right hand corner twice and the display became opaque, lighting up with tiles and icons indicating the computer had just been in hibernation.

"Where is the input surface?" Rome asked.

"It's a touch-screen," Rei said. "But if you really need to do some typing…" He pressed the upper left hand corner and two thin laser beams shot out and stroboscopically drew a keyboard on the dust-covered surface of the desk.

"Let me look," Rome said. Rei stood up and Rome sat down in his place. She scratched her head. "The keyboard must have gotten damaged from disuse," she said in a dead serious tone.

"Why do you say that?" Rei asked.

"Look at the layout of the letters," Rome said, pointing at the glowing red virtual keys. "Q W E R T Y," Rome read out loud. "A nonsensical arrangement."

Rei laughed. "Everybody says that before they learn to touch type," he said.

"What do you mean?"

"They're arranged in the order of convenience."

Rome shook her head.

"In my language, E is the most commonly used letter followed by T and the rest of the vowels. The people who designed the keyboard made it so that you did the least amount of work during the course of the day reaching the keys you use the most."

Rome started to speak then breathed a loud sigh. She knew better than to continue even asking. She faced the screen and gently touched it with her fingers. Very quickly, she absorbed the basic principles behind the operating system and was able to navigate her way through the folder structure. It was very similar to that found on the original 19 data slabs she had been given which had caused the whole Darwin mess.

The computer itself was sparsely populated and contained nothing like the crew manifest they were looking for. It consisted mostly of engineering diagrams, inventory lists and so on. Finally, Rome gave up.

"I don't think this computer has anything of importance. Most of its contents are designs and layouts for the starships next door as well a guide for managing…"

Suddenly, she stopped speaking. Pressed against the back of the desk was an assembly that she recognized. Standing upright was a docking block with one of the jet-black Essessoni data slabs mounted within. Rome reached to the back and slid it forward. Her eyes widened.

"Look, Rei," Rome said excitedly, shaking the assembly. "Volume 20 – Mission Parameters. So this is where they kept it." She pointed to the dock. "Is this your data reader?" she asked.

Rei nodded. "That's it," he said. "But I remember Bonnie saying the reader was on the fritz."

"I remember that too," Rome replied. "Can we at least try it? Can you activate it or attach it to the computer?"

"Sure," Rei said. He snapped the docking block to the other side of the computer. As soon as he did so, a new icon, like a piston without a rod, appeared on the desktop.

"I guess it wasn't on the fritz, after all," Rome remarked. "Imagine that. The Darwin people lying about something," she said sarcastically. She tapped the new icon and the cylinder opened up to show a folder and tree structure within. Rome tapped and swiped until she found what she was looking for.

"Look," she said. "Here is the orientation video, the Virus 5 video, the instructions on how to make more vaccine, specs for the canister we destroyed and so on. It's all here."

She spun in place and looked over the room. She pointed to the vats.

"They were preparing more vaccine," she said. "They really were moving up the schedule."

"By about a hundred years," Rei observed.

Rome furrowed her brow. A dark expression washed over her face. She shook her head and stood up.

"Well, they/re done now but this computer doesn't have what we need. Let's continue."

"I agree," Rei said. He pointed to the blank wall in front of them. "Let's check the next building."

They left the bio-lab via the front door and waited while MINIMCOM opened the doors to the second to last building. Rome pushed past him and started to enter but MINIMCOM barked out, `"Halt!"`

Rome pulled up sharply. "What is it?" she asked.

`"Allow me to illuminate the floor using ultraviolet."` With that, MINIMCOM lifted his hands, palms outward. Rei didn't see anything but with Rome's u-cones, she certainly did.

"Footprints," she said, pointing to the floor. Rei shook his head indicating he could not see them.

`"Two different pairs,"` MINIMCOM observed. `"However, they are old. They are buried under most of the dust."`

Rome surveyed the room. There were open air filing cabinets, white boards, peg boards made out of woven cane-tree bark and several desks. She determined that most of the activity by the parties unknown took place near the two desks pressed up against the side wall. She walked over to the first desk and found another computer frame propped upright. She doubled-tapped the upper-right hand corner of the frame and the computer awakened. She sat down and examined it closely, quickly moving her fingers about the screen. Finally, she turned in place.

"There's nothing on this one," she said. "It has no data, no documents, nothing."

Rei came over to where she was sitting and tried a different approach, using a sector editor to examine the contents of the directory. "It's been wiped clean," he said, finally. "Whoever was here, everything has been erased."

"Can you retrieve anything?" she asked. "I was able to, I don't know the proper word in English, 'un-delete' things on our storage units. Do you have the same ability?"

"No," Rei said. "This thing uses a secure delete which scrambles the sectors when a document is removed. There'd be no way."

"What if you deleted something by accident?" Rome asked.

"You'd better hope it was backed up," Rei said, knowing that Rome would be disappointed.

Rome shook her head. She surveyed the desk, moving papers aside. There was nothing of any importance and certainly nothing that looked like a crew manifest. She was about to give up when she looked to the right. The desk had several drawers built in. She pulled on the top one and found it was locked tight.

"MINIMCOM, can you open this?" she asked.

MINIMCOM made a noise that sounded like a tsk and with a sharp tug, snapped the lock and drew the drawer open.

Rome pulled out the yellowing papers stored there, examining each one. Once again, she found nothing of much importance. She was nearly at the bottom of the drawer when she felt something solid. She pushed the remaining few papers aside and found a slab that was similar to the black data slabs except this one was white. She lifted it up and inspected it from all angles. It was much lighter in weight than the jet-black slabs and had no label on it.

"Why is this one white?" she asked Rei.

"If those computers are the ones we brought from Earth, they have a limited internal storage capacity. That might be some sort of external storage."

"A backup?" Rome asked excitedly.

"Probably."

"Where would they have gotten it?" Rome asked, holding the slab in the air.

"I would assume we either brought them or they made it here," Rei answered.

"Would your data slab reader fit on this computer?" she asked.

"Yeah, sure," Rei answered.

"MINIMCOM, would you fetch the data reader from the other computer, please?" Rome asked the all-black livetar.

"Of course." Rather than walk back to the previous hut, MINIMCOM popped out of the room then popped back in with the data reader in tow along with the once-missing 20th slab still mounted within. He handed the assembly to Rome who pulled out the black slab and snapped the white one in its place. When it was snug, she slid it along the desk until it attached to the computer.

As before, a new icon appeared on the virtual desktop. Rome activated the laser-drawn keyboard and used it to examine the folder structure. There was a multitude of directory trees which bespoke of population projections, base construction diagrams, a Captain's log, provisioning and a variety of other topics repeated over and over. There was a main folder labeled Ark II. She abandoned the keyboard and used the touch screen to drill down until she found documents labeled Candidates, D Crew List and Full Roster.

"D Crew List," Rome said. "D for Darwin." She quickly tapped on the document and opened it up.

"This is it!" she said to Rei excitedly. "Look!" She drew her finger down the screen, counting each name. When she got to the bottom, she hit the PgDn key on the virtual keyboard and counted the rest of the names. She tilted her head.

"I count 111 names," she said, confused. "Something is wrong."

Rei bent his knees so he could peer over her shoulder. "Go back to the top of the document," he said.

Rome complied.

"There," Rei said, "at the top, right after Keller. Those two names, Fayed and Alexander; they were the pilot and copilot for the Ark II."

"What does MIA mean?" Rome asked, pointing to the symbols by their names.

"Missing in Action," Rei answered. "Those two were in the command module when we hit the asteroid. They got knocked into space along with Captain Keller. We've never found their sarcophagi so, officially, they are still missing."

"I see," Rome said. She scrolled down slowly. "Stanton, Pierre and Wright. Those are the three dead people we found back at the cave. Their names are marked with KIA. What does that mean?"

"Killed in Action," Rei replied.

"Then this is our list," Rome said. "It is complete and reflects the state of things after they arrived on this world." She whirled in place and looked up at the tall black livetar standing off to the side. "MINIMCOM, I would like you to take a snapshot of this list, please."

"Of course," MINIMCOM replied, stepping forward. "However, I think our OMCOM clone would be better suited `to store the data and collate the rest of the evidence we collect. After all, that is his specialization."`

"That's an excellent idea," Rome said. "Can you fetch his livetar?"

`"It would be my pleasure,"` MINIMCOM replied.

With a whoosh and a pop, OMCOM's two-meter tall, all-white livetar appeared beside them. The shell was the manifestation of their OMCOM clone which was buried 700 meters below Rome's library.

"How can I assist you?" the livetar asked.

"OMCOM," she said pointing, "on this slab is a crew manifest of the original occupants of Rei's Ark as well as a complete crew roster for the Darwin people. 111 in total. We know that three are dead. Two are missing out in space somewhere. Of the remaining 106 alive, 104 were transported to Helome. That means two were left behind but we don't know which two. With MINIMCOM's help, we should be able to identify more than half of those transported. But it is imperative that we narrow the list all the way down to the missing two. We believe they are the people who bombed our house and tried to kill Rei."

"Are they also the people that stole the two items from the library? The handgun and the invisibility cloak?" OMCOM asked.

"What would make you think that?" Rei interjected.

"As you are so fond of saying, 'there ain't no such thing as a coincidence'. What could be better for sneaking a bomb into someone's house, unnoticed, than an invisibility cloak?"

Rei looked at Rome. "He's right," Rei said. "I haven't had time to think about it but it makes perfect sense." Rei turned back to OMCOM. "Do you have any surveillance video or audio that might help us identify the thieves?"

"My workstations are continuously active, which means they were active during the time of the intrusion. However, I was under no instructions to analyze the recordings. I will set to work on that. With some interpolation and extrapolation, I might be able to get you some practical information to aid in your search."

"That is excellent," Rome said. "Please begin right away." She was about to pull the data slab out of the holder then she stopped. She closed the text file she had opened and returned to the one labeled Candidates. She opened up the document and found it was another list, this one consisting of four names. Two she had never heard of:

Andrea Grenmuller and Paul Chung. The third name was Wally Stanislaw who she knew. But it was the fourth name that shocked her. It was Rei Bierak. Rome tapped on the link for Rei's name. A balloon opened up with notations. As she read its contents, her eyes grew wider and wider.

"Oh, Rei," Rome cried out, sounding terribly depressed.

"What?" Rei asked staring at the screen. He saw his name listed. He read the notations out loud.

"Bierak, Rei – Engineer, Unranked. Has shown incredible resourcefulness beyond his test scores. Would make a great asset to the Project but has a strong moral streak that would interfere. He has married one of the Vook women and had a child by her. Best plan: have the wife and the child killed and frame the Vooks. His anger and indignation might be enough to swing him over to our side."

"Even then…" Rome whispered. "So devious. They truly were monsters." She turned in place and looked up into Rei's eyes. "Sometimes I have wondered if we did the right thing banishing them to Helome but after reading this…" She just shook her head.

Rei put his hand on her shoulder. "You can see why we have to stop them. Because they won't. No, we did the right thing," he said.

Rome lowered her head and placed it in her hands. She took a long time to compose herself. Finally, she sighed and stood up. She pulled the white slab from the reader and handed it to OMCOM.

"This is the place to start," she said. "After you have recreated the list of names, we will begin the process of elimination and hope that we can figure out who are the culprits. We are depending upon MINIMCOM's recordings and you and your skills."

"While I am honored by your confidence in my abilities, the fact is, you do not need me or MINIMCOM for that," OMCOM said. "The solution is trivial."

"It is?" Rome asked. "What? How?"

The livetar pointed to the sky. "Go to Helome and take roll. The two that are not present are the two you are seeking."

Rei just hung his head. "Duh," he said under his breath.

Chapter 6

THE MESMERIZING BLACKER-THAN-BLACK OF NULL-FOLD SPACE made it hard for Rei to not stare out the front cockpit. Rome never seemed to have a problem with it. Maybe it was her obsession with studying the virtual instruments. Maybe it was just the way her Vuduri brain was wired. Rei, on the other hand, could barely take it. Every time he glanced up, the non-existence of null-space seem to draw him in again. Rei found it almost impossible to pull his eyes away.

Luckily, with MINIMCOM's incredible speed, now 30% greater than what it was two years ago; it was only a six-hour trip from Tau Ceti to the Alpha Centauri system. Determined to not stare again until they got there, with yet another heroic effort, Rei tore his eyes from the front and closed them. "I'm getting a real déjà vu feeling," he said.

"What do you mean?" Rome asked, never lifting her eyes from the instrumentation.

"Last time we did this, didn't I tell you I thought we'd been neglecting Aason."

"Yes, I recall that," Rome said, looking up. "What's your point?"

"Well, here we are again, leaving him behind. In fact, we sent him away. Doesn't that make us bad parents?"

"Rei," Rome said sternly. "You know we sent him away for his own good. What kind of parents would we be if we did not?"

"I guess you're right," Rei said. He turned his head toward the front but refused to open his eyes. "I have been curious how Virga and the rest of them dealt with our, uh, present," Rei said. "And I did promise you we'd go back some day to check things out. Funny how things work out sometimes, huh?"

"Yes," Rome said in low voice. Her tone made Rei open his eyes again. He turned to look at her. She lowered her head so that she looked at him through the tops of her eyes. "However, I would like you to promise me that you will not be getting into bed with her naked this time."

Rei laughed a bit nervously. "Of course not," he said, seeing that Rome was serious. "I explained all that to you. It wasn't my first choice. I just didn't want them to hurt you. Or me, for that matter."

"Very well," Rome said. She looked back down at the virtual instruments. "We are nearly there, MINIMCOM," she said. "Will you be dropping out of null-space shortly?"

"`One minute, thirty-five seconds,`" the starship replied through the grille. "`I do know what I am doing, you know.`"

"I never doubted it," Rome said, smiling. She looked over at Rei and winked.

Very shortly thereafter, the shushing sound of the null-fold drive died away. Instantly, the darker-than-dark black of null-fold space disappeared and was replaced by the sparkling star-field surrounding the main star. Aleph was dead ahead and very bright as they were only 120 million miles away. Its beautiful golden color hid the dim stars behind it. Directly in front of them was the gleaming blue world of Helome.

"`They are aware of our presence,`" MINIMCOM said. "`However, there is no offer of handshake, just some coordinates. Is that where you want me to land?`"

"Absolutely," Rome said. "We have nothing to fear. Proceed."

"`Very well.`"

MINIMCOM's plasma thrusters roared to life, pushing Rei and Rome back in their seats. Rei felt the electrostatic push of his specially designed shirt give way slightly. It was as if his chest thinned. Meanwhile, the blue-white marble in front of them, flecked with puffy white clouds, quickly grew into a planet-sized sphere.

They entered a west-to-east orbit and MINIMCOM implemented the swooping and arcing of the Bessel function used to aero-brake their way into the atmosphere. They circled around the planet coming up on the same squarish-shaped continent they had landed on the last time they were here. Most of the vegetation was a deep shade of teal with sporadic patches of emerald green. To the south was a splash of colors that defied a singular description. Regardless of its color, the growth was lush and dense over the entire landscape. The only exception was the circles-within-circles shape of the Vuduri capital city. Farther to the south, the vegetation had thinned but there was no distinct pattern to the clearing.

"There's the twin towers," Rei said, pointing forward.

"`The coordinates they gave us are farther to the south,`" MINIMCOM countered.

"This is fine," Rome said. "Just land where they are requesting."

MINIMCOM looped past the city to the south about 50 kilometers. There, he found a small spaceport, sparsely populated with aircraft and very few spacecraft. MINIMCOM extended his landing gear and settled onto the hardened surface in front of a few low buildings. Behind them was an entire other row of buildings two stories tall. This landing strip seemed to be devoted to the complex rather than a general purpose spaceport.

Rei peeked out the cockpit and saw two people headed toward the rear of the ship. He stood up and held out his hand to Rome. Rome unbuckled and stood up, taking Rei's hand. She started toward the rear but Rei did not move.

"What?" she asked.

"Uh, ramps? Guns? Should we do something?"

"What do you mean?"

"You do realize that every single time we've ever gone anywhere and walked up or down a ramp, the people at the bottom or top are always armed and gunning for us?"

"You're being silly," Rome said, tugging on his hand. "We're in no such danger here. Let's go meet them."

Rei took a deep breath and followed her back along the corridor, past the cargo compartment and pressed the blue stud to lower the cargo ramp.

The beautiful, golden light of Aleph streamed in. Rei held his arm up to shield his eyes, blinking rapidly at the bright star. Since he had been forced to leave his sunglasses back on Earth before they launched, it never occurred to Rei to get a new pair. Rome wouldn't care. With her inner iris, she never had trouble with the sun. He decided someday soon, he would get MINIMCOM to rectify that: he'd get a replacement pair of sunglasses. At least Rome was patient enough to wait until his eyes adjusted. He and Rome descended the ramp together and were met by two people, a man and a woman, at the bottom.

"Hello," Rome said. "Do you know who we are?"

"Of course," answered the man in a hoarse voice. "You are Rei and Rome, the people who saved our race."

Rome smiled slightly. "Do you know where Virga is? We would like to talk to her."

"We will take you to see her," the man said. He turned and pointed to one of the heavy-duty flying carts used on Helome. "Please come with me."

Rei and Rome followed the two white jump-suited Vuduri to the flying cart. The woman took her place behind the wheel. The man sat in the front next to her. Rei and Rome clambered aboard and sat in the back seat.

With an easy motion, the cart lifted into the air and headed toward the south.

"No," Rome said. "Should we not be headed north?"

The man turned in his seat. "You requested an audience with Virga. She now lives in the southern territory along with the Essessoni."

Rome cocked her head. The words made sense yet they did not. She just leaned back in her seat and decided to enjoy the ride.

Rei did not enjoy it as much as she did. He kept glancing upward, searching for any signs of bat-wolves, even though he had been assured the last time he was here that they only came out at night.

They traveled along a barely paved road through thicker and thinner stands of the tree-analogs with the multi-colored trunks. Rei called them Crayola trees. Rome liked to squint her eyes so the colors blended forming a wavy rainbow.

At last they came upon a clearing, surrounded by a tall fence. The driver came to a halt and waited until the mechanical gate opened. Once it was fully open, she drove through. The man turned around to make sure the gate closed behind them. In the meantime, the driver flew the cart over a better-paved set of roads until they came to a village that reminded Rei of some of the more rustic places on Earth. The only difference was the dwellings were constructed out of Vuduri aerogel. In some places, the usual white of the aerogel had been stained with a brick color, not unlike the trick he used to make Rome's library appear more academic.

At last, they pulled up in front of a two-story house. The whole block consisted of detached dwellings which in itself was a departure from the usual rowhouse appearance of Vuduri housing. The man turned to them and said, "This is Virga's house. She is expecting you."

Rome waited but neither of their two Vuduri escorts made any move like they were getting out. Shrugging, Rome slid over and hopped out of the cart, followed by Rei. They walked up the front path and the door opened. Out came Virga to greet them. Her blonde hair sparkled in the golden rays of Aleph. It was still curly but was a little longer. If anything, she looked more beautiful than the last time they saw her. And also, she was very pregnant.

"Rome," she said, leaning forward and hugging Rome. Rome accepted the embrace as surprising as it was. Most Vuduri would never think to initiate physical contact but then the Vuduri of Helome were always a little different.

Virga released Rome and stepped to her left to hug Rei. She pressed her head gently against his chest. Rei was about to say something but Virga released him before she fell through his miniature PPT tunnel.

"How have you two fared?" she asked.

"We are well," Rome answered. "And I see you are doing well, also," she said, pointing at Virga's extended abdomen.

"My second," Virga said proudly. "My first was a beautiful, perfect little mosdurece boy. Not a trace of Onsira blood." She turned to Rei. "And we have you to thank for it."

Rei started to speak when a gruff voice emitted from the front door.

"Bierak!" came Captain Keller's voice. "How the hell are you?"

Rei was dumbfounded. "Captain Keller?" he asked incredulously.

"Just Maury, now," said the man striding up them. He looked ten years younger. "No more of that stuff for me on this world."

He put his arm over Virga's shoulder. "Why don't we invite these people in and find out why they're here?"

Virga nodded. She stood on her toes and kissed Keller on the cheek. Rei was dumbstruck. He looked at Rome whose eyes, if anything, were wider than his own. Shaking off their shock, they turned and allowed Keller and Virga to lead the way and the four of them retired inside.

The living quarters were an amalgam of a typical spartan Vuduri apartment, complete with workstation, sofa and table along with some Earth-style accoutrements including some photographs hung on the walls. Several of the chairs were clearly hand-carved, but exquisitely so, including one ornate rocking chair.

Virga left the room while Rei and Rome took seats on the sofa. Keller sat down in the rocker. Virga returned with a small tray and several squeeze-bulbs, some clear, some with a translucent brown liquid.

"We have water and beer," Virga said.

"Beer!?" Rei barked. "How? Where?"

Keller laughed. "We found some feral fields of barley and hops way up north on the site of the original settlement. Virga's people were kind enough to let us experiment a little." Keller leaned forward and grabbed one of the brown squeezebulbs. He lifted it up. "Try it and tell me what you think."

Rei snorted a laugh and reached down and grabbed one for himself. He took a healthy slug and said, "this is great!" He turned and offered it to Rome. "Do you want to try it?" he asked.

"I suppose," Rome said, suspiciously. She took a little sip, scrunched up her face and said, "This is horrid! How can anybody drink this?"

Rei laughed. "It's an acquired taste," he said.

"I will stick with water," Rome said and Virga handed her a clear squeeze-bulb.

"Captain Keller…" Rei started out but stopped when Keller held his hand up.

Keller took a good long draft of beer then set his squeezebulb down. "Before you say anything, there's something I need to tell you. I'm not the man you knew."

"You aren't?" Rei asked. "Ok, uh, go ahead."

"Do you remember when the Bethesda bomb went off?"

"Of course," Rei said. "How could anybody forget?"

"Well, I was stationed in Turkey at the time, fighting god-knows-who. Well, Bethesda, that was my home. My wife and two daughters lived there. They were incinerated, along with my parents and pretty much everybody that I ever cared about."

Keller sighed. "I was so angry, so blind with rage; I just wanted to kill everybody and everything that had even the remote chance of being related." He shook his head. "There was no way to grieve," he said. "The area was quarantined and off-limits for a hundred years. I wasn't allowed back. My bitterness made me an easy recruit for Darwin. I believed in what they wanted with all my heart and soul. I just wanted everyone who wasn't us to die. When I got to the stars, and there were already people there, I wanted them gone too. I held all of them responsible."

Keller leaned forward. "But you and your wife, you saved me. You showed me there was no point to it. It could never succeed. In fact, Rome, it was your final words to me before you shipped us off to this planet that rattled around in my brain and finally planted the seed."

"What did I say?" Rome asked, confused.

"You told me that Project Darwin *was* a success. You said that while it was survival of the fittest, it just wasn't the group I imagined."

He looked up and held out his hand. Virga came over and took it and sat down on the arm of the chair. "It wasn't until I got here and met these beautiful, beautiful people…"

Virga blushed slightly.

"…that I realized you were right. The Vuduri really are our children. They are the descendents of the survivors of the Great Dying. Our people really do live on in their souls. Once I understood that, I gave up the fight and decided to live. Virga, here, took me in. And I couldn't be happier. I have a beautiful little boy now and another one on the way." He patted Virga's tummy.

He leaned forward. "I let go."

Rei was speechless. He reached over and took Rome's hand. Finally, he found his voice. "Do all of you feel this way?" he asked.

"Most," Keller said. "But just in case…" He held up his wrist. There was a Vuduri tracking bracelet attached. "I told them not to trust us completely. This is just in case one of our group decides to try something stupid."

Virga stroked his cheek with her hand. "It is not too oppressive, is it, Maury?"

"Hell no," Maury laughed. "I kind of like the idea of being a kept man. It's for all our protection." He looked around for his little boy but did not see him. "The next generation, they'll be free to come and go. It'll be fine."

"So what is it you do around here?" Rei asked.

"I have my woodworking shop. Most of us have found gainful employment. We're building a new world. This one. It's enough."

Rome scooted forward a bit. "You said most of your people are this way. But not all?"

"No," Keller said. "There are some left who still harbor a deep resentment. But they are very few. We keep them off to themselves. Not exactly a prison. Call it a compound. The Vuduri have to make sure they don't get loose." He became silent and stared at Rei and Rome for a bit. "So what brings you folks here, anyway?"

Rome leaned forward. "Somebody tried to kill Rei with a bomb. We believe it is one of your remaining people who are still back on Deucado."

Keller sat back in his chair and frowned. He covered his eyes with his hand and drew it downward then he sighed. "I suppose it's possible," he said. "There's no way they could know what's going on here. I suppose they're still keeping up the fight."

Rei stood up and reached into his pocket. He drew out two sheets of paper and held them out for Keller.

"What's this?" Keller asked, taking the papers.

"It's the crew roster for the Darwin Project. I need to know which of these people never made it to Helome. They are the ones we're looking for."

Keller nodded and looked over the list. He flipped from one page to the other than back again.

"I know one of them," he said, finally. "Dan Steele. He's got to be back on Deucado. He never got caught. He'd definitely be up to the job. I mean, he's a natural born killer. He wouldn't know how to do much else."

"And the other?" Rome asked desperately. "Do you know?"

Keller flipped through the sheets again. "No," he said finally. "There are over a hundred of us here. I don't know every one of them."

"Is there anyone who does?" Rome posed forcefully. "Is there someone who could tell us who is the other missing person?"

"Let me think," Keller replied. He nodded his head. "Yeah, there's one," he said. "Bonnie Mullen. She knows every one of us here. She compiled the original list for Virga when we first arrived. She can tell you."

"Bonnie," Rei whispered. He looked up at Virga. "Can you take us to her?"

"Of course," Virga replied, rising up. She looked down at Keller. "You'll wait here?"

"Sure," said Keller. "My varnish is dry by now. I'm ready to do the next coat."

Virga nodded. "Very well. Rei, Rome, I will take you to see her but we should probably take your starship."

"Why?" Rome asked.

"She is one of the very few Essessoni we have allowed to roam outside of the territory. She is currently situated rather far inland." Virga put her hand up to her temple and after a moment, nodded. "Gemen, her companion, says she will receive you."

"Gemen, not Edgar?" Rei asked.

"No. Her former husband is one of the detainees who will not renounce their violent ways. He and Bonnie are no longer together."

"Huh," Rei observed. He stood up as did Rome. Keller joined them. He held out his hand.

"Bierak, you've always been a mystery to me but I've come to truly respect you and your wife. I hope you find out who it is and stop them. I mean that. You and your little lady deserve nothing less. You're both heroes to all mankind. Vuduri and mandasurte alike."

Rei shook his hand. "Thank you, sir," Rei said. "That means a lot to me."

"Virga will take care of you. She's really good at what she does."

Virga smiled. She kissed Keller on the cheek and then led the way out.

Chapter 7

THE LEADER OF THE VUDURI ON HELOME LED THEM TO A WAITING flying cart and they headed back the way they came toward the north, passing through the fence and on to the open road.

Along the way, Rei, who was sitting in the front seat with Virga, asked, "Where is this place we're going?"

Virga answered but kept her eyes straight-forward. "I suppose you could call it a farm or perhaps ranch," she said. "It was the place where we took the children who were born Onsiras to be raised."

"You segregated them?" Rome asked from the back seat.

"Yes," Virga said. "We could not bring ourselves to eradicate them but we feared having them grow up alongside us. This was the compromise the Overmind decided upon. It was our hope that our new breeding program would eliminate the need for such measures in the future."

"From what I can tell, the Onsiras are just worm-brains," Rei said. "Without MASAL, they're lost. Or at least irrelevant. Still, its your plan. From what you've seen so far, would you call the breeding program a success to this point?" Rei asked. "I did as you requested. I sent you the most primitive Essessoni I could find."

"Yes, you did," Virga said with a strange tone. They arrived at the small landing field where MINIMCOM was still parked on the taxiway. Virga pulled the cart out around back, past the low lying buildings next to the runway and down a narrow road to the tallest building in the cluster. She pulled up in front of the main door then she turned to Rei. "To the degree we originally imagined, it was a success. More than you realize. The very salvation of all Vuduri, even pure-bred, may lie there."

"What do you mean?" Rei asked. "I thought the plan was to produce mosdureces."

"It was but now we think there may be something better," Virga said mysteriously. "That is a science hall," Virga announced, pointing to the building on their right. "Would you find it a burden if we stopped in here for just a moment? I will present to you a rather perplexing mystery and it is possible that you may be able to help us clear it up."

Rei looked at Rome who shrugged. "OK," Rei said. "As long as it doesn't take too much time."

"It will not," Virga replied. She led them through the front entrance and up one flight of stairs until they came to a large room, set up somewhat like a classroom but with a variety of scientific equipment along the far wall. There was a long table in the front. Virga indicated the seats on the near side. Rei and Rome sat down. Virga closed her eyes and a projector, hidden in the ceiling, lit up the front wall and displayed a map of the human genome. Rei quickly counted 22 pairs of chromosomes plus one X and one Y chromosome; 23 chromosome pairs in all.

"This is the chromosomal layout of a normal 23-chromosome male mandasurte," Virga said. She blinked and all but the X and Y chromosomes disappeared. They nestled themselves in the upper left hand corner of the screen. Below them, a second partial map appeared. This one had two X chromosomes plus two additional pairs of chromosomes to the right of the double Xs.

"This is a normal, full-blooded, Vuduri female with 24 pairs of chromosomes. In fact, this is me." She turned to face Rome. "As you are aware, the 24th chromosome does not split during meiosis. Propagation of the 24th chromosome is mitotic so a normal Vuduri couple would each require a diploid complement to produce full-blooded children."

Virga turned back to the screen. This time, the additional chromosomes slid to the upper right-hand corner of the screen and another map appeared. This one had an extra pair of chromosomes, even shorter and stubbier than the Y chromosome lined up to the right.

"20% of the Essessoni that you sent us have the exact genetic complement we expected. They are identical in every way to a 23-chromosome mandasurte. But the other 80% have this extra chromosome pair, a portion of which is reminiscent of our 24th, but they are not DNA in the truest sense. They are a form of peptide nucleic acid and they do not have telomeres on one end. They are quite odd. We call them the 25th chromosome for lack of a better name."

"Uh," Rei started to speak. Rome interrupted him.

"What is the significance of this?" Rome asked.

65

"The significance is this: this genetic material, this extra pair, would prevent the expression of the Onsira phenotype, even in a full-blooded diploid Vuduri. If we could figure out a way to introduce it to the Vuduri population in general, no Onsira would ever be born again. Mosdurece or not."

"If this is the case, why have you not done so already?" Rome asked.

"We have tried," Virga said, sighing. The projector shut off. "However, we cannot keep the genetic material from disintegrating outside of the cell wall. In other words, we cannot figure out a delivery system."

Rei looked at Rome who nodded. Rei touched his temple. With a whoosh and a pop, MINIMCOM's all-black livetar appeared, holding a white bottle which he handed to Rei.

"What is this?" Virga asked.

Rei unscrewed the top and spilled the contents onto the table. "This is your delivery system," he said.

Virga reached over and picked up one of the white pills. "What are these?" she asked. "Where did you get them?"

"These are the pills OMCOM made back at Skyler Base to help my crew overcome 14 centuries of degeneration in their backs. Our instructions were to give one to every member of my crew but some of them evidently refused. I guess that's the 20% you're calling the normal ones."

Virga held the pill up to the light. "Do you realize what this means?" she said, almost giddily. "This is the salvation of the Vuduri." She looked down at the pile of pills. "We do not need all of these," she said. "We will be able to replicate them." She looked up at Rei and Rome. "You must take the rest of these to Earth. There must be uncounted Onsiras loose there. This would put an end to any possible threat from them forever."

Rei gathered up some of the pills and put them back in the bottle, leaving a pile on the table. "I guess we could," he said. "But we're not really supposed to go there. We were banished, you know."

"Yes," Virga said. "Our opinion now is the same as it was the first time I met you. The Overmind of Earth treated you horribly. You two are heroes many times over. They should be honoring you, not exiling you." Virga cocked her head. "Rei, the last time you were here, you told me that MASAL injected you with his version of the 24th chromosome. Did you take one of these pills?"

"Uh, no," Rei said. "I sort of took a different kind."

"What do you mean?" Virga asked.

"Well, old OMCOM had other plans for me. The pill he gave me was yellow and I guess you'd say I got some superpowers from them."

"You did mention that to me the last time you were here but I did not pursue it. What kind of powers?" Virga asked.

Rei tapped his ear. "Besides fixing my back, it gave me super-hearing, kind of like sonar vision. He also built a cell-phone into our heads so Rome and I can talk."

"Rome has this too? Is it like our PPT resonance?" Virga asked.

"No, this one is based upon EM, not gravitic modulation," Rome said. Then she added in a bit of a huff, "It ruined my bloco!" She tapped her temple then she shrugged. "No matter. Rei and I have found our communication channel very useful at times."

"I am fascinated. Would you mind if I took a genetic sample?" Virga asked. "For comparison with a normal Essessoni?"

"What's involved," Rei asked skeptically.

"Just a swab from the inside of your cheek. Nothing invasive," Virga indicated with a vague wave of her hand.

"We gotta get going," Rei said.

"It will only take a minute," Virga pleaded.

"OK," Rei said. "What do you need me to do?"

"Just stay there," Virga said. She walked over to a rack of equipment and retrieved two sticks with a fluffy swab on the end. She returned and stood before Rei. She put her hand under his chin. "Open your mouth," she requested, "and I will just run this along the inside of your cheek."

Rei complied.

Virga turned to Rome. "Do you mind if I take a sample of your DNA as well?"

"No," Rome said, "I do not mind." She opened her mouth and Virga ran the soft end of the other swab the inside of Rome's mouth as well. She then carried the swabs over to a squat, metallic box and inserted them into small holes which looked like they were designed for exactly that purpose. An indicator light turned red, then amber, then green. Virga turned back to Rei and Rome and the projector lit up again.

Virga gasped. Her connection to the Overmind actually wavered slightly.

The middle row showed the normal complement of 22 chromosomes plus an X and a Y along with a much larger 24th chromosomal pair, very similar to a Vuduri 24th chromosome but slightly different. To its right was a much fuller version of what Virga called the 25th chromosome. It was larger than any of the others including chromosome pair 1. But this was not what made Virga gasp.

Beneath Rei's chromosome map with its X and Y chromosomes lay Rome's map. She had no less than three pairs of the 24th chromosome plus a full 25th like Rei's. In that brief moment, the Overmind of Helome realized that Rome was the most genetically complex human being in existence. It had trouble grasping the full implications.

At last, Virga recovered. In a very quiet voice, she said, "I thought you were mosdurece. You were to have had a single pair, yet you have a triploid complement of the 24th chromosome plus the same 25th as Rei. Can you explain this?"

"Yes," Rome said, without a hint of modesty. She pointed to the screen. "The first pair was my genetic inheritance from my mother. That pair allowed me to be connected to the Overmind of Earth and on Tabit until I was Cesdiud."

Virga's shoulders sagged but she said nothing.

"The second pair was given to me on Deucado by Pegus in order to re-establish a PPT connection to my son. It is still active. I still communicate with the Overmind there."

"Go on," Virga said encouragingly.

"The third pair was a prosthetic version of the 24th chromosome given to me by MASAL, when he kidnapped us on Earth. He wanted to take me into his samanda or at the very least convert me to an Onsira but he was unaware of OMCOM's 25th chromosome," Rome pointed to the screen. "It allowed me to prevent them from even starting a resonance in the first place."

Virga turned to Rei. "And you? You are Essessoni. You were injected with this prosthetic chromosome as well?"

"Yeah," Rei said. "For a minute or two, I really was connected to MASAL but then they decided they hated me and kicked me out, Cesdiud."

Virga just shook her head.

"It was actually sort of fun while it lasted," Rei said. "It gave me a little sense of what it must be like to be Vuduri, but… oh well."

Virga turned back to Rome. "And your son? Was he conceived before or after you were genetically modified?"

"He is a mix of both," Rome said. "His PPT resonance is very strong and he has our 25th chromosome. I suspect that when I was injected on Deucado, the new pair crossed the placental barrier. However, he has an Essessoni father so he would never let go of his individuality. He can talk to the Overmind on Deucado but he would never submit. Even in the womb. He is neither Vuduri nor Essessoni. He's something else."

Virga looked back up the screen. "If you ever had another child, he or she would have triple PPT resonance plus your OMCOM's enhancements." She just shook her head. "This child would be very powerful."

Rome gave Rei a knowing look but said nothing. OMCOM had already requested they produce a daughter and the time was drawing near. Rome put it out of her mind.

"We will not be alive to produce any more children if we do not capture the people who would kill us. Can we go see Bonnie now?"

"Of course," Virga said. She gathered up the pills lying on the table and placed them in a jar by the side of the sampling equipment. "Thank you very much for these. They are invaluable. I will take you to see her right away."

Chapter 8

MINIMCOM SOARED EAST OVER THE BEAUTIFUL, SNOW-CAPPED peaks of the central mountain range that ran the length of the squarish continent. Like everything else on Helome, they were more spectacular than anything Earth had to offer. They were taller than the Rocky Mountains with small plateaus of the Crayola trees interspersed. There were crystal clear mountain lakes and rivers and to the far north, there were glaciers. Their craggy tops displayed every manner of color including deep purples, blues and slate gray. As they drew closer, Virga indicated a small, grassy field that lay within the tall fence-lined area that really did look like a ranch and that is where MINIMCOM set down.

After exiting MINIMCOM, they walked across the fresh field to the Vuduri version of a log cabin. It was constructed out of stained aerogel but still looked more rustic than futuristic. Two people came out of the house, a man and a woman. The woman waved to them and came trotting over. It was Bonnie Mullen but she was much thinner than she had been on Deucado and looked much older. She was dressed in a traditional white Vuduri jumpsuit but somehow it looked right on her. She hugged Rei and Rome briefly.

"It's so good to see you both," she said with a faint smile. There was a hint of sadness around her eyes that didn't match.

"You're not mad?" Rei asked. "I wasn't very nice to you right there at the end."

"Nah," Bonnie said. "It was my own fault. You did the right thing." She paused for a moment then said, "Where are my manners? This is Gemen," she said, pointing at the Vuduri man. "He doesn't talk much, as you can imagine."

"Hello," Gemen said and that was all.

"I am glad you are not upset that we sent you to this world," Rome threw in.

"Oh, no," Bonnie said. "It gave me a chance to get away from Edgar. That's all I really wanted. Needed, really. I didn't care where." She turned and waved. "Let's go into the house." She led them up the two front steps and into the large, single room dwelling.

Rei looked around the house. "Where's your baby?" he asked.

Bonnie's expression turned very dark. She looked away and pressed her hand up to her eyes. She took a deep breath and turned back to them.

"I had a lot of complications. The baby was stillborn. I was bleeding out so they had to give me a complete hysterectomy. My days as a brood mare were over. At least, that's what I thought. " She waved around the room. "It kind of left me with nothing to do. Feeling very empty inside." She frowned. "Not a pun." She pointed out the window. "They had no need for an Essessoni historian on this world so they let me come here, to help with the Onsira ranch." As she was saying it, her breath caught.

"You take care of Onsiras?" Rome asked. "How?"

"What do you mean how?" Bonnie replied "They were babies. You feed them, you clothe them. You make sure they wash behind their ears." Once again, her breath caught. This time, however, it took her longer to regain control. Finally, she continued. "They really were kind of sweet, in their own weird way. I know they appreciated our care." She looked over Gemen who smiled slightly. "Loved us, in a way. I think, maybe, we loved them back. I always thought I didn't want kids. It turns out I just didn't want them with Edgar. Those little buggers were my life…"

"You keep talking about them in the past tense," Rei said. "What's going on?"

Bonnie looked at Virga who nodded. She stood up and stared out the window. "The little ones, especially, even though they were Vuduri or Onsira, or whatever. They still needed taking care of. They understood nurturing. I can't really say that I understand the Overmind all that much but whatever it is, they had some sort of one going here. There was definitely a presence that guided them as a group. Almost like a herd. Sometimes, I think I was even able to communicate with it, whatever it was." Bonnie pointed out of the window into the fields beyond.

"Then one day, a Vuduri woman came to visit. She said she was from Earth and she was here to make sure the Onsiras were being treated humanely. I took her on a tour of the ranch and she seemed to find it OK. She said everything was in order and then she left."

Bonnie turned back to Rei and Rome, tears streaming down her cheeks. "The next morning, when we woke up, they were gone."

"Who was gone?" Rome asked.

"All of them. All of my babies," she said. "Not one trace." Bonnie fell back into a chair and put her face in her hands. From the way her head was bobbing, it was obviously she was crying but no sounds were emitted. She took a deep breath and looked up. The look of grief was etched in her face. "Gemen and I are still waiting, still hoping. Maybe they'll come back some day but it's been a year. I don't think they're coming back."

"This woman," Rome asked. "Did she have a name?"

"Yes," Bonnie replied, eyes unfocused. "She said her name was Sussen."

"Sussen!" Rome hissed. "Her eyes! Did she have one light eye and one dark eye?"

"Yes, as a matter of fact, she did," Bonnie said. "How did you know?"

Rei spoke up. "She was the spy sent to Deucado to make sure they kept the Ibbrassati oppressed until the asteroid came and wiped out the planet. She was an agent for MASAL. She left just before we did to warn MASAL that the inmates were taking over the asylum."

Rei turned to Rome. "I guess she made it back to Earth but then to come here? Why bother?"

"The Onsiras," Rome said. "It means they are not giving up. They are marshaling their forces."

"Still," Rei said. "The Overmind of Earth and the regular Vuduri would never let them rise to power. They vowed to protect the mandasurte. There's nothing to worry about."

"I agree with Rei," Virga said. "When the Overmind of Earth established the static PPT tunnel to Helome, it was not just a tunnel. It was a gate as well. Its purpose was to create a world with just pure-bred Vuduri. No mandasurte were to be allowed."

"MASAL would have been proud of you," Rei said sardonically.

"No," Virga said. "We learned our lesson. Our genetics betrayed us. Even with your magic pills, we will never segregate or discriminate again. Essessoni and mandasurte are welcome here, even if we do not need them for genetic reasons anymore."

Bonnie held up her wrist and waved her tracking bracelet at Virga. "Uh, welcome?"

"The bracelets will be removed some day," Virga said. "But first we must make sure that there are no more Erklirte hiding among you."

Bonnie turned to Rei. "Do you remember that day you sent me away? You asked me when I found out the principles behind Darwin, did I disagree with them?"

"I expected you to say no," Rei said with an edge to his voice. "At least I was hoping you would. You couldn't do it though. That's why I sent you away and that's why Virga has you on a leash."

"I've thought about that ever since that day," Bonnie said quietly. "And I can tell you now that I did not agree with killing everyone. What I wanted more than anything was a place to live, a place to raise children on a world without planet-sized storms, without overcrowding, without unending terrorism. First Deucado and now this world, Helome, is all of that and more. My heart is with the future so my allegiance to Darwin is over."

"That's great," Rei said, standing up. "That's just what I wanted to hear." He pulled out the creased set of papers from his pocket. "The reason we're here is because there are still two Darwin members running around on Deucado. They tried to kill us by blowing up our house."

"Oh my god!" Bonnie said. "Was anybody hurt?"

Rei made the horse lips sound. "Yeah but we're over it." Rei handed the papers to Bonnie. "Captain Keller identified one of the two as Dan Steele. That's a complete list of all the members of Darwin. Can you tell me who else is on that list but never got brought here to Helome?"

"I'll do my best," Bonnie said. She read down the list and stopped when she got to the bottom. "David Troutman," she said. "He never made it to Helome so I guess that means he's your other missing person. He's a chemical engineer and munitions expert. If anybody could build a bomb, he could." She flipped the papers over to the second page, just to be sure. She flipped the pages back and tapped the top sheet with her finger. "He's definitely your man. And Steele, he's just..." Bonnie shivered then took on a quizzical look. "You know, it's kind of funny, now that I think about it."

"What is?" Rei asked.

"When Sussen was here, she asked me how an Erklirte came to be in charge of the children. I told her how you and Rome got wind of Project Darwin and how you sent us into exile here."

"Did she say anything else?" Rome asked her.

"No," Bonnie replied. "She did ask me if there were any more Darwin people left on Deucado. At the time, I wasn't sure. She dropped the subject after that."

Rome looked at Rei who nodded.

"Thank you, Bonnie," Rome said. She stood up. "You've been very helpful. I just have one more question."

"What?" Bonnie inquired.

"Now that we know who we are looking for, can you give us any guidance as to where we should start looking?"

"That I couldn't tell you," Bonnie answered. She looked out the window as if the answer was blowing in the wind. Suddenly, she nodded. "But I bet Nick Greer could. Troutman used to hang around with him. He might be able to tell you something."

"Where do we find Greer?" Rei asked.

Bonnie lowered her eyes to the ground. Rei looked over at Virga. She had a sad expression on her face.

"What?" Rei asked. "Where is he?"

"As I told you," Virga said. "There were a few recalcitrants who remain uncooperative to this day. Greer is one of them."

"So what did you do with them?"

"They built a prison," Bonnie answered for her. "They pretend it isn't but it is. Keller even supplied the Vuduri with the design. They had no idea how to build one. That's how serious Maury was about reform. It's ways away from here."

"A prison, huh," Rei said. "Can you take us there?" he directed at Virga.

"Yes," Virga said. "I will take you but I do not think Greer will be very communicative."

"Let me go with you," Bonnie said, stepping forward. "He might talk to me." She looked over at Virga. "Is that OK?"

Virga nodded.

Bonnie turned to Gemen who had remained silent up until this point. "Goodbye, honey," Bonnie said to Gemen and she kissed him on the cheek. "I'll see you later."

Gemen sighed and lifted his hand to wave farewell.

Chapter 9

MINIMCOM TRANSPORTED THEM BACK OVER THE MOUNTAINS TO the prison compound to the north of the Vuduri city. There was simply no other way to describe it. The Vuduri had nothing like it. Keller must have had direct experience with one based upon its layout and security measures. There were tall fences with a peculiar local bush whose every branch was studded with razor sharp thorns. Inside that was a metallic fence with barbed wire running along the top. There was only one entrance and that was through a sally port. MINIMCOM landed in the parking area outside the sally port. The four humans had to enter by foot along with MINIMCOM's livetar.

The guard station at the first door opened the gate and let them through then closed the gate behind them. Rei looked around and up. The sally port had 40-foot high walls of thick steel gate with even more barbed wire all around. Virga led them to the internal entrance where another guard let them through. The courtyard opened up to an inside out cell block, each with its own entrance. In some ways, it resembled standard Vuduri housing.

"They keep Edgar down there," Bonnie said with disgust, pointing to their left.

"Do you see him often?" Rome asked.

"No," Bonnie said. "I came by once. That was enough. He…" Bonnie stopped short. She shook her head and refused to offer any more explanation. They let it go.

Virga led them along the walkway to the farthest "apartment" to the right. She knocked once on the door then opened it up. The room reeked of smoke.

On the inside, it really did look like a prison cell. There was a single bed along one wall, a small refresher, a desk and not much else. Nick Greer was sitting at the desk, smoking a cigarette. Virga left the door open to air the place out.

"Bierak," Greer said, looking up. "And all the bitches. What do you want?"

As the room was constructed out of standard Vuduri aerogel, the walls glowed softly with a light blue radiance that came from no particular source. Somehow, the light became brighter. Rei could see that there was a pair of tracking bracelets attached to Greer's legs connected by a loose chain. Greer pushed an ashtray forward with the stump of his right arm and stubbed out the cigarette with his left hand.

Rei walked over to where he was sitting. "There are two members of Darwin still running around on Deucado. Troutman and Steele. Bonnie said you knew Troutman. Can you tell us anything that might help us track him down?"

"Why should I help you?" Greer sneered. He stood up suddenly and waved the stump of his arm in Rei's face then pointed at MINIMCOM's livetar. "Look what your robot did to me. I'm nothing but a useless freak now."

Bonnie came over to where he was standing and put her hand on his shoulder. "Nick, you were going to shoot Rome. I saw you. Self-defense is self-defense. The war is over. Captain Keller said so. You heard him. Everybody has to let go. You included. Why won't you help them?"

"I just won't," he said. "You all sold out. I'm not going to. Not to my dying day."

"Please," Rome said from behind Rei. "Your two compatriots would have killed all of us, including my son, if not for good fortune. We do not want to live our lives in fear."

Greer just shook his head then an evil grin spread across his face. His teeth were yellowed by the layers of two years of heavy smoking. He held up the stump of his right arm. "I'll tell you what," he said snidely. "I'll tell you whatever you need to know as soon as you give me my right hand back."

"That's it?" Rei asked. He looked over at MINIMCOM who nodded. "OK, deal," Rei answered.

"Wait. What?" Greer said, stupefied. "You can do that?"

MINIMCOM strode over and gently guided the dazed-looking Greer back to his seat. MINIMCOM laid out the man's left arm and hand along the desk then placed the stump of the right arm next to it. The livetar took a cast of the left hand and projected a thin membrane, a mirror image of the hand and attached it to the right arm. The animated shell then illuminated his shoulder lamps to get more light.

The actual operation took little less than an hour. It was more complex than Rei's back reconstruction but far less delicate so MINIMCOM was able to move faster. The livetar injected the membrane with a passel of VIRUS constructor units which formed cages in the shape of the bones. No need to inject anyone else. MINIMCOM simply used a second group of constructors inserted into Greer's own remaining left hand as a model and built the reverse. He built it from the inside out. Using his .01% rule, MINIMCOM transported bone cells, muscle, ligaments and tendons as well as circulatory vessels. Once the interior was complete, MINIMCOM coated the membrane with more muscle and skin then removed the flap of scarred epidermis that encased the former stump to allow blood to flow.

"I will be transporting the neural cells to the proper location," MINIMCOM said. "However, you should not expect the hand to be fully functional initially." MINIMCOM circled his hands over both sets of fingers.

"Ow, ow," Greer said, "it feels like it's burning."

"Those are the nocioceptors coming online," MINIMCOM said. "The proprioceptors and afferents will connect last." MINIMCOM applied pulses of the miniature null-fold to ensure that all the "wiring" was complete.

Greer looked at the brand new hand in amazement. He tried moving the new fingers and they flexed slightly. A broad smile crossed his face.

"You should not expect it to respond normally for a while," MINIMCOM said, slowly closing the hand into a fist then gently opening it again. "I was able to connect the neurons to the proper areas of your brain but the final fine-tuning will require that you exercise the hand every day."

Greer turned the hand over and back. "How long?" he whispered.

"It will take about a month to get all the 'wiring' complete," MINIMCOM said. "You should have full strength by then as well."

Greer stood up. MINIMCOM produced an elastic ball and placed it in the palm of the new hand.

"Squeeze that for a few minutes every hour or so," MINIMCOM said. "It will hasten the regrowth of the peripheral nerves and help you build up strength. The hand will be completely functional before you know it."

Greer flexed his fingers around the ball then eased up on the pressure. He laughed and shook his head. "I knew you guys were from the future but how come nobody told me you could do this before?"

Rei looked over at MINIMCOM. "Up until about a week ago, we didn't know he could do it either. Now will you help us?"

"Sure, sure," Greer said, distracted by the new limb. "What do you need to know?"

"We need to find Troutman and Steele. Where should we start looking?"

Greer looked around the room at each of the people there as if he were seeing them for the first time.

"Steele, I can't tell you," he said. "But Troutman and me, we were on the crew that brought down the ingots and metal rolls, maybe once a month."

"Why'd you even bother with that?" Rei asked. "You knew the Vuduri could synthesize any materials you needed."

"We had to hide the fact that we were building the base so we smelted just enough ore to make it look like we were doing something up there. Ionelli, Troutman and me, we liked playing hoker and Keller wouldn't let us play at the base. So when we came down, we joined the game going in New Ark City."

"What is hoker?" Rome asked.

"House poker," Rei answered.

"I know what a house is," Rome responded. "But what is poker?"

"It's a card game," Rei said. "So who'd you play hoker with?" Rei directed at Greer.

"Paul Chung and a couple of other people. We played at Chung's house," he said. "You know him? He was one of the regulars."

"That was one of the names on Keller's candidate list," Rome interjected.

"Why him?" Rei asked. "Why his house? I'd have thought you guys didn't want to socialize with us."

Greer laughed.

"What's so funny?" Rei asked.

"For him, we made an exception. He lifted one of the Vook food synthesizers."

Rei shook his head. "So what? Anybody could have one who wanted one."

"Yeah, but nobody else made vodka. His was awesome. His house was the closest thing we ever found to a bar," Greer said. "So, in answer to your question, I'd start there. If anybody back on Deucado knows where Troutman is right now, it'd be Chung."

Rei looked at Rome who nodded then he looked back at Greer. "Thanks," he said. He bent his head toward Greer's new hand. "And you're welcome."

Greer held up his two perfectly matched arms. The flesh on the new right hand was paler than the one on the left. A few days in the sun would rectify that. Greer turned them back and forth. Then he threw the elastic ball down to the ground and caught it with his new right hand on the bounce up.

The four humans and one livetar turned to leave when Greer shouted out, "Wait! Virga!"

"What is it?" Virga asked.

"What Bonnie said," Greer asked. "Does that offer still stand? I think I'm ready to let go now. Can you guys find something for me to do rather than sit around here rotting all day?"

"It can be arranged," Virga answered in a level tone. "However, you will have to disavow your previous commitment to violence and promise to contribute to the betterment of our society."

"I will, I will," Greer said, shuffling forward.

"I will send someone," Virga said. "You will be watched very closely but we will give you your opportunity."

"Thank you," Greer said. He sounded heartfelt. "And Bierak?"

"Yes?" Rei asked.

"Thank you, too. I guess I should have listened to you a long time ago."

"It's never too late," Rei said. "Good luck with your new life."

Greer nodded and they left.

After exiting the sally port and climbing aboard MINIMCOM, Rei and Rome took their places in the cockpit. Virga and Bonnie joined them.

"It's a kind thing you're doing," Rei said to Virga. "Giving him another chance like that."

Virga nodded. "I have not and never will berate you for the class of Essessoni you sent to us," she said. "After all, I did say to you the more primitive the better. The more we can use, the quicker we can heal."

Rei blushed a little bit. "Well, they were useless to us and you did ask. I couldn't think of anything else to do with them."

"It is fine," Virga said. "We are not displeased. As you can see, the vast majority of them have had an epiphany and have settled in nicely here. That prison block back there only has six residents although now it would appear that number will dwindle down to five. It is a small price to pay for the benefits we have derived."

"OK," Rei said. "Well, we got what we came for. We'll take Bonnie back to the ranch, drop you off then head back to Deucado."

Bonnie stepped forward. "About that…" she said.

"Yes?" Rome asked.

"What did Keller say about your plan?"

"He was behind it," Rei answered. "He said he hoped we caught these jokers."

"That's what I figured," Bonnie said. "So I was thinking, what if I came with you?"

"Back to Deucado?" Rome asked skeptically.

"Yes. Like I said, my days as a brood mare are over." She bit down on her knuckle and continued. "I don't think any of my babies are coming back. It's been a year." She looked at Rei plaintively. "I really am kind of useless on this planet. I know what Steele and Troutman look like. Maybe I can help you track them down."

Rei looked over at Virga. "Do you mind?" he asked.

"She is one of yours," Virga said. "If you trust her, we have no objections."

Bonnie pressed the issue. "I really have nothing to do here other than looking after the ranch. They don't need me for that." She bent her knees slightly to look Rome in the eye. "After we catch the bad guys, maybe I could come work for you, at your library. It's what I was trained to do."

Rome pointed to the back of MINIMCOM, the starship. "You do not wish to return here? What about Gemen?" she asked. "You two seemed to have some sort of connection."

"Gemen?" Bonnie said. "He's sweet but he is Vuduri. He won't care." She turned to Virga. "Will he?"

Virga touched her index finger to her temple. She nodded once. "He does care but he understands," Virga said.

"You promise to be good?" Rei asked.

Bonnie put her hand over her heart. "I swear it, Rei. I just want to do something with my life. This seems like it."

"OK then," Rei said. "Let's get going."

Intermezzo 1

January 24, 2067 AD
Just outside Philadelphia, Pennsylvania

25-YEAR-OLD REI BIERAK WAS DRIVING ALONG PA ROUTE 3 between secure zones, inside the walled highway leading to the West Chester Dome. The fact that it was even called a dome was a testament to the dreams of the residents there. It was their hope and desire that someday the structure would become fully enclosed. Only then would they have protection from the pollution and the increasingly brutal storms that had been invading the East Coast.

Even though it was January, it was a warm night. The sun was just setting. Rei adjusted the driver's side visor to block out the orange-red orb hanging low in the sky. As he drove along, he couldn't shake the idea that today was his last day on Earth. Technically, this was not true. Tomorrow, he would be flying to Houston to go into quarantine. Assuming he tested clean for 30 days, he'd begin the agonizing two-week protocol of dehydration prior to being placed in cryo-hibernation. Once frozen, he and his sarcophagus would be transported and stored aboard the orbiting Ark II which was in its final preparations for its 240-year voyage to Tau Ceti.

Rei was on his way back to Raul and Sally's house, having borrowed Raul's truck to get rid of the very last of his earthly possessions. The potential colonists were only permitted to bring 20 kilos of belongings. After accounting for all of his clothes, his tablet computer and his transit, Rei had elected to take a straight razor, some polymer books and his sunglasses. With just those few items, he was right at the weight limit already.

The road dipped down, going under an extended overpass. Rei was just emerging from the tunnel when he noted a group of horseback riders just ahead moving along the bridle path on the other side of the retaining wall. Suddenly, there was a flash. A loud and powerful explosion rocked the truck. Impossibly, Rei could see the carcass of a horse flying up in the air and over the retaining wall. He slammed on his brakes but he couldn't avoid it. The brown mass hit the hood of the truck and smashed through the window. In the mean time, Rei threw his arms up to protect his face and it was only by the sheerest of luck that he managed to keep his foot on the brakes until the truck came to a complete halt.

The force of the horse's body hitting the truck did not set off the crash curtain. After all, who would build a truck that could detect dead horses landing on the hood? There was shattered glass everywhere. Miraculously, Rei was not hurt, just completely shaken. After taking a few minutes to inventory his limbs and innards, Rei composed himself and pressed the activator on his cheekbone earpiece and called emergency services.

It turns out he didn't have to. The National Guard was already on its way. By the time they got there, Rei had extricated himself from the cab of the truck and was leaning against the side, away from where the explosion had occurred. The soldiers did a preliminary sweep of the area but there wasn't much left of the horseback riders and certainly no sign of the terrorists. Raul's truck was ruined, however. One of the guardsmen who had field medical training insisted on checking Rei out despite the fact that the young man assured him he wasn't injured. As expected, the medic didn't find anything serious. After the soldiers finished their cleanup, a pair of them gave Rei a ride to Raul and Sally's house where his parents and Raul and Sally anxiously awaited him.

"Oh, Rei," his mother Ruth said, grabbing a hold of him as he came in through the door. "We were so worried!"

"Thanks, Mom," Rei said, closing the door behind him. "It was pretty scary but I'm OK." He looked up at Raul whose bushy eyebrows and forehead were furrowed in a frown.

"Sorry about the truck, Raul," Rei said. "I'll pay for whatever damages there are. I gave my Mom all my money. You can take it from that stash."

"Do not worry about it, man," Raul said with a slight Brazilian accent. "My IED rider is up to date. It will all be covered. I am just glad you are OK."

Rei's father, Edward, put his hand on Rei's shoulder. "You gave us quite a fright, there, buddy," the older man said. "Your last day as a free man was almost your last day, period."

Rei laughed cynically. His parents parted and Sally Reynolds, the one-time love of Rei's life, stepped forward and gave him a hug. Sally was short, just a few inches over five feet with shoulder length brown hair, flecked with strands of gold. "Reinard Bierak," she said. "Leave it to you to almost go away and miss your own going away party."

"Yeah," Rei said, addressing the group. "That would be pretty sleek irony, huh?" He smiled sheepishly.

"I wouldn't call it that," Sally replied sarcastically but with no edge to her voice.

Since he was nearly two hours late, Rei's parents rushed him to the dining room table where the four of them had prepared what they called his last supper. Every inch of the table was covered by casseroles and serving dishes. It was literally every food that Rei ever liked or claimed he liked. There was pizza, ribs, steak, fried chicken, turkey legs, corned beef, egg rolls and other foods uncounted. The festive meal included wine, no pruno tonight, and a lot of laughing, mixed with the occasional tear.

For dessert, Ruth Bierak and Sally brought out three cakes, each with twenty five candles. Ruth made Rei blow out every one of the candles for each birthday they would never spend together. One cake was chocolate-covered banana cake, Rei's favorite. One was chocolate, chocolate-chip with fudge icing aka Death by Chocolate. The third was a cheesecake drizzled with strawberry syrup. Rei elected to have a healthy slice of each one even though he knew he'd catch holy hell at the Mission Center for gaining weight.

After dessert, Rei's parents ushered him into the spacious living room and made him sit by himself on the loveseat. Raul and Sally sat down on the sofa and held hands while Rei's parents stood before him. Rei's mother had her arms hidden behind her back.

"What's up?" he asked trying to peer behind his mother.

"We got you a little going away present," his mother said bringing her hands forward. She was holding out a box, roughly four by six inches, wrapped in gold foil. She handed it to Rei.

"Oy," Rei said, hefting the present. "You know I'm so close to my weight limit as it is," he opined. "What is it?"

"You know we'd never spoil a surprise," Rei's father said. "There's only one way to find out so go ahead and open it."

Rei tore open the paper. Inside was a shiny white cardboard box. Inside the white box was gray foam packing. And in the center of the foam packing was a gleaming, dark silicon blue rectangular object. Rei took it out of the box and inspected it along all sides.

"Is this what I think it is?" he asked, with a broad smile on his face.

"Yes!" his mother said. "It's a custom-built solid-state music slab, completely solar-powered. The earpieces clip on magnetically. It has no moving parts and they assured us it would survive for a thousand years. It's all your music in one tidy package!"

Rei jumped up and hugged his mother and father. "This must have cost you a bloody fortune," he said giddily.

"Well, actually, you paid for it, buddy," Edward said. "We didn't need your cash. We wanted to put some of it toward something that will remind you of us whenever you get to where you are going."

"This is amazing," Rei said. Then he frowned. "I think this is going to put me over, though, weight-wise," he muttered.

"It's already taken care of," his mother replied reassuringly. "We called down to Houston and gave them the exact weight of the slab and the headphones. They said you'd be over by not even fifty grams. They suggested you get rid of your sunglasses and that would be enough. What do you think? Is that OK?"

"Sure," Rei said. "This thing is worth a hundred pair of sunglasses." He sat down to examine the present more closely. He reached into the box, fished out the set of earbuds and placed them in his ears. He held up the other end of the cord, examining it closely. He found that merely waving the connector near the proper junction point on the slab caused it to snap in place magnetically. Rei pressed the upper right hand corner of the device and the front face lit up. The dim integrated menu displayed a variety of ways to access the music. He studied the symbology then instructed the slab to pick a song at random. Immediately he heard the stirring tones of "I Know You're Out There Somewhere" by the Moody Blues. As the music rose, he pressed the volume up control until it was blasting in his ears.

"This is so sleek," he shouted without realizing it. Everyone laughed at his inappropriate tone. Seeing their mirth, Rei grinned then removed the earbuds. He detached the connector and carefully placed the slab back into the foam packing along with the earbuds.

"Thank you, so much," he said in a normal voice. "I'll treasure this always."

"We're very proud of you, son," his father said. "Use it in good health."

Rei stood up and hugged his parents again.

After tolerating his hug for a moment, his mother spoke up. "Sit, sit," she commanded. "We have one more surprise for you. Compliments of Raul."

Rei looked over at Raul who saluted Rei with two fingers as Rei's mother left the room. Ruth soon returned with a small tray holding a chilled 375 ml bottle of ice wine and five champagne flutes.

Rei's eyes opened wide. "Ice wine?" he asked incredulously. "How did you…"

Raul smiled and leaned forward. "I may not have learned all the ways of your country yet but I am very familiar with how the black market works."

Ruth set the tray down and picked up the beautiful cobalt blue bottle. "It's from a winery on Lake Keuka in New York State," she said. "With all the global warming, Raul tells me they only had three bottles left in the whole world."

"Raul!" Rei said disapprovingly. "You shouldn't have."

"Well, I did," he said. "It is my pleasure. It is one of the perks of being a doctor. You may as well enjoy it."

Ruth made great ceremony out of pouring the slightly thickened pale yellow liquid from the sapphire bottle. Sally had contributed by putting the flutes in the freezer earlier to chill. Despite his protests, Rei had to admit the smuggled ice wine was exquisite. They took turns toasting each other and carrying on about a variety of topics until the bottle was long gone.

A little while later, Sally stood up and motioned to Rei to follow her out onto the deck. She walked to the railing and rested her elbows on the composite material crafted to look like weather-beaten wood. Rei came out and stood next to her, leaning up against the side, facing her. Tall bushes, co-mingled with gnarled trees formed a buffer between Sally's house and the neighbors on the far side of the woods. Fireflies flickered in the trees in an asynchronous pattern. Global warming had messed up their mating cycle so thoroughly, they came out year round trying to find a partner. It was an odd but beautiful sight.

"It's so weird," Sally said glancing up to look at the three-quarter Moon. "I don't even know how to feel. After today, none of us will ever see you again."

"It is weird," Rei said. "For me, it's kind of bittersweet. I mean, I have an adventure ahead of me but everyone I know, my parents, my friends, you…" Sally turned to look at Rei. He stooped down slightly and stared into her dark brown eyes intently. "I know you're married to Raul now," he said, "and I wish you two nothing but happiness but still…"

Sally snapped her fingers up to her lips. That stopped Rei from continuing. "There's no sense in rehashing the past," she said. "You wanted to go. I didn't. It's that simple. My father was thrilled to get you into the program after I told him about you. He said they would always have room for someone as brilliant as you."

"Aw, gee, Sally," Rei said. "You're going to make me blush."

"It's the truth, though. Getting the right mix of volunteers was important to them. You deserved it."

"Thanks," Rei said. He held his hands out, palms up. "In fact, I keep wanting to say I can never thank you enough but of course, when you think about it, it's literally the truth. It's almost like I'm not even here anymore." Rei sighed a long sigh. "Getting back to what I was saying earlier, I still remember there was a time when I thought you and I would spend the rest of our lives together."

"Come on, Rei," Sally chided. "Don't go all gloomy on me. You know what happened in Brazil. It changed me. It would change anyone. It gives you a different perspective. I almost died. After that, I decided I wanted to live my life in the here and now. Not betting it on some uncertain future. "

Rei turned and looked up at the sky. "I know. And I know we both agreed this was the best way. It's just that I'll never love anyone again the way I loved you. That part of my heart is kind of broken permanently."

"No it isn't," Sally said. "You're too good of a person to go through life without somebody to love." She pointed up in the general direction of the Moon. "Maybe the woman of your dreams is up there, waiting for you. Waiting to love you."

Rei focused on where Sally was pointing. On this night, the constellation Orion the Hunter was just to the southeast of the Moon. Light pollution from the city drowned out many of the stars that would have been seen in an earlier age. But Alnitak, Alnilam and Mintaka, the three stars in a row marking Orion's belt, were still very recognizable.

"The star you're pointing to is the grip on Orion's shield," Rei said, trying to be analytical. "I don't remember its name… Tabit maybe? But we're not going anywhere near there." He turned his head, scanning the horizon. "There," he said, pointing to the southwest. "That constellation down there, just over the trees, it's called Cetus the Whale. The bright star right in the middle is Tau Ceti. *That's* where we're headed. Ain't nobody there. And if they are, they're little and they're green."

Sally shrugged. "Says you." She paused for a moment as if she were listening to an inner voice then she took in a deep breath. "I know you didn't believe me when I told you this before. But almost dying made me a little bit psychic somehow. I'm telling you, I think your dream girl is waiting for you up there, somewhere. You just have to go and find her." Sally smiled warmly. "Or maybe she'll find you!" she added.

Rei laughed. "Wouldn't that be a hoot? We go to the stars and when we get there, there are already people? Nah," he said, shaking his head. "I'm just hoping for some grass and trees to start a colony. At this point, I think we'd settle for air."

"They wouldn't be sending you if they didn't think you had the odds stacked in your favor," Sally said. "You and the Arks are mankind's best chance just in case something really bad happens down here."

"And you're mankind's best hope as a cure-all for all the new diseases popping up," Rei said. He put his hand on her shoulder, stroking it gently. "You and your incredible adaptive immune system."

Sally's face reddened. Rei wasn't sure if it was embarrassment or something else. "I know," she said. "Sometimes I can't figure out if Raul is my husband or my doctor or my epidemiologist. They take blood samples, like, every week." She held out her forearm and showed Rei the bandage across the crook of her arm.

"So we're both trying to save mankind," Rei said. "Each in our own way."

"Maybe we are," Sally nodded but she did not appear to be completely convinced.

Rei held out his arms and Sally came forward. They hugged each other tightly for a long time as only former lovers could. Rei could feel every inch of her body against his frame. Out of sheer habit, he ran his hand down her back but had to stop himself before he went too far. The body pressing against him was once his but it would never be again. She belonged to someone else now and that was that.

As much as he did not want to, he forced them apart. As they let go, Sally put her palm up to his cheek and said, "I will always love you, Rei Bierak. I wish for nothing but good things for you, now and forever. No matter where you end up."

Rei reached his hand behind her head and tilted it forward so he could kiss her on the forehead. In every real way, Sally was his past. He let go and took one last look up at the stars. They were his future. That was where his destiny lie.

"Thanks, babe," he said, "same for you. But dead man walking here. I gotta get up early tomorrow. Let's go in so I can spend some time with everyone. For the last time. And thanks for having us over."

Sally nodded gamely. "It was the least we could do." She took Rei's hand and led him back into the house. For Rei, tomorrow was bearing down fast and while he did not realize it, everything he thought he knew about the universe was about to change forever.

Chapter 10

UPON ARRIVING IN THE GENERAL VICINITY OF DEUCADO, MINIMCOM dropped out of null-fold space and it wasn't long before he used a single, normal PPT tunnel to close the remaining distance to the planet. They entered into an east-to-west orbit and MINIMCOM instructed everyone to buckle in for re-entry. He was about to use his direct entry method of jumping to the surface when his preparations were interrupted by OMCOM.

"Rome. Rei," OMCOM's voice came from the grille. "Welcome back. While you were gone, I was able to utilize my workstations to piece together most of the details concerning the raid on Rome's library."

"Thanks but we don't need it anymore," Rome said. "Our mission was successful. We were able to get the names of the people involved." She turned and looked back at Bonnie who was strapped into the new chair that MINIMCOM had built for her. MINIMCOM had called it the 'navigator's chair' although Rei was fairly certain it was their computer friend's attempt at humor. Rome continued, "And Bonnie Mullen has returned with us. She even knows what they look like."

"We're headed to someone's house right now who might know where to find them," Rei added. "So we're good."

"Still, the information that I have acquired could be crucial to your investigation," OMCOM insisted.

"Thank you, OMCOM," Rome said, trying to put the computer at ease. "We will come see it right after we stop at Paul Chung's abode. Our sources tell us this is our best lead in tracking them down."

"But you really should look at what I have synthesized first," OMCOM said, uncharacteristically insistent. "It may have a bearing on what you do next."

"Look, OMCOM," Rei said firmly. "Rome said we'll come take a peek. Let us do our work first then we'll come see you."

"Very well," OMCOM replied. Rei could have sworn there was a hint of disappointment in OMCOM's voice but that would be impossible since their clone did not even have a personality module. A decisive click indicated OMCOM was no longer connected.

After punching a hole in the atmosphere of Deucado, MINIMCOM emerged within a waterspout over Lake Eprehem which died away as soon as the tunnel closed. The starship headed east, taking them to a landing strip on the outskirts of New Ark City.

One would think that Vuduri City would be the most futuristic and to some degree, it was. However, despite the fact that they had built their new city in a Star of David pattern instead of concentric rings, it was still just a Vuduri town. Ibbra City was sort of a mess. It had the widest variety of people but the construction styles were haphazard and mixed. It was actually Deucadia, home of the Deucadons, that was the most like you'd see on The Jetsons. While they had lost or forgotten much of the Essessoni technology, they had come up with some spectacular replacements and also had the largest group of any race on the planet.

New Ark City, on the other hand, wasn't really a city at all. It only consisted of some 400 individuals and was mostly residential. The Essessoni had the best all-around engineering skills and didn't mind borrowing liberally from Vuduri and Deucadon technology but nonetheless, it was more of a bedroom community. Its major advantage was that it was centrally located, conveniently placed near Rome's library. More importantly, Rome simply liked living there.

As they were leaving the ship, MINIMCOM spoke up through the grille.

"**Will you be requiring a livetar to accompany you?**" he asked.

Rei looked at Rome who shook her head.

"Don't think so, buddy," Rei said. "This should be pretty easy."

"**Very well,**" answered their friend and protector. "**You know where to reach me.**"

The three humans left the starship and it only took a few inquiries to find out where Paul Chung lived. Rei, Rome and Bonnie piled into a community aircar. Rome decided it would be easiest on Rei's back if she drove. Rei protested mildly but quickly surrendered the driver's seat to his wife. They traveled down a series of roads until they got to a sequestered area which the inhabitants had come to refer to as Fox Hollow. This was an odd name indeed as there were no foxes on Deucado but there were no rules here. That was what they called it.

As they drove up the ceramic-laden street, Rome pointed at the houses.

"Why are these houses so large?" she asked. "What would you do with all those rooms?"

Rei laughed quietly to himself. "Back on Earth, by the time we left, all the wealth of the world was in the hands of very few individuals or corporations. Most people struggled just to get by. Ever since we got here, everything has been handed to us. Some people had a harder time dealing with it than others. On this world, I guess this group of people wanted surroundings that make them feel rich, even though everything is free."

"I don't understand," Rome said.

"Everybody needs a touchstone," Bonnie offered.

"What is a touchstone?" Rome asked.

"It's a thing, metaphorically, that lets you measure the worth of something. I guess these people measure their worth by how large of a house they own."

Rome started to speak then decided to let it go. For as long as they lived, there would always be concepts and habits of Rei's people that she would never comprehend.

They drove down a wide street to a large cul-de-sac and circled around, stopping in front of the house identified as the Chung's. All three hopped out and walked up to the front door. Rome reached up and clanked the knocker several times.

A woman came to the door. She was fairly short, not much taller than Rome with blonde hair, cut in a page-boy style. She looked at the three of them. Her eyebrows raised when she saw Bonnie standing there. "Can I help you?" she asked.

Rei took one step forward. "I'm Rei Bierak, this is my wife, Rome and this is Bonnie Mullen."

"I know Bonnie," the woman said.

"Hi, April," Bonnie said. "How are you?"

"I'm fine," April Chung replied. "And as for you, Rei, I know who you and Rome are. Everybody knows who you are. What is it you want?"

"We're here to see Paul. Is he home?"

"No," April replied. "He's working today. He'll be home later if you want to come back."

"No, it's rather important," Rei said. "Where does he work?"

"He runs the lunch wagon down by the power plant," April replied. "They love his food and he enjoys making it."

"Oh, yeah," Rei said. "I probably should have known that. I think I've seen it." He put his hand on Rome's shoulder to guide her around. "Thanks, April," he said then he turned to walk away.

"Goodbye, April," Bonnie said then she followed them back down to the aircar.

As they were driving back the way they came, Rome asked, "Why do you even have a power plant? Isn't each house and building self-powered with a PPT generator like ours?"

"No," Rei answered. "With the rapid growth of Ibbra City and Deucadia, it was easier to build a central facility and just run cables there. We call our settlement New Ark City but you know it isn't really a city. Our people just want to help and this was something everybody needed and appreciated."

"It still makes no sense," Rome protested. "It is completely inefficient."

"It's the way they wanted it. I'm sure someday everybody will go back to being self-sufficient but maybe for now it's the Ibbrassati and Deucadon touchstone, like Bonnie said," Rei replied.

Rome shook her head. Rei persisted. "It makes them more comfortable."

"It's still inefficient," Rome grumbled as she crossed her arms across her chest. "If there is a single problem or interruption of energy flow, hundreds, thousands are affected instead of just one or two."

"Honey, that's the way they wanted it so that's the way they got it," Bonnie said. "To each his own."

"I suppose," Rome said, under her breath, deciding to focus on their destination.

Rome piloted the little aircar through the central industrialized section of New Ark City until they came to the power plant. It was a city block-sized building, built out of white Vuduri aerogel. Huge, thick cables exited from the side and disappeared into the ground. The air itself had a faint hint of ozone.

Looking around, Rei said, "I don't see the lunch wagon anywhere. Why don't we go inside and ask where it is?"

Rome and Bonnie concurred so the three of them entered the building through the wide set of doors on the side. Inside the building, the piercing odor of ozone was overwhelming. Rome fanned herself, trying to blow the smell away. Bonnie inhaled deeply, almost as if she relished it.

Rei was pleased to see that there were several Deucadons, clearly distinguishable by their distinctive dress, working alongside his fellow colonists. The Deucadons had spent half a millennia perfecting conduit technology and it was heartening to observe them giving of their expertise to his compatriots. At the core of the plant was the hydra-like form of a multi-branched PPT generator.

"I've never been here before," Bonnie said. "What is that thing?" she asked, pointing toward the waving conduits and tubes that resembled an upside down root system.

"That's a Vuduri power plant," Rei said. He turned to look at Rome. "Hey, this is just like the one you had back at Skyler Base. Doesn't that kind of debunk your centralization theory?"

"No," Rome said, still waving at her face. "That was the power plant for that building. If we had another building, we would have built a second plant."

"Oh," Rei said.

"How does it work?" Bonnie asked.

Rei pointed to the thick tubes, conduits and dense wires that split into branches which split into branches and so on back to the far wall. "If this were a lung, those thinner branches would be like the capillary system and those tips, the ones that are kind of blurry, would be the alveoli."

"I still don't understand," Bonnie said.

"The way the original OMCOM, we call him Planet OMCOM now, explained it to me; the tips of the tubes use Casimir pumps to produce a froth of unstable PPT tunnels. They only last long enough to split the neutral energy into a bit of positive and negative energy then they disappear. The wires and conduits collect the positive energy and run it down...somewhere."

"What happens to the negative energy?" Bonnie asked.

"OMCOM told me they just disperse into the atmosphere. I suppose it just moves air molecules from one place to another. No harm done."

"So you get free energy out of nothing," Bonnie said. "I'd always heard about it but never saw it up close. Isn't all that negative energy dangerous, though?"

"OMCOM did say that there would be a price to pay some day but he never told me what it was."

In front of them sat several two-story tall cylinders which Rei assumed were analogous to capacitors. He looked around and saw huge coils he figured were stationary magnetos. The magnetos would be responsible for converting the energy into electricity then conditioning it into the electrical stream that ran through the cables and out to the other communities.

The plant foreman saw them and came over to them. A quick inquiry indicated Paul's lunch wagon was on-premise but was located on the other side of the building. The three of them walked across the main floor and exited through a second set of doors on the far side of the plant.

In front of them was Paul Chung's lunch wagon. Rei chuckled to himself how closely it resembled one from his time on Earth. It even had wheels. The entire vehicle was plated in diamond-patterned shiny aluminum and looked fresh and clean. If nothing, Paul had a sense of humor because there was no earthly reason why he would fashion it so, otherwise. They walked up to the large side window and a man stepped forward to greet them. He had vaguely Asian features and although he was hidden from the waist down, Rome could tell he was a bit shorter than Rei.

"What can I get you folks?" he asked pleasantly. "Oh, Bonnie, hi," he said, somewhat surprised to see her.

"Hi Paul," Bonnie said. "This is Rei Bierak and Rome, his wife."

"I know who they are," he said. He nodded toward them. "So what can I do for you?"

"We're looking for David Troutman," Rome said, speaking up. "Do you know where we can find him?"

A dark fleeting expression passed over Chung's face. "No!" he said insistently. "What would make you think that?"

Bonnie spoke up. "Nick Greer said that you guys had a hoker game going back at your house and he and Troutman played with you sometimes."

"Yeah, sure," Chung said, "but that was a long time ago. Right after you guys," he pointed at Rei, "rounded up those Darwin people, he took off. I haven't seen him in ages."

"Are you sure?" Rei asked. "Do you have any idea where he might have gone off to?"

"No, none at all," he said. He looked off into the distance. "I thought that the rest of the Darwins turned themselves in. Wasn't he with that group?" He directed his question at Bonnie.

"No, he never made it," she said. "He's still here on Deucado."

Chung started to speak then stopped himself. His expression soured. "I'm a little busy right now. If you don't want anything to eat, why don't you get going? They're going to be taking a break pretty soon and I have to get ready."

Rome stepped forward and placed her hands on the counter. "Please," she pleaded. "It's very important. We think he tried to kill us. We do not want that happening again. What about Dan Steele? Do you know where he is?"

Chung's eyes widened and he shivered. "Sorry," he said. "Can't help you." He turned quickly and moved back into the dark interior of the truck, leaving Rei, Rome and Bonnie just standing there. "Good luck with your search," Chung called out as he disappeared into the recesses of his mobile kitchen.

"I don't understand," Rome said, craning her neck forward, trying to see in.

Rei put his finger up to his lips and waved for the two women to follow him. They circled around the outskirts of the power plant's main building back to where they had left the aircar parked.

"OK," Rei said. "Now you can talk."

Rome searched Rei's eyes. "He understood that we are in danger. Why would he just push us away? Why not try to help us?" A tear came to her eye.

Rei just shook his head. "It's obvious to all of us that he knows something but for whatever reason, he doesn't want to talk. We have to find another way."

"What other ways?" Rome turned to Bonnie. "You knew these men. Do you have any other ideas?"

Bonnie addressed Rei. "On all the police shows, whenever they were looking for someone, they used a sketch artist to draw pictures of the suspects. Then they canvassed the neighborhood. Do you think we can find somebody who could do that? I could describe to them exactly what Troutman and Steele look like. We could start with that."

"I'm pretty sure that can be arranged," Rei said, nodding.

Chapter 11

TRUE TO REI'S WORD, ON THE WAY UP TO ROME'S LIBRARY, MINIMCOM took Bonnie's description of Troutman and Steele and developed what Bonnie thought was a perfect likeness of each. David Troutman was tall, a full two meters, with red curly hair and a freckled complexion. Dan Steele was shorter, only six feet tall, a light-skinned black man who was powerfully built; all wiry muscle. MINIMCOM synthesized three photographs of their face and frame and Rei, Rome and Bonnie each took a set.

When they got to the library, MINIMCOM landed at his own private airstrip and instantiated a livetar who accompanied them across the broad central boulevard and into the parking lot in front of Rome's building. To their left were the commissary, dormitory and combination lecture hall/theater; the three buildings which were designed to be part of the original complex. Behind them stood the smaller geology lab and off in the distance, the new general science building loomed upwards, nearly finished.

They walked up the stairs to Rome's library and entered the main door. MINIMCOM indicated they should head to the left to the wing which was evolving into a small museum. Inside the room, on the right-hand wall were two full-sized Vuduri workstations. On the left hand wall was a glass case holding the Essessoni data slabs, the Deucadon's memory stick, Trabunel's journal and a stack of Vuduri data cubes. These original sources formed the foundation of Rome's historical studies. In a special pressurized case sat Silas Hiram's journal, a present from the Overmind of Helome thanking them for delivering the genetic material in the form of the Darwin contingent.

In a case at the back of the room, the hook that had been used to display Hanry Ta Jihn's handgun sat empty, along with another hook that had been used to hold up one of the Deucadon's invisibility cloaks. The other cloak remained where it had always been.

As they entered the room, OMCOM's livetar appeared with a whoosh and a pop.

"Thank you for making the time to come see me," the livetar said. Rei thought he caught a touch of sarcasm in the livetar's voice. Maybe some of Planet OMCOM's personality was beginning to seep through after all.

The all-white being took them over to one of the two workstations.

"The video cameras and microphones on these two workstations were active the entire time before, during and after the raid or whatever you wish to call it. I think burglary is the proper word although that typically implies breaking and entering. Since the library is never locked, there was no actual breaking in."

"Can you get on with it?" Rei asked with a hint of impatience.

"Of course," the livetar replied. "Unfortunately, the video feeds themselves were at the wrong angle. I could not get any images that I could present to you. I was only able to get a sense of where the persons were located in the room at any given point in time by the change in lighting and shadows. I have constructed an animation."

OMCOM showed them a floor plan of the library. A yellow dot appeared at the front door then extended to become a yellow line, indicating the path the intruders took. They didn't meander. They headed right for the museum area that Rei, Rome and Bonnie now occupied and went directly to the display cases.

"As you can see, they were very purposeful in their actions. They came in, they removed the objects then retraced their steps back outside."

"Not very useful," Rei said. "It just confirms your suspicion. They came here to steal and they got the gun and cloak."

"I agree that tracing their paths, in and out, of itself, is of no consequence," OMCOM said. "However, I was able to use the acoustical inputs to create essentially a three dimensional construct of the group as they entered the room. Very similar to your sonar vision, Rei."

"What do you mean by group?" Rome asked. "There were just the two of them, right?"

"No," OMCOM said. "There were three of them." The acoustical renditions showed three people moving through the room as gray specters. Two of the shapes appeared normal height or thereabouts. The third person was very short.

"Three?" Rei sputtered. "The tall one must be Troutman. The medium sized one must have been Steele. But who was the third?"

"I was able to use a series of transforms to extract their voices. She did not say much but I can play it for you."

"Sh, sh, she?" Rome stammered. "It was a woman?"

"Yes," OMCOM said.

The livetar played the recording. The woman only said two things. The first time OMCOM played the recordings, it was not very clear. After a few adjustments, the sound of the voice sharpened up. The woman's voice said, "You will only need one cloak."

OMCOM's animation indicated one of the two taller beings reaching in the case. At that point, the woman said, "Put the handgun back. It belonged to Hanry Ta Jihn. You do not need it."

One of the two men growled at her that they did and that was the end of it.

Rei sat down heavily at the seat by the workstation.

"You heard that, right?" Rei inquired of Rome. "The accent?"

"Yes," Rome said sadly.

"What?" Bonnie asked. "What's so special about that woman's voice?"

"She's Vuduri," Rei said. "Our two would-be killers have a Vuduri woman helping them."

Rome strode over to the other workstation and sat down.

"What are you going to do?" Bonnie asked.

"I am going to contact the Overmind," Rome said defiantly. "If she is Vuduri, he will know who it is."

Bonnie started to speak but Rome held up her hand. She closed her eyes and put her fingers to her lips to make sure that everyone remained quiet.

"Hello," Rome said.

"Hello, Rome," the Overmind answered back. Over the last year or so, it had grown in strength and vitality as the number of Vuduri on Deucado had increased and they found a way to work with it without becoming a slave to it. *"I was very sorry to hear what happened to Rei. I am glad he is now up and around."*

"Thank you," Rome replied. *"That is very kind."*

"Do you know who perpetrated this assassination attempt?"

"Yes. Two Essessoni," Rome said. *"They were part of the Darwin group."*

"You have identified them? This is good," the Overmind replied. *"Have you located them yet?"*

"No," Rome said.

"Is there anything I can do to help?"

"Perhaps," Rome replied. *"That is why I am contacting you. There is something I need to ask you."*

"Anything."

"We have reason to believe they were being aided by a Vuduri woman. Were you aware of that?"

"No," the Overmind replied, *"but if she was disconnected, how would I be?"*

"Please reach out and see if any of your communicants have any knowledge of this or who this woman might be. Whatever her motivation would be for aiding them, it would be impossible to keep it a secret from other Vuduri."

There was a small delay and then the Overmind spoke up again. *"I am sorry to report to you that there is no hint of such a woman. It is possible that she has remained disconnected since the act was perpetrated."*

Rome opened up her eyes and stared around the room at the humans and livetars.

"The Overmind has no knowledge of such a woman," she said. "He was unable to detect a person with motives before the crime or since."

"How can that be?" Bonnie asked. "I thought you were all mind-connected?"

"They are," Rei said. "And they can't lie. But they sure can keep secrets."

Rome held her hand up and closed her eyes again.

"Is there anything at all, anything amiss that you could tie into this? Our lives depend upon it."

"No," the Overmind replied. *"You and Rei are beloved across this entire planet. There is not a single Vuduri here who has ill will toward you. From my understanding, the same is true of the Essessoni, Deucadons and the mandasurte. No, whoever this is, she has had no experiences that she has shared with me or any of the Vuduri. That or she was never a part of my samanda to begin with."*

"Not part of your samanda?" Rome scrunched up her face. *"How could that be?"*

"I cannot answer your question," the Overmind replied, *"but it is the only explanation I can postulate that fits the facts."*

"Hmm," Rome said. *"I will have to think about that."*

"I am sorry that I cannot be of more help," the Overmind said wistfully.

"I appreciate your efforts," Rome said sadly. *"We will have to find them another way."* With that, Rome disconnected. She looked up at Rei. "The Overmind has nothing to offer. He speculated that perhaps this woman never belonged to his samanda in the first place."

"How could that be? Do you think she was Cesdiud?"

Rome shrugged. Rei looked around the room and stopped when he made eye contact with Bonnie. "You mentioned the police shows we used to watch. What would they do now?"

"They'd haul the first witness back in and hook him up to a lie detector," Bonnie said. "Try and catch him with an inconsistency. That's all it usually takes to break them."

"What is a lie detector?" Rome asked, standing up.

"It's a machine they hook up to you and it records the person's vital signs during an interrogation. Inside a person's head, there are all sorts of things happening that might indicate their words were not the truth."

"Inside their heads, you say?" Rome offered. "Like the Espansor bands?"

"The bands are way better," Rei said. "I wonder if we could make Paul Chung put one on and you could question him."

OMCOM stepped forward and said, "You may not need to."

"I don't understand," Rome replied.

"Rome, within your head are all the components that make up the Espansors. You could effectively build a one-way device with just your brain alone."

"How?" Rei asked skeptically. "How would she do that?"

"If Rome uses two sets of non-matched PPT transceivers, she could bathe her subject, or their brain more specifically, with enough gravitic radiation such that her EM link could pick up the electrical activity in the subject's brain and use a feedback loop to cause an equivalent resonance in her own brain. It would be identical to the Espansor bands but without any hardware. She would become what your people refer to as a telepath."

"You do know I only have one functional set of PPT transceivers," Rome pointed out.

"I can reactivate a second set," MINIMCOM said matter-of-factly. "It would not be a problem."

"No, you cannot," Rome countered. "Once they are deactivated, they can never be reactivated again."

"With your Vuduri technology, that may be true," MINIMCOM corrected her. "But with my null-fold, I have the capability of reactivating them again.

"Impossible," Rome scoffed.

"Not impossible," MINIMCOM replied. "Back on Helome, when I was in the science lab with you and Virga, I saw your genetic chart. You actually have the potential for three sets of autonomous PPT transceivers. Not only can I reactivate your original connection to the samanda of Earth, I could even activate the PPT transceivers that would connect you to MASAL's samanda."

"I'll pass on MASAL's, if you don't mind," Rome said with some disgust. She cocked her head. "You can really do that? Reactivate me?"

"Are you sure you want to do that?" Rei asked. "When Estar did it to me, it hurt like hell. And I remember the scream you let out when Pegus reconnected you."

"The normal method of activating transceivers is based upon negative energy generators," MINIMCOM explained. "My null-fold splits negative energy into a real and imaginary component. It is the imaginary component that causes the pain. The real part should be painless. May I?"

Rome thought about it for a moment then nodded. The livetar stepped forward and put his hands over her temples. After a moment, he stepped back. "It is done," he said. "You now have two completely functional sets of PPT transceivers. You are the first Vuduri in the history of mankind who can now connect at will to two different worlds. If you were to go back to Earth, you could join the Overmind there."

"Really?" Rome said, putting her hands to her temples. "I don't feel any different. OMCOM, are you saying I can now perform the functions you ascribed."

"To evolve into a true telepath, you must train yourself," OMCOM offered.

"How would I train myself to do something that has never been done before?"

OMCOM stepped forward. "The methodology is very straightforward. You must find a willing subject and they must allow you to guide their thinking completely. The simpler the better. You will then use your heightened senses until you are able to lock into their thoughts. Once you do that, they will not be able to mislead or tell untruths."

"A living lie detector, huh?" Rei said admiringly. "That is so sleek!"

"Where would I find such a willing subject?" Rome asked innocently, ignoring Rei's comment.

Both livetars lifted their arms and pointed to Rei.

"Me?" he asked. He shrugged. "Sure, why not?"

"How do I do this?" Rome asked.

In answer to her question, OMCOM took Rome aside and whispered to her, giving her very detailed instructions. Rome's eyebrows shot up in surprise. She whispered back to OMCOM. Eventually she nodded, indicating she got it.

Rome had a strange look to her eye as she had Rei grab the remaining invisibility cloak. The three humans then left for the quick journey back to New Ark City.

Chapter 12

AFTER ARRIVING IN THE VICINITY OF BINODA AND FRIDONE'S HOUSE, MINIMCOM landed nearby and lowered his cargo ramp. Rei and Rome walked down the ramp, accompanied by OMCOM who decided to send his livetar along. They all agreed it would be best if Bonnie remained onboard MINIMCOM.

After a quick bite to eat, Rome led Rei into her parents' bedroom, walking him over to the bed. Gently, she had him sit down. She knelt down in front of him and took his hands in hers then looked up into his eyes.

"Bonnie is spending the night in MINIMCOM," she said. "OMCOM's livetar is standing guard by the door and has set up surveillance devices around the perimeter of the house. We are safe and alone for the evening."

"OK," Rei said, smiling. "Now what?"

Rome picked up each of Rei's hands and kissed first one then the other very tenderly.

"Mau emir, I love you more than anything and I know that you love me."

"Of course," Rei said uncertainly. "What's that got to do with you learning to be a telepath?"

"No Vuduri could ever understand this but our love travels in all dimensions. Our minds, our hearts, our bodies."

Rei nodded.

"When we make love, it is not simply a sex act; it is the very definition of our expressing our love for each other via the flesh. As my lover and my friend and my Asborodi Cimponeti, you are always so careful to show this to me in, how should I say this, taking care of my needs?"

"Well, sure," Rei said.

"In order for me to train my brain to use these new capabilities, I need your brain absolutely blank. You need to think only the most primitive of thoughts and I must be able to control them. OMCOM was very explicit regarding the training. He and I agreed that sexual pleasure is by far the simplest to effect. I must do things that I know will bring you pleasure and I must sense that pleasure. "

"Well, I think I can cooperate," Rei said with a goofy grin on his face. "We've done this before."

"No. This time must be different. Tonight, I need you to think of nothing else other than yourself. You cannot think about me at all." Rome squeezed Rei's hands for emphasis.

"What do you mean? How do I not think about you?" Rei asked, gazing down at his beautiful wife.

"You can think about me but I do not want you to consider my needs whatsoever. You must allow me to attend only to your own pleasure. You must be completely and totally selfish."

"Why?" Rei said with some protest. "I don't know if I can do that."

"For this to work, you must. It is only for one night. Please? Can you do this for me?"

Rei cocked his head, looking at Rome askew. "Let me get this straight. You're demanding, for your training, that I just lie back and let you do all the work?"

"Exactly," Rome said with a smile. "Do you think you can do that for me?"

Rei laughed. "I'll muddle through it somehow."

"Excellent," Rome said. She stood up and helped Rei to his feet. Very carefully but very sensuously, she removed Rei's electrostatic blouse to reveal the miniature PPT tunnel underneath.

"Don't stick your hands in there," Rei said, pointing to where his chest should have been.

"We must remove the vest," Rome said. "You can be without it for one night."

"OK," Rei said, "but be very careful. I don't want you losing a limb."

"I will be careful," Rome replied. She unclasped the leather-like thongs along the sides and Rei helped her lift the vest up and over his head and put it off to the side. Rei started to unclasp his pants and Rome slapped his hand away.

"Allow me," she said as she began to flood his brain with gravitic radiation emitting from her dual set of active PPT transceivers. "Everything must be so I can measure the effects."

"OK," Rei said, shrugging. He watched in amusement as Rome removed his trousers. After that was complete, paying extra attention

107

to make sure he did not flex his back, Rome had him sit back down on the edge of the bed.

Rome removed her jumpsuit in the closest thing she could do to approximate a striptease. Noting that it had the desired effect, she knelt down and began her training in earnest.

To her credit, despite the distractions, Rome was every bit the scientist, performing tiny experiments and noting the results. She had been inside of Rei's head so many times, she was already familiar with the terrain. But this was different. Unlike with the bands, she found she could direct Rei's thoughts with very simple actions. It was fascinating to her to see that things she always thought Rei enjoyed, some of them were very pleasurable and others were not as important. She discovered some things that even Rei did not know he enjoyed. She was able to sense when certain motions strained his back which allowed her to alter her actions instantaneously to reduce the strain.

Even as she was applying her ministrations, Rome knew this would ultimately be the end of the Vuduri in their current form. The very best of them had tried to eschew the flesh. They tried to deny their animal origins and this was a complete mistake. Humans were human and they had to embrace every part that defined the species. To reject the physical, as most of the Vuduri had done, was to reject their humanity. Rome knew that she had to communicate this to them, to take them back to something less and at the same time, something more. But that would be another day.

As she tried different lovemaking positions, frequencies and intensities, Rei's brain gave her animalistic feedback in a way that his voice, his utterances, his touch never could. Rei's mind blazed with love and affection for his wife, combined with exploding sensations. Rome was so far inside his brain, it was almost as if she was making love to herself.

After a while, Rome had all the information she needed but she did not stop. Just like with the bands, there came a point where there was no longer a conscious difference between them as their souls intertwined and merged. What could not be possible with any other human being was routine territory to Rome; not that that made it any less remarkable. The man beneath her was her gift from the heavens. What they had was beyond love. They were one. Forever and always.

***

Some time later, after it was all over, a fully-trained Rome lay next to Rei, on her back, staring up at the ceiling. She was breathing heavily but that did not prevent her from holding Rei's hand tightly. One of the things she discovered was that she needed physical contact with her subject to truly delve into their minds at its fullest.

"That was amazing," Rei said, also completely out of breath. "I've never experienced anything like that before in my life." He turned toward Rome. "You were incredible."

Rome twisted toward Rei and smiled. "I have accomplished my goal but I must say that I enjoyed it as well." She became silent for a moment then shook her head. "I thought of what it all means when we started. My people, the Vuduri, have no idea what such ties can represent. The emotional and the physical. It's such a loss. Some day they must learn if they want to have meaningful lives."

Rei reached up and kissed her hand. "Their loss, my gain," he said.

Rome shrugged. "Are you ready to go to sleep now?" she asked.

"Sure," Rei said in all sincerity.

Rome's eyes widened. She was still holding Rei's hand and his thoughts were crystal clear to her. "You want to go again?" she asked incredulously, propping herself up on her elbow. "Really?"

Rei smiled sheepishly. "I guess you really can read my mind, huh?"

***

The next morning, before heading out, a tired Rei and Rome sat at Binoda's dining table, having coffee.

"It's great that your parents learned to like coffee," Rei said, holding up a cup. "Saved me a lot of effort."

"I agree," Rome replied. "Now that I am a living lie detector, as you put it, how do we go about exploiting this ability to find the people trying to kill us?"

"Well, like Bonnie said, the first thing we do is go back to see Paul Chung. We all know he has more information than he let on."

"Of course," Rome said. "We will be able to get the absolute truth from him."

Rei looked at her and wagged his finger. "Uh, before we start," he said, "you probably need to know a little something about the lie detectors we had back in my day. They were called polygraphs and they weren't foolproof. People used to get away with lies all the time."

"What do you mean?" Rome asked him. "If that was the case, they couldn't have been very good in the first place."

"No, there's kind of an art to lying. This isn't anything a Vuduri could understand. You're all so used to having people inside your brains, you never perfected the method." Rei looked around. "Here, I'll show you," he said. "Put your hands on the table."

Rome did so.

"Now ask me something simple, like, what's your name?"

"OK," Rome said. "What is your name?"

"Brave Counsel," Rei answered.

Rome screwed her face up in surprise. "Your name is Rei Bierak," she said. "I know this."

"You think you do. Now take my hands, turn on your lie detector and ask me the same question. Make sure you are good and connected."

Rome reached forward and flipped her hands upside down, palms up. Rei put his hands within hers.

"You're in my brain, right?" he asked.

Rome nodded. "I feel the connection."

"Good. Now ask me the exact same question again."

"What is your name?" Rome asked, closing her eyes to concentrate on Rei's answer.

"Brave Counsel," Rei answered again. Rome opened her eyes in shock. "You are telling the truth. I, I don't understand."

Rei smiled. "My given name is Reinard, which means brave counsel. I think it's German. My parents were always a little weird that way."

"But I asked you your name. How could you answer the wrong thing?"

"I didn't," Rei said. "I chose to interpret your question differently than you intended. I answered the question I made myself believe you were asking and I answered it truthfully."

Rome harrumphed. "If I can't tell if you are telling the truth about such a simple thing, of what use is this new ability."

"We'll figure that out. Let's try another one." Rei pulled his hands away from Rome's. "Ask me what girl is the love of my life."

Rome's face lit up. This one would be easy. Rei put his hands back into hers. "What girl is the love of your life?" Rome asked.

Rei leaned forward and stared into Rome's eyes. "It was Sally Reynolds," he answered, deadly serious.

"What!?" Rome cried out, completely taken aback. She knew categorically that Rei was telling the truth. "Not me? I am not the love of your life?" Tears started welling up in her eyes. She tried to pull her hands away from Rei but he tightened his grip on them.

He said, "of course you are. I said 'was', not 'is'. And besides, you asked me what girl. Romey, trust me, you are every bit a woman, not a girl. I simply answered the question I made myself believe you asked."

Once again, Rome realized he was telling the truth.

"What do I do?" she asked sadly. "How can I know anything if the way I ask a question allows the other person to lie or mislead?"

"From what I can tell, you shouldn't be asking any questions at all. Just say words. Let their minds work against them. Their thoughts will betray them."

"I don't understand."

"I'll give you an example. Ask me if I know your father."

"Of course you do," Rome said huffily.

"So ask me then."

"Do you know my father?" Rome squeezed Rei's hands tightly.

"No," Rei answered in all earnestness. Rome was shocked. Rei was telling the truth.

"This is not possible!" she exclaimed. "I know you know my father."

"Because once again, you don't know how I interpreted the question. From my perspective, when I think about it, nobody *really* knows anybody. Well, maybe except you and me. There's too much depth. People only scratch the surface. Even me and your father."

Rome was breathing heavily. "I thought this was going to be the answer to all of our difficulties."

"It will be. It's easy," Rei said. "Look into my mind and just say your father's name."

Rome looked at him warily and said, "Fridone." And there it was. The image of her father appeared within Rei's mind along with the warmth of his affection for the man. Instantly, several flashbacks came to Rei of the times they had spent together. Some good, some under not the best of circumstances."

"Now," Rei said, as he saw Rome nodding. "Do I know your father?"

"Yes," Rome said, beaming. "I see now. I do not ask anything. I just give you reason to think about something."

"Exactly," Rei said. "We Essessoni have spent our whole lives learning how to live within our heads. You have to come in without them putting up a guard. That way they can't use their skills or defenses."

He pulled his hands out from Rome's and touched his temple. MINIMCOM's livetar appeared with Bonnie standing right next to him.

Bonnie looked around to get her bearings. "What's the plan?" she asked. "Did it work?"

"Here," Rei said, pulling out a chair. "Sit down for a moment."

"Sure," Bonnie said.

"Do you want a cup of coffee?" Rei asked.

"I'd love one," Bonnie said. Rei got up and left the table. He returned a moment later with another cup. After Bonnie prepared her coffee and took a sip, she set the cup down.

Rome reached forward and held her hands out, palms up. "Will you put your hands in mine?" she asked. "I have found this works best if I am in physical contact with my subject."

"Sure," Bonnie said and she did so.

Rome looked at her face and said one word, "Edgar." Bonnie frowned but said nothing. However, what had transpired was vividly clear to Rome, like a movie of the mind. The depth of Edgar's depravity shocked Rome. It took a moment for her to recover.

"The first time you went to see him in prison, he raped you," Rome said sympathetically. "Even after all you had been through. I'm so sorry," she said.

"How did you know?" Bonnie asked, pulling back. "I never told anyone."

"I am practicing my new skills," Rome answered matter-of-factly. Then, with more sympathy in her voice, she said, "that is why you never went back to see him again."

Bonnie sighed. "He was a pig. I hope he rots in that cell."

Rome nodded. The images she saw in Bonnie's mind matched her words exactly.

Rome squeezed her hands in support. "Now, another name," Rome said. "Sussen."

Immediately, the image of the Vuduri woman with the mismatched eyes became clear. Bonnie thought back to the day Sussen supposedly came to 'inspect' the Onsira ranch. Rome felt Bonnie's overwhelming sadness upon discovering the children were gone the next day. Bonnie knew in her heart that Sussen was responsible for stealing them away. She just could never prove it. Gemen was gone that day. There was no evidence that Sussen was ever there. Virga and the rest of the Vuduri gave Bonnie the benefit of the doubt but nothing was ever done.

"I believe you," Rome said. "Did you see her ship? Was it large enough to transport all the children at one time?"

Bonnie cocked her head. "What? How did you? No, I never saw it," she said. It was crystal clear that she was telling the truth. Again, waves of sadness echoed in Bonnie's mind as she thought back to how much she missed her babies.

Rome gave Bonnie a moment to compose herself. "I would like you to try and lie to me now," Rome said.

"Huh?" Bonnie replied. "Why?"

"Rome needs to experiment," Rei offered.

"OK."

"How do you feel about Gemen?" Rome asked.

Bonnie tilted her head. "Nothing, really," she said. "He's deadly dull as a partner."

Rome looked into Bonnie's heart and saw that this was not the truth. Bonnie actually was very fond of Gemen but only as a friend. They had slept together a couple of times but he was so reserved, he did not fill the void in Bonnie's heart. That had been fulfilled by taking care of the Onsira babies. Rome watched as the play of emotions swirled around in Bonnie's brain. Everything in Bonnie's world led back to that singular event.

Rei was right. It was all so clear to her now. Rome just had to raise the idea of something and let the person's thoughts flow naturally. Pointed questions would not work with the Essessoni. But the power of suggestion would.

Rome looked over to Rei and nodded. *"I understand now,"* she said to him silently. *"This will work."*

"Awesome," Rei said mentally. Then out loud, he said, "Ready to get this show on the road?"

Rome nodded enthusiastically.

Chapter 13

THE VUDURI CALENDAR DID NOT ACKNOWLEDGE SUCH THINGS AS weekends. For the most part, they defined their lives in terms of their jobs and there was no reason to take a day off. However, the Essessoni had no such restrictions. Since the Vuduri week was normally ten days long, the Essessoni had arbitrarily picked Iodemi, Nifemi and Tazemi, the last three days of the Vuduri week as their weekend. They used those days to rest, relax and recreate.

Today was Iodemi so when Rei, Rome and Bonnie went searching, their best guess to find Paul Chung was going to be at his home. MINIMCOM flew them directly there, landing right in the middle of the large cul-de-sac. Thoughtfully, he turned on his stealth shield so as to not frighten the other residents. The starship instantiated a livetar who accompanied the three humans down the cargo ramp and up the walkway to Paul Chung's house.

Rei lifted the knocker and rapped three times. This time, it was Paul Chung himself who answered the door.

"You three again?" he said. "What is it this time? I already told you I didn't know anything."

"May we come in?" Rome asked.

"Why?" Paul asked, placing his hand across the doorway rather aggressively.

Rome pointed inside. "While you say that you do not know where Troutman or Steele are located now," she said, "it is possible that you might have some information that we could use. Information you may not even be aware of."

"I'm sorry, but I don't think I can help you," Chung said, not budging.

MINIMCOM strode forward, gently pushing Rome aside. He leaned his head down until it was inches away from Paul's face. "`May we come in, sir?`" the livetar asked in a loud voice. Somehow it didn't really sound like a question.

Chung looked up at the two-meter tall living shell, dressed all in black. There was nothing but darkness behind MINIMCOM's eye slits and that somehow made him appear even more menacing. Paul decided discretion was the better part of valor. "What the hell," he said, "come on in."

He stepped aside and the party of four entered. Chung led them to the dining room and waited patiently while the humans took a seat. Paul himself sat down at the head of the table with Rome to his left. Once he was settled, MINIMCOM came over to stand by his right side and remained standing. Rome leaned forward and put her hand on his shoulder then spoke in a low voice. "Troutman," she said.

"Troutman what?" Chung replied but his mind was already awhirl with thoughts and memories. Rome had to fight from grinning. It was like one of Rei's movies. Chung's mind played out his history and events so clearly, it was amazing. Finally, Rome understood his reluctance to cooperate.

"He threatened you, didn't he?" Rome asked. "No, wait. It wasn't him. It was Steele! You saw both of them, didn't you?"

Chung's eyes grew wide. "How did you…" he stopped speaking.

"Is your wife here?" Rome asked, louder this time.

"Yea…yes," Paul replied.

"April?" Rome called out. "Can you come out here please?"

The petite blonde came into the room from the kitchen. "I thought I heard someone at the door. What's going on?"

Rome stood up but kept her hand on Paul's shoulder. "Your husband used to play hoker, house poker with David Troutman and several others." Rome looked down at Paul then back to April again. "After the Darwin people were exiled, Paul claims he never saw them again. But both Steele and Troutman were here not too long ago."

Chung started to rise. MINIMCOM placed his hand on Chung's other shoulder and gently pushed him down again. The livetar's hand was like a rod of steel.

"Paul, is this true?" April asked accusingly.

"Yes," Chung said sadly. "Steele said he would hurt you and Perry if I told anybody anything. I'm sorry."

Rome looked up at April. "We intend to track them down and apprehend them. We need Paul to give us as much information as possible. It will help facilitate matters."

"Steele?" April said, shivering. "I only met him once. He was awful."

"Yes," Rome replied. "We have heard. Once they are in custody, they will be extradited off this world. They would never be a danger to anyone again. The quicker we find them, the quicker this will happen. So for your own safety and that of your son, please encourage your husband to cooperate."

April walked over to Paul. MINIMCOM stepped back out of her way.

"Paul, honey," she said. "These people have risked their lives ten times over to save us, our world, the whole human race. I think we owe it to them to help them."

A tear came to Chung's eye. "I just wanted to make sure you were safe," he said. He hung his head. "OK," he muttered reluctantly. "I'll talk."

"Thank you," Rome said, sitting back down. However, she did not remove her hand from his shoulder.

Chung looked down at the table. Finally, he raised his eyes up to regard the group. "After the whole Darwin thing went down, Troutman disappeared. That part is true. And at the time, I really did think he was with the group that surrendered. But a few months ago, in the middle of the night, he came here."

"Why?" Rei asked.

"He said they were getting into some things that he no longer wished to be a part of. He asked me if he could hang out here for a few days until things blew over."

"I didn't know that," April said. "I never saw him."

Paul looked up at his wife. "That's because Steele was at the door no more than an hour later," he said. "He barged right in and grabbed Troutman. He took him into the other room…" Chung pointed to the living area. "The discussion got pretty heated and in the end, Troutman went with him."

"Did they say anything that could help us locate them?" Rome asked.

"I couldn't make out most of what they said but they did mention Ur several times."

"Ur?" Rei asked. "The resort city?"

"Yeah, that Ur," he said.

"I didn't think any of the Darwin people ever ventured that far south," Bonnie interjected.

"What was their reason for mentioning it? Were they going there?" Rome asked.

"I can't tell you. They didn't know that I heard them and I wasn't about to ask. As they were leaving, Steele told me to forget that I ever saw them. That's when he threatened me and my family. He said they needed to disappear and I'd better not be the reason why people found them."

"And you didn't see fit to mention this to anyone?" Rome asked. Chung's mind churned over his worries regarding the safety of his family.

"No, I figured what harm could two men do?" he answered. Rome knew better. Chung was conflicted the whole time.

"That is not the truth," Rome said. "But I do understand. You cared too much about your family to take the chance."

Chung looked at Rome for a long time then down at her hand. "How are you doing this?" he asked. "I mean, I know you Vuduri have your voodoo but it doesn't work with us Essessoni, does it?"

"Rome is very special," Rei said proudly. "Anything else, sweetheart?" he directed to Rome.

Rome looked at Paul intently then shook her head. "Those are the salient facts we need. That's all he knows."

"OK then," Rei said, standing up. Everyone else took that as their cue to get up as well.

"Thank you, Paul," Rome said, rising in place. She stepped behind her chair and pushed it in, under the table. Suddenly, she snapped her fingers. She reached over and touched Paul's cheek. "One other thing," she said. "Do you know if Troutman or Steele established a relationship with a Vuduri woman?"

"Not to my knowledge," Chung replied, ignoring the fact that Rome appeared to be caressing him. "As far as I knew, neither of them cared too much for your people."

Rome nodded to Rei that it was the truth. "We have enough," she said. She walked over to April and held her hand out. April Chung took Rome's hand and shook it. The information flowed like a torrent into Rome's brain.

"Everything will be alright," Rome said, reassuringly. "You and your husband and child will be safe. No one will know that you provided this information. And after we capture these two men, it won't matter in any event."

April nodded. "I know you'll take care of them. We all believe in you."

"Thank you," Rome said, releasing her grip and they left the house.

As soon as they got outside, Rome tugged on Rei's shoulder.

"What?" Rei asked.

Rome asked, "Do you think I have a fever?"

Rei bent over and kissed her on the forehead. "No," he said. "You're fine. Do you feel sick?"

"No," Rome said. She furrowed her brow. "Do I radiate more heat than a regular Essessoni?"

Rei pulled his head back, confused. "No more than anybody else," he said. "What's going on?"

Rome shook her head. "Even during his most stressful times, Paul kept thinking to himself that I was really hot compared to his wife. What does that mean?"

Rei and Bonnie laughed.

"Why is that funny?" Rome asked.

"It means he thought you were really attractive," Bonnie said.

Rei held his hand up. "Yes, Romey. Sexually."

"I don't understand," Rome said. "I…" She stopped short. "Oh!" She cocked her head. "Do you think I'm 'hot'?" she asked her husband.

"Romey, if you were any hotter, you'd be incandescent," Rei said with a smile on his face.

Rome nodded definitively. "I don't know why it matters to me. It shouldn't but it makes me feel good."

"It should, honey," Bonnie said. "If I had your body and face, I'd be running this world."

Rome shrugged. She pointed and they headed toward MINIMCOM.

Chapter 14

AS MINIMCOM FERRIED THE GROUP TO THE SOUTH AND WEST, REI looked over the likenesses of Troutman and Steele that MINIMCOM had fashioned. "If you ever decide to retire as a starship, and renounce your career as a surgeon, you could go to work as a sketch artist for the police," he addressed toward the grille.

"Thank you," MINIMCOM replied. "I would say you flatter me but in this case, you are correct."

"Police?" Rome asked.

"Oh, yeah," Rei said. "Ain't got none of those, do we?"

As instructed, rather than flying over the huge crater lake, MINIMCOM flew low along the shore, curving around until he was headed due west. They passed the vineyard that some of Rei's compatriots had established then they passed over a rocky stretch. Far off in the distance was a tiny object, rising above the horizon that Rei figured was "The Hand" of Ur. It was supposed to be spectacular but he had never actually seen it up close.

"We have to comb the entire city of Ur," he said. "They couldn't operate without somebody seeing them. Maybe they had help down there."

"Do you think it might have been one of the other people on that list we found?" Rome asked. "After all, it was entitled candidates."

"I don't know," Rei answered, "My name was on there and I wasn't of much use to them."

"What about the others?" Rome asked.

"We can check." Rei addressed the grille mounted on the front of the console. "OMCOM, do you read?"

"Yes," came a deeper voice.

"On that list we found called Darwin Candidates, besides me and Paul Chung, what were the last two names?"

An image of the Darwin list appeared in the central display.

"Wally Stanislaw and Andrea Grenmuller," replied the computer.

Rei rubbed his chin. "I didn't really know Andrea, what does it say about her?"

Even though the contents of the entry were displayed on the screen, OMCOM read it out loud. "Grenmuller, Andrea," intoned the library computer. "Brilliant mathematician. Would be really useful in helping solve engineering equations for new Vook materials. DT assigned to swing her but was rejected. May try again later."

"DT?" Rome observed. "That sounds like they are referring to a person. Could that stand for David Troutman? What else does it say about her?"

"That is the only entry on her," replied OMCOM.

"Any hint where, or when?" Rei asked. "Some way we can locate her?"

"I said that is the only entry on her," OMCOM insisted in a slightly imperious manner.

Rei let out a burst of air. "OK, the other one, Wally Stanislaw. I know him. He always seemed like a stand-up guy to me. What does it say about him?"

"Stanislaw, Wally," read the library computer. "Excellent geologist. Skill set vastly superior to anyone on staff. Has been approached obliquely about joining the plan but seemed fairly resistant. Would be a great aid to the mining program. Re-approach in a year."

Rome tapped the display. "I know him as well. I recognized his name immediately."

"How do you know him?" Rei asked.

"He was one of the very few Essessoni who came to me for language lessons. I taught him Vuduri."

"And that's it?"

"No," Rome replied. "OMCOM, isn't he one of the scientists you're supporting in the geology wing?"

"Yes," replied OMCOM. "He has his own subscription channel. His research regarding the geophysical history of the planet has been extremely illuminating. He has found a wide variety of interesting objects buried deep under the ground. He believes there may have once been other kinds of life forms on this planet."

"Really?" Rei asked. "How come nobody ever mentioned this before?"

Rome turned to her husband. "Several scientists have approached me about having their own research resources within OMCOM. I have said yes on each occasion but I have not been monitoring the information flow very closely."

"Well, it's probably a dead-end anyway," Rei said. "He doesn't sound like he had much interaction with them in any event."

"If you would prefer, you can ask him yourself," OMCOM offered. "I see from MINIMCOM's coordinates that you are within a few kilometers of his current research site."

Rei looked at Rome who shrugged. He turned to Bonnie. "What do you think?"

"I think no stone unturned," Bonnie replied. "How could it hurt?"

"OK," Rei said. "MINIMCOM, can you take us to where Wally is working?"

"**Already there**," MINIMCOM replied. "**Just buckle in for the landing as this is somewhat rocky terrain.**"

Rei and Rome buckled into the pilot and co-pilot's seat respectively. Bonnie strapped herself into the "navigator's" chair that MINIMCOM had constructed for her. MINIMCOM's nose dived down and he leveled off just above the surface. He gently lowered himself to the ground and the whole space-plane shook as it crushed some boulders beneath the landing gear. MINIMCOM flashed the coordinates of the research site which Rome committed to memory. After settling down, the group of three left via the rear cargo ramp.

To the south, as far as the eye could see, the ground was a barren, clay-colored landscape with boulders and rocks strewn everywhere. There were a few deserts on Deucado and this was the edge of one of them though it was because of the rocky nature of the ground, not due to lack of moisture.

Rome led the way followed by Bonnie with Rei bringing up the rear. They came to a campsite, or at least the Vuduri version of a campsite with several tents that resembled teepees and a much larger "building" covered by a white material. They approached the white building, entering by the door flap and standing there were two men conversing over a large flat table. To the far left were three others, a mix of Vuduri and Essessoni, working with hammers and chisels and brushes and something that looked like a pen-light.

The two nearer men looked up. One of them was Deucadon.

"Rei!" the young man exclaimed.

"Steben!" Rei called out. He trotted over and the two of them hugged although Rei pulled back before Steben could apply substantial pressure. "I haven't seen you in like forever," he said.

"Yes, it has been a long time," replied the young man, just a bit shorter than Rei. His peach-fuzz beard was just coming in.

"Bierak," said the other, taller man.

"Hey, Wally," Rei said.

"What brings you and your lovely wife here?" the scientist asked.

Rei waved to Bonnie and Rome who came over to join them.

"Steben," Rei said. "This is my wife, Rome and this is Bonnie Mullen."

"Hello," Steben said cheerfully. "I've heard a lot about ya," he directed at Rome.

"Likewise," Rome said. "And as I said, I've already met Wally."

Wally nodded. "Hello, Rome," he said. "How have you been?"

"I've been better," Rome answered. "We've had some things happen that were not so good."

Bonnie interjected. "Wally, I think you and I met once before. Rome told us you've been working through her library?"

"Oh, yes," the scientist replied. "Rome's library computer has been amazingly helpful in our work here."

He held up a pencil-sized tube, reminiscent of a laser pointer from an age long gone. "Rome, next time you speak to OMCOM, tell him thanks for these miniature PPT throwers. They've been incredibly handy in carving things out of the rocks without disturbing them. Way better than anything we have."

"I will do that," Rome said.

Rei looked around the tent. "What are you doing here, anyway?" Rei asked. "OMCOM said you may have found evidence of other kinds of life? On this planet?"

"Oh, it's more than that," Wally said. He led the group across the tent to the far side where there was a cane-tree pinup board. There were some diagrams and a photograph of a large outcropping.

"Look at this," he said, pointing to a gray vertical bar with a series of white lines cutting through it. "This is a cross-section of the iridium density of a series of core samples. We've been working on a huge fault, chasm really, that goes back almost 50 million years as far as we can tell."

"What are those lines?" Rome asked, pointing to the strips.

"Those are the iridium densities that are significantly above normal. Depth is fairly tightly proportional to time."

"Iridium comes from meteors and the like, right?" Bonnie asked.

"Exactly," Wally said, his eyes gleaming. "Asteroid class. This poor little planet has been absolutely pummeled by things falling out of the sky for as far back as we can tell."

"What about that gap?" Rome asked, pointing to one section of the graph that had no lines cutting through it.

"That," Wally said, tapping the region that Rome was referring to, "is the most amazing period of time in this little world's history that we've discovered so far."

"Why?" Rei asked.

"Because they had about a three million-year window where there were no extinction-level events. Plenty of time for life to branch out and create some variety. I'm supposed to be a geologist but I'm taking a little spin as a paleontogist."

Rei pulled his head back. "Paleontology? As in fossils? There's never been any fossils reported so far. There's nothing to fossilize."

A big smile crossed Wally's face. "You're wrong," he said. "We've all been wrong." He pointed to the image of the ground pinned upon the board. "Come with me," he said. "Let me show you what we found at that dig."

He and Steben walked to the back of the tent. Propped up in the corner sat a large flattened piece of stone.

Rei saw lines criss-crossing the stone. There was a straight vertical line and four lines radiating from the sides plus another, fifth line, off angle near the top. It reminded Rei of the figurine drawn when children play hangman.

"What are we looking at?" Rei asked.

Wally bent over and lovingly stroked the stone. "This, my friends, is a genuine Deucadon fossil. Of a vertebrate. It is nine million years old but it absolutely had a spine."

"Wow," Rome said spontaneously. "We have never seen any evidence of vertebrate life here. Not the falling blankets, the swishies, nothing."

"More than a vertebrate," Wally said. "Sentient."

"Sentient?" Rei sputtered, "here, on Deucado? How can you tell it was sentient and not just another dumb animal?"

Wally tapped the left upper line which ended in a four-fingered gripper, very similar to those found on the falling blankets. There was a round, cylindrical gap and a squarish object beyond that. "Look in his hand, Rei," Wally said. "That's a hammer!"

Rei's jaw dropped open. Before he could say anything, Wally reached over and tapped the right paw in which another long cylindrical carving appeared. "And that was a chisel. This thing carved rocks!"

"Holy Mackerel," Rei said. "What happened to them?"

"We can only guess," Wally said. "Tell them, Steben."

"Yes," replied the young Deucadon. "Dr. Wally asked for permission to go down to our underground city. Bukky said 'twas all right. I was his tour guide."

"I've been there, too!" Rome interjected proudly.

"Yes. The caves we inhabited. And the magma tube we tapped into, to use its power. They were already there when our people first arrived."

"I thought Bukky told me you built them," Rome asked.

"Naw, we fashioned them to our likin' but they were already there."

"So what's this got to do with anything?" Rei asked.

Steben walked away. He opened a small chest and retrieved some objects. He returned with two metal rods in his hand. He held them out for Rei, Rome and Bonnie to see. They were chisels.

"When our forefathers got down there, during the buildin' phase, they found many of these. And the hammerheads, like there in the fossil," Steben said, pointing up. "We have always held the belief that the caves were somehow built. The ceilings were always too smooth to be natural."

"Yes!" Rome exclaimed. "This is the very thing that I noticed in the Cathedral," Rome said. "Do you remember me mentioning it to you?" she directed to Rei.

"Yeah, I do," Rei said. He looked at the chisels in Steben's hands and back up to the fossil. "What does it all mean, Wally?" he asked.

"I don't know yet," Wally said. "But it is an amazing coincidence, don't you think?"

Rei took a deep breath. He rubbed the back of his head where MINIMCOM had fused his skull not two weeks earlier. "This hurts my head," he said. "It's, it's beyond sleek. It's mind-blowing."

"We think so, too," Wally said proudly. "We're going to keep going but there is a lot more to this little planet than we thought."

Rei stood there, lost in thought. Bonnie nudged Rome who, in turn, nudged Rei.

"Oh, yeah," he said. "This is amazing stuff but it isn't really why we came."

"Sure," Wally said. He pointed and Steben left them to return the chisels to their packing case. "So why *are* you here?" Wally asked.

"You know that somebody tried to kill me," Rei offered.

"Yeah, I heard," Wally replied showing the proper amount of concern. "But you seem OK to me. Do you know who did it?"

"Yes," Rome interjected. "It was the two remaining members of the Darwin group named Dan Steele and David Troutman. Do you know them?"

"Darwin, huh," he said, looking right at Bonnie.

Rome pulled the two pictures out of her pocket. "Here are their images," Rome said. "Do you recognize either of them?"

The scientist studied the pictures for a minute. He pointed to the picture of Steele. "I'm assuming that's Steele. I have no clue about him. I've never met him."

"What about David Troutman?" Rome asked.

Wally Stanislaw tugged at his chin. "Yeah, him, I've met. He came to see me, oh, maybe three years ago."

"Why?" Rei asked.

"He wanted me to come work for his mining group. At least that's what they called it. Of course, that's before we even knew Darwin existed."

"What happened?"

"He had some cockamamie excuse about having to mine certain metals and they needed help finding the right kind of ore."

"Well, that's right up your alley, right?" Rei asked.

"Yeah, but his whole story didn't make any sense. I mean, hindsight is 20/20 and all but even then they couldn't come up with a rational explanation. The Vuduri have been more than generous in giving us whatever we needed. He couldn't explain why that wasn't good enough so I told him to get lost."

Rei pointed over his shoulder. "Well, he wasn't one of the ones deported so he's still running around. Have you seen him since?"

"It's possible but I can't say for sure," Wally replied, handing the pictures back to Rome. "The last time I was in Ur, I bumped into a really tall guy, way too tall to be Vuduri. Same color hair. Ginger. But this guy had a beard and was wearing a hood. He didn't act like he recognized me. From the way he was dressed, I figured it was one of the Deucadons but it might've been him. I'm not certain."

"That makes perfect sense!" Rei exclaimed. "There's no reason why he would stay clean-shaven. If you don't want to be recognized, growing a beard would be the first thing you do. Then dress like the natives."

Rei turned to Rome and Bonnie. "Let's get going." He turned back to Wally. "Thanks, Wally, for the info and congratulations on your discovery. We'll be sure to check up on it once we get back home. Steben!" Rei added. "Good seeing you again, buddy."

"Same here," Steben replied, returning to where they stood.

And with that, Rei, Rome and Bonnie left.

Chapter 15

MINIMCOM APPROACHED THE RESORT TOWN OF UR FROM THE EAST, flying very low. The azure waters of Lake Eprehem stretched north as far as the eye could see and off to the horizon to the west. A lazy band of clouds drifted over the center part of the water. Rei watched with a sense of wonder from the cockpit window as The Hand came closer and closer. Because of that one geological structure, Ur was easily the most spectacular location on all of Deucado, perhaps on all the worlds of Man.

The Hand was like nothing Rei had ever seen anywhere. Everyone had always assumed it was a meteor that hit Deucado and caused the crater that became Lake Eprehem. The truth is, it was a comet with an iron-nickel core. When the comet crashed down and created the gigantic depression, the metallic core continued on and punctured a pocket of magma. The magma bubbled up to the surface forming a tower that reached nearly a half a mile high. The metal core also hit another band of magma which seeped up to the surface and formed a spurting magma geyser. At regular intervals, like an evil cannon, it would shoot great globs of molten rock up and over the top of the tower that stood before it. In its fluid state, the entire structure bent over toward the impact crater. More shots of magma coated it to form a solid platform at the top, a half mile wide. By the time it cooled, the newly formed mountain was hanging out over what would become the largest lake on all of Deucado.

Much of the water filling the lake came from the comet which quickly condensed. The rest came thanks to the dust and dirt the explosion shot up into the atmosphere which caused Deucado to experience years and years of torrential downpours. As the rains fell and Lake Eprehem filled to the brim, the overhang, now called The Hand, hung farther and farther over the lake.

"Look at that thing," Rei said, more or less to himself.

"It is amazing," Rome replied, more or less answering him.

Rei squinted and could see partial concentric circles with The Hand essentially in the middle. It reminded him of a Vuduri city but that wouldn't make any sense because what would the Vuduri be doing in Ur? When the Essessoni had arrived, they brought their social conventions with them. Even though none of them wanted for

128

anything, they still felt the need to take vacations and Ur was certainly the most satisfying vacation spot on the continent. A resort town sprung up around the giant structure and a portion of it on top as well. The Vuduri would have no use for a resort.

The waters washed up enough sediment to form a beautiful beach underneath. On top of The Hand were several buildings including a few eating establishments and what Rei had heard was a fledgling casino, each offering spectacular views. Although Rei had never been here personally, he always intended to bring Rome and Aason here one day. Circumstances could have been better, though.

MINIMCOM settled down in a clearing within the clump of cane-trees just outside the city limits. The three humans had lowered the cargo ramp and were getting ready to disembark when MINIMCOM addressed them from a grille in the cargo bay.

"**Will you be needing a livetar?**" the starship asked.

Rei looked at Rome who shook her head. "Not this time, buddy," he said. "I think we need to keep as low of a profile as possible. We don't want to spook them. I think your presence would make us stand out too much."

"**Very well,**" MINIMCOM replied, not bothering to hide his disappointment.

"In fact," Rei said. "Rome, why don't you go grab the other Deucadon cloak? I may have to make myself hidden during our search as well. They obviously know what I look like."

"Of course," Rome said. She returned in just a minute with the Deucadon invisibility cloak draped over her arm. Rei took it and fastened it around his neck.

"Ready as we'll ever be," he said.

The three of them walked down the ramp. When they got to the bottom, Rei put his hand up to his temple and thought, *"Why don't you make yourself scarce for now. No reason to alert people."*

MINIMCOM did not answer but he did raise his cargo ramp and lower the hatch. As soon as the seal was complete, MINIMCOM activated his stealth shield, shimmering for a moment then disappearing completely.

"**Be careful,**" was all the starship said.

"We will, buddy. Thanks," Rei replied. *"We'll call you if we need you."*

As they exited the cane-tree forest and embarked upon the road leading into the town proper, Rei could not help but notice that other than The Hand, even Ur looked ordinary. Each of the side roads curved off to the side. There was no doubt about it. The streets were concentric circles. There were some side roads and the tops of some dwellings peeked up over the trees but nothing stood out.

So far, on Deucado, each of the four races had kept to themselves. The Vuduri remained in Vuduri City, the Deucadons in Deucadia, the Ibbrassati in Ibbra City and Rei's people gathered in New Ark City. But Ur was something different. It was the first place where all the races co-mingled and lived together. The design of the city proved that the Vuduri were involved as well.

"Hey Rome," Rei said, coming to a stop.

"Yes?"

"I'm certain that the Vuduri had a hand in helping them build this city. Its design is basically the same as every other Vuduri city I've ever seen. Concentric circles."

"Vuduri City, here on Deucado, is made up of overlapping triangles."

"Oh yeah," Rei said. "I guess that was their one creative outburst. But why do you think they leant a hand here? Ur doesn't seem like the kind of place they'd go."

Rome looked up and down the streets. "The Overmind here is committed to blending each of the races and building a stronger world. The architecture is probably its way of contributing to the spirit of Ur."

Rei shrugged. "I guess that makes sense," he said and he started walking again. On some streets, it was easier to see the housing. Most of the residences, at least here on the east side, were built out of standard Vuduri aerogel. There were some deviations, probably introduced by the non-mind-connected races. But even so, there was a homogeneity about it. Up ahead, everything changed.

As plain as the little city looked, The Hand was anything but. Its looming physical presence was almost too much to comprehend. Its base was huge, almost a mile wide. The way it projected from the ground, it almost looked like it had been grafted on. Its graceful arc began and it narrowed somewhat as you got closer to the top. From where they stood, they could not even see the upper section which extended quite a distance over the lake. The view from the top must be awe-inspiring as well, Rei thought to himself.

Rome stumbled as they walked along. Rei grabbed her arm and helped her right herself. "Are you OK, honey?" he asked.

"Yes," she replied. "But that." She pointed up. "The Hand. It is stupendous. I cannot take my eyes off of it."

"I agree," Rei said. "It seems like the overhang goes off forever." He forced his eyes back to the ground.

Bonnie added, "In our time, when people went to New York City for the first time, they did the same thing, tripping over themselves, staring at the skyscrapers. There's something hypnotic about being close up to really gigantic structures."

"I will try to get used to it," Rome said, "but I don't know if I will be able to."

"Well, we have business now. We'll come back some day and take it all in properly."

"Agreed," Rome said and she charged forward.

The circular streets and residential area curved around to the left. Going the other way, starting right at the edge of the shadow of The Hand, there was an open area that was a combination of farmer's market and bazaar. As they walked along, both Rome and Bonnie gawked at the wares set out on the various tables. At one point, Rome walked over to one table and picked up a bright red fruit. She showed it to Rei. "This looks delicious," she said. As she started to bite into it, the merchant, clearly Deucadon, said, "hold on."

"What?" Rome asked.

"That will be two Deucats," he said, stroking his beard.

"What is a Deucat?" she asked.

"It's money, coin," he said, rubbing his two fingers together. The merchant eyed Rome up and down.

Rei came over to where she was standing. She set the fruit down and turned to her husband. "You explained to me about money once," she said. "But why would we need it here? I don't understand."

Rei regarded her confusion then turned to address the merchant. "What's up with that?" he asked. "This world has unlimited free energy. Molecular sequencers. Anybody can have anything they want. Why *do* you want money?"

The merchant shrugged. "Around here, there are so many different people and races, it's the only way we can gauge value. And, ya need it for the casino." He pointed straight up. Seeing no reaction, he shrugged. "If ya don't have any money, then there is nawt anythin' I can do for ya. Ya can move along."

"Money is stupid!" Rome exclaimed.

"It is only stupid if ya do nawt have any," the merchant smirked. He tapped the bowl holding the rest of the fruit several times.

Rome put the fruit back and stared at the merchant, scowling. Rei saw her disappointment and moved to the edge of the table.

"Can I see one of these Deucats?" he asked. "I've never seen one before."

The merchant reached into a leather-like bag attached at his waist and pulled out a single silver coin. He handed it to Rei who hefted it then flipped it over in his hand. It was about the size of a silver dollar and by its weight, probably contained about the same amount of precious metal. On the obverse, there was an image of Deucado, pock marks and all. On the reverse, was an image of The Hand, engraved in the center. The rim was serrated and along the edge was inscribed the legend One Deucat in English and Vuduri.

Rei handed it back to the merchant and turned to Rome.

"Let me have your ring," he said.

Rome quickly hid her left hand behind her back. "Why?" she asked suspiciously.

"I just need to borrow it for a few minutes," Rei insisted. "I'll give it back, I promise."

"Very well," Rome said unenthusiastically. She used her right hand to gently twist and remove the diamond engagement ring off of her left ring finger. The ring had been Rei's gift to her on their one year anniversary. It was among her most prized possessions because of what it represented. Reluctantly, she handed the ring to her husband.

Rei held the ring out to the merchant. "How much will you give me for this ring?" he asked.

"Rei!" Rome shouted. "No!"

"It's OK," Rome," he said. "I know what I'm doing." The merchant took the ring from him and held it up to the light.

"It's a six carat flawless diamond with two one-carat diamonds on the sides. Mounted on a pure platinum base."

The merchant's eyes grew wide. "This ring, it is very valuable," he said. "I would nawt have enough to pay ya. Maybe up top? At the casino?"

"Not necessary," Rei said. "Would you say that ten Deucats is a fair price?"

"Ten Deucats?" the merchant sputtered. "It is worth a hundr'd times that much, a thous'nd."

"OK then," Rei said. "I'll sell it to you for two Deucats."

"Rei?" Rome whined, "what are you doing?"

"Shhh," Rei said. "Two Deucats?"

"Of course, of course," the merchant said. He reached into his bag and pulled out two silver coins.

"So here's the deal," Rei said. "You're giving me two Deucats. I'm going to go away for a little bit and when I come back, I'll give you ten Deucats to buy the ring back. OK?"

The merchant narrowed his eyes.

"Look, you're making back five times your investment in just a few minutes. You agreed it was worth at least ten Deucats. Do we have a deal?"

"Ya," said the merchant. "We can do this."

"Great," Rei said and he held out his palm. The merchant dropped two silver coins into his open hand.

Rei turned to Rome and Bonnie. "I'm going to go down the road for a few minutes. You two stay here and keep an eye on this guy. Make sure he doesn't do anything funny or take off."

"Where are you going?" Bonnie asked.

Rei just winked at them. Rome nodded.

"It is alright, Bonnie," Rome said. "I know where he is going."

Rei dashed off back the way they came.

Rome grabbed Bonnie's arm and pulled her over to sit on a bench that she spotted just behind the merchant's table. They watched the merchant turn the ring over and over in his hand. He even tried to slip it on one of his fingers but the ring was too small. They just sat in silence for about ten minutes until Rei came jogging back from down the road. In his hand was a leather-like sack similar to the one the merchant had on his hip.

When he arrived at the table, he took a moment to catch his breath then reached into the bag and brought out ten coins, placing them on the table.

The merchant picked up the coins and examined them closely. He even tried to bend one. He looked at Rei and his full sack and slid the pile of coins back toward him.

"I've changed my mind," the merchant said. "The deal is now one hundred Deucats."

"What the hell are you talking about?" Rei growled at him. "A deal's a deal. You agreed to ten Deucats. Where's your integrity?"

"Sorry," the merchant said with a slightly crooked grin. "The deal is now one hundred Deucats or I keep the ring."

Rei started to clench his hand into a fist. Rome's lilting voice entered into his head.

"He'll take twenty five," Rome said. *"He just wants you to bargain with him."*

Rei turned to look at her. *"How do you know?"* he asked her.

"I can read his mind," she replied, smiling.

"I thought you had to touch someone to do that."

"For deeper thoughts, yes. For something this simple, no. Offer him a few more Deucats and let him fight you down to twenty five. We have to be on our way."

"OK," Rei said. He turned to the merchant.

"Do you know who we are?" Rei asked, angrily.

"Of course," answered the merchant. "Everyone knows who yar. Yar possibly the most famous people on all of Deucado. Ya can certainly afford it, judgin' by the size of yar bag."

Rei took a deep breath. "I'll give you fifteen," he said.

"I will take naw less than fifty," the merchant countered.

"Twenty," Rei said.

"Forty," offered the merchant.

"Twenty five and that's my final offer," Rei said. He raised his fist in the air. "Otherwise, I start beating you."

The merchant smiled. "Ya drive a hard bargain but twenty five it is." He held his hand out, palm up, showing the ring to Rei.

Rei let out a short burst of air then reached in his bag and brought out fifteen more coins. The merchant grabbed the Deucats then handed Rome's ring back to Rei. Rei gave it to Rome who quickly placed it back on her finger, breathing a sigh of relief.

"We're done here," Rei said and started to turn away. Suddenly, he turned back. Defiantly, he grabbed the fruit that started the whole exchange. "With your compliments, right?" Rei asked, still slightly miffed at the man.

The merchant shrugged reluctantly. Rei handed the fruit to Rome and they left the merchant's table to continue the search.

"Where did you get the money?" Bonnie whispered as they were walking away.

"I happen to know a magician," Rei answered cryptically. "He can make anything happen. This wasn't even a challenge. In fact, it made him laugh, it was so easy."

"OK," Bonnie replied, shrugging.

"Anyway, from the look of things, we're gonna need some money anyway."

"Why?" Rome asked.

"Because it's obvious, we're too recognizable." He pulled the hood of his cloak over his hair. "We're gonna have to find something to cover you ladies up. I don't want Troutman or Steele to get tipped off before we find them. The less attention we draw, the better."

Rei looked around and spotted a stall where an Ibbrassati woman was selling clothing. After a little modeling session, Rome selected a brown cloak. Bonnie selected a beige one. Rei purchased them from the woman manning the stall as Rome and Bonnie donned the cloaks. Bonnie pulled up her hood. Rome was about to do so when she said, "Wait!"

"What?" Rei asked.

Rome walked around behind the display and pulled out the new picture of Troutman, the one MINIMCOM had sketched with a beard. She showed it to the Ibbrassati woman but did not say a word. She put her hand on the woman's shoulder and only then asked her if she had ever seen the man in the picture.

The woman studied the image for a bit but claimed she did not recognize him.

"Thank you for trying," Rome said and she put the picture back in her pocket. The three of them started walking away. It was only then that Rome pulled up her hood.

"So what's the plan?" Bonnie asked as they moved through the crowd. "Canvassing the neighborhood?"

"Not necessary," Rome said with a smile. "I have discovered there is something in between the truth and lies. Sometimes a person cannot clearly recall something and discards the idea because they are not sure. Even though she said she did not know, I know that she did. She has seen Troutman."

"She did?" Rei exclaimed. "Where?"

Rome pointed to the gigantic stone prominence over their head. "Up," she said. "We must go to the top of The Hand."

Chapter 16

THERE WERE SEVERAL WAYS TO GET TO THE TOP OF THE HAND. Technically, it was possible to walk up. The first people to arrive at Ur had actually carved out a series of stairwells, switchback-style, to make it possible to go to the top by foot. But most found that too tedious. Some industrious soul had built a dumb-waiter style elevator to the top that now served as a cargo lift. After the casino was built, a much nicer, glass-enclosed elevator was constructed to ferry people topside in elegant fashion. The elevator was mounted on the western side of the gigantic tower.

It cost Rei, Rome and Bonnie one Deucat each to take the ride to the top but it was money well spent. The three of them stared out the window at the majestic vista as they rose to the plateau on top. As they got higher, if anything, Lake Eprehem seemed to get larger and stretched out forever in front of them.

As they stepped out of the elevator onto the rocky surface, one half mile in the air, Bonnie grabbed onto Rei's arm.

"What is it?" Rei asked.

"I don't know," she said. "It's just that being up here makes my knees rubbery."

"We'll hold on to you," Rome said, going around the other side and taking Bonnie's arm. "Let's go."

To the west and north, the view was completely unobstructed. Along the leeward side, to the east, there were some restaurants and an inn. They walked past all of the structures to the very tip of The Hand. Rei's guess was they were on the 'ring finger' of the titanic structure. Thoughtfully, somebody had constructed a railing to prevent people from tumbling over the edge. Rome leaned over and looked straight down, one half mile, into the deep blue waters of Lake Eprehem. From their vantage point, it looked like they were suspended in space. The lake appeared to stretch forever in all directions.

"Sleek," Rome said. "It is beyond beautiful. Who knew our little world contained such a treasure?"

Rei smiled at her use of the word sleek. "It is sleek," he said. "Someday, we'll come back here for a proper vacation but for now, we should get to the business at hand."

Rome looked around. There weren't many people on top this day. "We go door to door?" she asked.

"No need," Rei said, pointing at the glittering façade of the largest building on top. Its shiny exterior would shout casino on any world. "We go to the casino. If Troutman came up here, chances are that'd be where he was headed."

"What is a casino, anyway?" Rome asked as they approached. "What is its purpose?"

Rei laughed. "Its purpose is for people to lose money."

"I don't understand," Rome said. "Why would they go to the trouble of acquiring it, just to lose it?"

"It's for gambling," Bonnie offered, trying to clear things up.

"And what is gambling?"

"There are games of chance in there," Bonnie said, pointing forward. "People bet. Some people win. But mostly, in the end, everybody loses."

"This is like our card games?" Rome asked. "We never played for anything other than the joy."

"Yeah," Rei said, "but some people find more joy when they win money."

"Back to money again," Rome said. "The whole concept is starting to make me angry. I only went along with it because we had to get on our way. I think I am against it just on general principles."

"I agree with you," Rei said, as he opened the front door. "My people brought a lot of cultural hang-ups with us and that is not one of the good ones."

They entered inside and were immediately assaulted with flashing lights, bells and assorted sounds going off and a smell that reminded Rome of Nick Greer's cell back on Helome.

To their left was a bank of slot machines. They were sparsely populated with a couple of Essessoni and Deucadons. To Rei's surprise, he saw not only some Ibbrassati but also two people who were clearly Vuduri. He stared at them. There was no doubt about it; they were playing the slots. The whole picture was surreal.

"Where do we start?" Rome asked, interrupting Rei's reverie.

"Let me find somebody," Rei said and he charged forward. He found an Ibbrassati woman dressed in some sort of costume which Rei figured meant she worked there.

"Hello," he said to her.

"Hello," she replied. Her eyes widened a bit when she realized who she was talking to. "What can we do for you? Are you here to play?"

"Not really," Rei said. He looked up and around and immediately spotted several security cameras. "Is there somebody we can talk to about people coming and going? Maybe look at your security footage?"

The woman shook her head. "No, that is off-limits to everyone," she said. "You're not allowed."

Rei frowned. "You know who I am, right?"

"Of course," she said. "But you still aren't allowed. We must respect everyone's privacy."

"Is the owner here or a manager or something?" Rei asked.

"I cannot say," she replied. "Management doesn't mix with the patrons."

"Sure they do," Rei insisted. "It's important."

"No, sir," the pretty little Ibbrassati said. She turned to walk away. As she left, she said, over her shoulder, "If you are not going to play, you may as well leave." She waved to a rather large Essessoni who was standing to the rear. He started making his way over to where Rei and Rome were standing.

"What do we do?" Rome asked. "Why would she not cooperate with us?"

"Who knows?" Rei said. "Casinos operate by different rules." He did a slow sweep around the place with his eyes. He could see some narrow windows, in the rear, mounted at the very top of the main hall. He squinted, trying to peer behind them but they were tinted so he didn't have much luck. He looked down at the variety of table games in front of them. To the far left was a large wheel. It was spinning slowly and whenever it came to a stop, some people would shout and others would throw their hands in the air.

In front of them were some long tables. There were other people there, including yet another surprising number of Vuduri, watching a man throw marbles along the length of the table. There were five white marbles and one black. There were holes in the table and the person throwing the marbles looked like they were trying to get the marbles to go into the holes. Judging from the operator, it must have been some sort of Deucadon game of chance.

To Rei's right were other table games and suddenly, he had an inspiration. He tugged on Rome's elbow and drew her away from the main part of the room. Bonnie followed.

"You said down below you can read people's minds without touching them, right?" Rei asked in a low voice.

"Yes," Rome answered in kind. "Superficial thoughts only, though."

Rei pointed to the card table on the far right. "What about what cards each person is holding in their hands? Do you think you could tell me that?"

"I suppose," Rome said, "if they were concentrating on them."

"That's kind of cheating," Bonnie said, "Don't you think?"

"Exactly," Rei said. "What better way to get management's attention?"

Bonnie cocked her head in confusion but then she nodded definitively.

"OK," Rei said to Rome. "Let's try," He took Rome's hand and led her to a table where there were four people and a dealer playing hoker.

Hoker or house poker was a simple variation of regular five card draw. The only difference was the house participated in the hand instead of merely dealing. The dealer would look at each card before handing it to the players and they would keep every fifth card. To stay in a round, a player had to bet a certain amount. Since the house had a distinct advantage, to make the game more fair, a player could withdraw from each round by surrendering half of their pot. If the dealer drew three of a kind or two pair before the players accumulated something better, the house won. A player could lay their hand down at any time and if they beat everyone, they won everyone's chips including those that belonged to the house.

It was a simple game and went very fast. A good player could lay down their hand or surrender early and do well. A bad player would wait too long and the house would win.

Rei brought Rome right up to the edge of the table. Bonnie stood directly behind her.

"Undo your jumpsuit a little bit," Rei thought to Rome. *"Show a little flesh. It'll distract people."*

"What!?" Rome exclaimed, slightly insulted.

"Trust me," Rei answered. *"Then look in their minds and see if you can tell me what every player has in their hand,"* Rei asked Rome mentally.

Rome did as Rei requested then she started with the first player on the far right. *"Two queens, a seven and a four,"* Rome replied.

"Great," Rei answered. *"And the next one?"*

"Three eights and a six."

"And the next?"

"A four, a five, a six and an eight."

"Same suit?"

"Yes," Rome replied.

"OK. Great. Forget the last one. See what you can do with the dealer," Rei instructed. *"That's the most important one."*

"The dealer has three tens and a jack. She's getting ready to deal."

The player with three of a kind said, "Call" and he laid down his hand. All the other players turned their hands over. The dealer smiled and flipped over her cards and the man who had called slapped the table.

"Damn!" he said. "I thought I had you." The dealer calmly collected all the chips and swept them into a receptacle. A helper pulled them out and organized them into the little trays in front of the dealer, sorted by color. The man who lost the hand got up and left the area.

"OK," Rei said out loud. "I'll give it a try."

"Are you sure that is wise?" Rome asked. "This seems like a triviality. Don't we have more important things we should be doing?"

Bonnie leaned over and whispered, "If he's going to do what I think he's going to do, it's exactly the right thing."

Rome looked at her then looked at Rei and shrugged. Rei sat down and pulled out his bag of Deucats. "What's the table minimum?" he asked.

"Five Deucats," answered the dealer. Rei pulled out fifty of the silver coins and placed them on the table. The dealer pulled them forward, counted them, and handed Rei a stack of chips.

"Tell me every card as they are drawn," he said to Rome. *"And keep track of what the dealer has. That's the most important thing."*

"If you say so," Rome replied and they begun.

It's amazing what you can win if you cheat. Nearly every hand, Rei laid down his hand early or surrendered. Slowly but surely, his pile of chips grew larger and larger and larger. Every tenth hand or so, he'd turn in a stack of chips for a chip of larger value which he would hand to Rome. Rei was like a chip-collecting machine. The stack of chips he handed to Rome eventually became so cumbersome, she had to take off her cloak and use it as if it were a sack.

It didn't take long until the other players left the table in disgust only to be replaced by a series of gawking onlookers. Soon it was just Rei and the dealer. That was when he really kicked it into high gear. He bet a hundred, then two hundred, then five hundred Deucats per hand. With relentless precision, his pile of winnings became uncountable, especially because the bulk of it was hidden in Rome's bulging cloak.

Each time Rei won, the steadily-growing crowd shouted and cheered. At one point, the dealer was breathing heavily and asked to be excused. The heavy-set Essessoni who they had spotted coming from the rear sat down to take her place. As he sat down, he pulled the deck closer to him and centered it.

"Rei!" Rome said insistently. *"He just put four cards on top of the deck that he was holding in his palm."*

"Do you know what they are?" Rei asked, frowning.

"Yes," Rome replied. *"An ace, a king, a four then another king."*

"The bastard," Rei said. *"He was going to sucker me into losing."*

"Hey," Rei said out loud, pointing to the deck. "I saw you palming those cards. You just rigged the deck."

"I did not," the new dealer said with a straight face. "You're crazy."

"I saw you and I'll prove it," Rei said. He turned back to Rome. "Dump all your chips on the table," he commanded.

Rome shook her head and lifted her cloak, spreading its contents all over the table.

"Double or nothing," Rei said. "I tell you what the next four cards are, the ones you were palming. If I'm right, you match my pot and I win. If I'm wrong, you can have them all."

The dealer put his finger into his collar in a vain attempt to loosen it. He turned in his seat to look up at the tinted windows but got no indication. He turned back to Rei. "All right," he said. "First card?"

"Ace," Rei said. The dealer flipped the card over and an ace of diamonds appeared. The crowd applauded.

"Next card?"

"King," Rei replied. The dealer flipped the card over and it was the king of spades. This time, the crowd shouted then applauded.

"Next card?" the dealer asked nervously.

"Four," Rei said. "So I'd have nothing at this point." The dealer flipped the next card over and it was the four of hearts. The crowd went wild, roaring its approval.

Rei reached into his sack of Deucats and dumped the rest on the table.

"Rei!" Rome suddenly interrupted. *"He's going to take two cards. It won't be the king."*

"Right," Rei answered. Then out loud, he said, "Stop right there and get your hands away from the deck. Get somebody else to turn the card."

"No," the dealer said. "That's not the deal." The crowd's agitation was palpable.

"Yes it is," Rei insisted. "I said the next four cards. You already palmed four cards and now you're going to lift two. If you won't get somebody else, I'm going to turn the last card over myself."

"You can't do that," the dealer said. He reached down beneath the table and drew out a weapon. He placed the plasma blaster on the table. "House rules," he said. "I say how this goes down." The crowd murmured and quickly moved back, clearing out a wide buffer between themselves and Rei, Rome and Bonnie.

Rei touched his temple and suddenly, with a whoosh and a pop, MINIMCOM's livetar appeared. But this livetar was much larger than normal. It was nearly eight feet tall and appropriately proportioned. Across one of the livetar's arms was a hybrid rifle. The barrel and stock looked normal but the end looked more like a shower head. The business end, the one that resembled a shower head, was studded with little tips that glowed bright red.

"You think you can threaten me?" Rei said angrily, standing up. "You can shoot me. You can probably kill me. But you can't kill him," Rei said, jerking his thumb toward MINIMCOM. "He isn't even alive. Tell him what you got there, buddy."

"This is a PPT blunderbuss," MINIMCOM said. "It will puncture you with thousands of tiny holes. You will not die right away but you will die as sure as there are stars in the sky. And I am told it is a very painful death."

The dealer's eyes grew wide. Rei took advantage of his frozen reactions and said, "King." He reached forward and flipped the card over and it was, indeed, a king of clubs. From a distance, the crowd went crazy.

The dealer leaped up and in so doing, knocked his chair over backwards.

"Pay me," Rei said, pointing to the pile of chips and money on the table. The dealer turned back and stared up at the tinted windows in the back helplessly. There was a discernible motion. The Essessoni dealer turned back and said, "The owner would like to see you, first, if you don't mind."

"That's more like it," Rei said, standing up. "My rather large and well-armed friend here…" he indicated MINIMCOM's larger livetar. "…will make sure you count it correctly." MINIMCOM took one step forward and lifted the rifle head slightly in response.

"Sh, Sure," the dealer said. "You go back through that door." He pointed to the far right rear of the room. "Someone will meet you at the stairs."

"OK," Rei said. "Bonnie, can you stay here and watch him too? Make sure he doesn't cheat us any more."

"Sure, Rei," Bonnie said, her eyes wide with amazement at what just transpired.

"Come on, Rome," Rei said, reaching down to take Rome's hand. "Let's go find out what's going on."

He led Rome through a winding path around the rest of the tables until they got to the hallway at the rear. "How did you know this would make the owner agree to see you?" she asked.

"Because casino owners hate to lose," he said. "It isn't anything you could understand but this whole place is about separating people from their money. What happened back there is like their worst nightmare."

At the base of the stairwell, an Ibbrassati appeared but this one was dressed in Essessoni-style clothing. The man did not speak while he escorted them up the stairway. He ushered Rei and Rome into a hardwood-paneled office that would have been right at home anywhere on Earth. It looked odd, here on Deucado. At the desk was a woman with dark hair and bangs. She stood up.

The Ibbrassati closed the door but remained in the room, standing at attention.

"You two don't need any introduction," she said. "But I do. I'm Andrea Grenmuller." She leaned over the desk and held out her hand.

Rei reached forward and shook her hand. "Sit down," Andrea said, indicating the two chairs in front of her desk. "Very impressive display," she mused admiringly. "I had no idea you were so good at cards."

"I'm not," Rei said, sitting down. Rome sat down next to him. "I cheated," he answered proudly.

"And you're admitting it?"

"Yeah, sure," Rei said. "I don't want your money. You can have it back."

"You don't want it?" Andrea asked incredulously. "Then what do you want?"

"Information," Rei said, leaning forward. "About David Troutman and Dan Steele."

Andrea narrowed her eyes. "What if I said I didn't know anything about them?"

Rei turned to Rome who nodded. She stood up and walked around the desk. Andrea watched her skeptically while Rome gently rested her hand on Andrea's shoulder.

"She's lying," Rome said. "She knows Troutman very well."

Andrea looked at Rome's hand then up at Rei. "So that's how you cheat? You read people's minds?"

"I can't," Rei said. "But she can. You might want to rethink the games you offer by acknowledging that the people here aren't all like us."

"OK. Point taken. What do you want to know?" Andrea asked.

"Anything. Everything," Rei said. "Troutman and Steele tried to kill us with a bomb. I want to find them before they take another shot at it."

Andrea leaned back in her chair. She sighed. "I heard that, but David's not a bad person," she said.

"He's bad enough to try and blow me up," Rei shot back with an edge.

"That was Steele's influence," she said. "David just wanted to…" She didn't finish the sentence.

"How do you know Troutman?" Rei asked.

"He and I, well, we've slept together a few times. He used to bring me the silver ingots I needed to make the coins."

"You're minting the money?" Rei inquired. "Why? On this world, we get everything we need for free. Why bother?"

"When you mix four races," Andrea said, "not everybody values things the same way. By implementing a simple standard of exchange, the people down there…" Andrea pointed toward the tinted window mounted on the far wall. "…they can agree on what's what. It levels the playing field. The market down below sets its value. We just use them as a way to get people in here."

"Why?" Rome asked, still standing over Andrea. "Why all of this?"

Andrea looked up at her. "I'm a mathematician by trade. When we got here, nobody needed me for anything. I had to find something to do with my life. On Earth, we had to work just to survive. Here, we don't. So I decided to do what I've always wanted. And I've always wanted to own a casino." She waved her hand outward in a general gesture. "So I built this one. And that's why we make the money. You can't gamble if you don't have anything to gamble with."

Rome lifted her hand from Andrea's shoulder. "Money is stupid," she said. "I have only been exposed to it for a short time but I can tell you it brings out the bad in people."

Andrea looked up at her. "You're probably right," she said. "But I don't make anybody come in here."

"Troutman," Rei said, drawing her attention again. "Where is he?"

"I don't know," Andrea replied. Rome put her hand back on Andrea's shoulder. "Speculate. Where do you think he is?" Rome asked.

"Every time we were together, we went back to my place," Andrea replied. "If I had to guess, I'd say he lives to the west. He always told me his place was way too sloppy to let me see where he lived."

Rome looked at Rei and nodded.

"What about Steele?" Rei asked. "Do you know where he is?"

"No," Andrea replied. "I was told he came in here one night a while back but I wasn't even around. David said I was lucky."

Looking around the room, Rei spotted a tiny video camera mounted in the far corner, where the walls met the ceiling. "I saw you had cameras downstairs," Rei said, pointing. "Do you keep video records?"

"Yes," Andrea replied. "We tape everything."

"Can I see the videos?" Rei asked. "Maybe we'll spot something."

"You'd have to go through several month's worth," she said. "I don't really think that's practical."

"Maybe for you and me," Rei said. He leaned back in his chair. There was a whoosh and a pop and a more normal-sized MINIMCOM livetar appeared.

"Buddy, can you watch some video for me at high speed and see if you spot something. You know who we're looking for."

"Of course," the livetar replied.

"OK," Andrea said. She stood up and walked around her desk and over to the far side of the room. She pressed a button and a large flat screen display lit up, segmented into four quadrants of video. She tapped a few keys on a keyboard and the display changed. MINIMCOM's livetar walked over and stood in front of the display.

"Begin," he said.

Andrea pressed a single button and the images started flying by at super-speed. MINIMCOM remained motionless. Rei didn't even know how the livetar transmitted what came in through the eye slits but however he accomplished it, MINIMCOM seemed to know what he was doing.

After few minutes, MINIMCOM raised his hand and said, `"Stop."`

Andrea typed on the keyboard and the images froze. MINIMCOM bent his bullet-shaped head forward and pressed a few keys. When he rewound back to where he wanted, he expanded the image in the upper-left-hand quadrant so that it occupied the full screen.

`"This is what you seek,"` he said. Rei and Rome came over to join Andrea in front of the monitor. MINIMCOM pressed a key and the video began playing back at normal speed.

MINIMCOM pointed to a figure dressed in dark clothes, entering the field of vision from the left-hand side. `"That is Steele,"` the livetar said. `"Although he has his face obscured, I was able to get a sufficient match using biometrics."`

They watched as the furtive figure sat down at one of the hoker tables. He tossed a few coins down and received chips. For a short while, he played the game like a regular person, winning some hands, losing others.

"Look!" Rome shouted, pointing at the screen. A very short woman, Vuduri most likely judging from the white jumpsuit, sat down next to Steele. "Can you zoom in on her face?" Rome asked.

MINIMCOM tapped on a few keys and the interaction between Steele and the woman took up the entire screen. However, the woman was wearing a cap and a visor that looked like a wraparound frameless pair of sunglasses.

"Why would a Vuduri woman be wearing sunglasses?" Rei addressed toward Rome. "Your internal iris would make it unnecessary."

"Either she is mandasurte, dressed like a Vuduri, or she did not want anyone to see her face," Rome answered. "I suspect the latter."

In the video, the woman leaned over and whispered in Steele's ear. He snapped his head back and looked at her intently. She pointed toward the front door. Immediately, Steele grabbed his chips and followed her out of the camera's field of view.

"Any audio?" Rei asked. "I need to know what she said to him."

"No," Andrea replied. "Only video. Sorry."

Rei stroked his chin. He stared at the image on the screen. "I know it seems like we found something but I don't think we did. Maybe that he met our mystery woman here." He turned to Andrea.

"Can you tell me who the dealer was? Maybe he or she heard something."

"It was me," answered the Ibbrassati who, up until now, had been standing silently by the door.

The three people turned toward him.

"Can you tell us anything about this?" Rome asked.

"Not much," replied the man. "The woman was definitely Vuduri. I could tell from her dismissive attitude toward the mandasurte. I, too, found it strange that she would wear darkening glasses. Our casino is not that brightly lit in the first place."

"Did you hear what she said to him?" Rei asked.

"No," replied the man. "The room was very loud and she was whispering to him. I am sorry but I did not hear a single word. But whatever she said must been interesting to the man you were watching. He left the game immediately."

"Did you ever see her again?" Rome asked.

"No," replied the man. "In fact, I never saw either of them again."

Rei sighed. He looked at Rome.

"When was the last time you saw Troutman?" Rome asked.

"I haven't seen him in over a month." She looked at the readouts on the screen. "In fact, I probably only saw him once more right after this video was made."

"OK," Rei said. "Thanks, Andrea. This has been sort of helpful. And you said you think Troutman lives on the western side of the city?"

"Yes," Andrea replied sadly. "But I'm not sure how I feel about you finding him. He's not a bad person."

"I have no intention of causing him harm," Rei said. "Unless he gives me a reason. By rights, since he tried to kill me, I should be able to do anything I want to him. But I just want my family to be safe."

"I understand," Andrea said. "I guess in that case, I do hope you find him."

Rei turned to his livetar friend. "Thanks, MINIMCOM. We'll go collect Bonnie and head toward the west. Why don't you go back to the ship and we'll stay in touch."

The livetar nodded his head and disappeared.

Chapter 17

"ARE ALL MEN OBSESSED WITH SEX?" ROME ASKED REI MENTALLY AS they left the casino.

Rei laughed out loud and then thought back, *"Of course."*

"That's what I have come to realize," Rome replied. *"First Paul Chung, then the merchant below and the way the men at the card table were ogling me. What they were thinking!"*

Rei had a hard time holding back laughter. When he was able to compose himself, he said, *"If you're going to dive into people's heads, you have to be prepared for what you find there. Our people are used to their privacy. They're not like the Vuduri where somebody is always peeking in. Sometimes we don't think the greatest thoughts."*

Rome sighed. *"I suppose you are right,"* she replied. *"I have to keep that in the forefront when I am probing their minds."*

Rei tried steering the trio toward the elevator but Rome resisted. She looked longingly at the spectacular vista before them. She had vowed several years ago to always take the time to appreciate the beauty that nature provided her. Within her, a tug of war raged on but finally, practicality won. First things first. They had a job to do. Reluctantly, she turned away and followed Rei and Bonnie back the way they came. After the elevator ride back to the ground, the three of them ducked into an alleyway to strategize.

"Did you find anything out?" Bonnie asked Rei and Rome.

"One thing, yes," Rei answered. "The thing we know is that Troutman probably lives to the west."

"So that eliminates half the town," Bonnie said dismissively. "That still leaves us with the entire other half to search."

"I think I may have a method," Rome said. "We now know that even if I am not in direct contact with them, I can still read people's minds. At least at the superficial level. I think that if we walk toward the edge of town, each of you should take turns bumping into people. This will get their attention. Immediately show them a picture of Troutman and Steele. It will only take me a moment to determine if they have seen them or not. That should help us home in on the proper direction."

"That's a pretty sleek idea," Rei said. "Like a human GPS."

"A GPS?" Rome asked.

"Never mind," Rei said. "Let's get going."

They wandered through the western side of the marketplace with Rei and Bonnie pretending to bump into people. Rei carried a picture of Troutman. Bonnie carried a picture of Steele. Even as they were excusing themselves, Rome was able to get flashes of recognition. No one had seen Steele but Troutman stood out because of his height. Rome had Bonnie switch pictures. They quickly discovered that if they moved in one direction, fewer people showed any recognition. If they turned another way, more people showed flashes of recognition. Rei's description of Rome as a human GPS device turned out to be more accurate than any of them realized. They soon found themselves on the far western side of the city, well out from beneath the shadow of The Hand. Even though the streets were built the same as on the eastern side, the construction technique for the residences here quickly degraded. In fact, while there were many homes here, they steadily decreased in attractiveness as they got closer to the edge of town. Unerringly, their technique took them closer and closer until they got to one of the last streets, right on the outskirts of Ur. Most of the people here hadn't even bothered to use aerogel to construct their dwellings. They were more like sophisticated shacks. The one or two properly built homes stood out like sore thumbs.

Rome pulled a Vuduri gentleman aside and even though no words were spoken, mentally, she had a conversation with him. He pointed to the third house on the left. Rome thanked him and returned to Rei and Bonnie.

"He saw Troutman enter that house this morning," Rome said. "To his knowledge, he is still in there."

"How do we grab him?" Bonnie asked. "If we go right up to his door, he'll see us and take off."

"Yeah," Rei said. "Let me think about this for a minute." He surveyed his surroundings. "You ladies stay here," he said. "Let me scout around." He drew the Deucadon cloak over his head, drew his hand down the front and promptly disappeared.

"Where are you going?" Rome asked him mentally.

"I'm just going to do a quick recon," Rei replied. *"I'll be back as fast as I can. OK?"*

"Of course," Rome replied. She and Bonnie backed up a little bit and removed themselves off to the side.

Rei was gone for some time. Rome thought she heard a whoosh and pop off in the distance but could not be sure. At last, Rei returned, making himself visible again. He pulled down his hood and spoke in conspiratorial tones.

"Here's the deal. There are two entrances to his house," he said quietly, pointing at the dwelling identified as belonging to Troutman. "There's one door around the back. I've got that one taken care of. Romey, you stay out of sight till we go in. Bonnie, I want you to pull your hood up like you're hiding your face and go right up to the front door. Your cover story is you snuck back here from Helome and want to hook up with the Darwin people again. I'll be there with you."

"Won't that give things away?" Rome asked sharply.

"Not if I'm invisible," Rei said. "After we take him down, Romey, you come in and do your telepath thing with him so we can find Steele. Everybody okay with the plan?" Rei looked at each woman. Both Rome and Bonnie nodded.

Rei drew his hand along the cloak and disappeared again. Bonnie pulled her hood over her head and walked slowly toward the house. Rome dashed past her and went around the side of their target house to hide.

After making sure that Rome was out of sight, Bonnie knocked on the door.

"Who's there," came a gruff voice from inside.

"David, it's me, Bonnie Mullen," Bonnie whispered.

The door opened a crack. Light streamed into the room and Bonnie could see Troutman was just behind the door. She pulled her hood back a little so he could see her face.

"What the hell are you doing here?" he said.

"Just let me in," Bonnie pleaded. "I need to get off the street."

"OK," Troutman said and he opened the door wider. Bonnie pretended to trip and bumped into the door, forcing Troutman to open it wide for just a minute. As soon as Bonnie was inside, Troutman slammed the door shut.

The tall man walked over to the window and pulled the threadbare curtains aside to look out. "Did anybody see you come here?" he asked.

"No," Bonnie replied. "I've been real careful."

She looked around the house. It was tiny, just two rooms. In the corner was a workbench with wires and electronics and a pile of something that Bonnie assumed was an explosive. It was a typical bomber's lair.

"How the hell did you escape?" he asked. He pointed to a table covered with litter. He shoved a clean space and pulled out a chair. "Sit down," he said. "Do you want anything to drink?"

"No," Bonnie said, "but thanks." The room smelled strongly of body odor. Troutman clearly didn't take much care of himself.

He sat down next to her. "So what gives?" he asked. "Where did you come from?"

"Well, when they rounded us up, they shipped us off to Alpha Centauri."

"Jesus H. Christ," the tall man said. "Alpha Centauri?"

"Yeah," Bonnie replied. "The Vooks call their world there Helome. I gotta tell you. It's actually quite beautiful there, not like this dump. You'd be surprised."

"OK, I believe you," he said. "Then what?"

"You know the Vooks. They asked us if we were going to be good. We said yes so they pretty much let us do what we wanted. I got a job running a farm which was pretty peaceful. But Keller started plotting how to get back."

"Keller, sure," Troutman said, nodding. Then he tilted his head. "How *did* you get back here?"

"I know it's going to sound stupid but I just asked. The Vooks there, they didn't care. Keller put up a stink for me so they let me hitch a ride on a ship back to this dopey planet."

"So how'd you find me?" he asked. "How did you even know where to look?"

"Well, I started with the fact that you and Steele were never caught..."

Troutman bristled when she mentioned Steele's name. "So I figured you'd be easier to track down. You do kind of stand out."

"Yeah...but still," Troutman said. "Really, how did you figure it out?"

"Well, as soon as I heard that somebody tried to kill that idiot Bierak..." There was a rustling sound in the corner of the room.

Troutman looked up but saw nothing. He turned back to Bonnie who continued. "I figured it was you two. I remembered that you used to play cards with Paul Chung so I went to his house. He told me where to look."

Troutman slammed the table with his fist. "Dammit," he said. "If Steele finds out Chung said anything, he's going to be in for a world of hurt."

"Yeah, so where is he?" Bonnie asked. "Steele."

"Why do you want to know?" Troutman replied back.

"Because if we're going to take over this world, we need to band together. I figured three of us have a better chance than two."

"Steele doesn't want to be found right now," Troutman said with a bit of fear in his voice.

"Come on, David," Bonnie said. "You can tell me."

"No," Troutman said. "We have to lay low for a while till things cool down."

"Please," Bonnie pleaded. "It's important."

Troutman's eyes narrowed. He looked around the room and then back at Bonnie. "You still never told me how you found me. And there's no way you could know it was me and Steele that planted the bomb. It could've been anyone. Something doesn't smell right." He meant that literally. From the corner of the room was the odor of a clean, well-groomed person, not the squalid smell he had long since become used to.

"You can say that again," Bonnie said, trying to be funny. Troutman didn't laugh. "No, really," she said. "There's nothing going on." She looked at Troutman but he seemed distracted.

"Actually, there is," Rei said, appearing suddenly in the corner.

"Bierak!" Troutman shouted. He leaped up and took his chair and flung it at Rei who ducked in time. The chair crashed to the wall then the floor. In the mean time, Troutman bolted toward the back of the house. He got to the back door and whipped it open, only to see MINIMCOM's two-meter tall all-black livetar standing there. Before Troutman could even turn, MINIMCOM lifted his arm, brought his hand down on the crown of Troutman's head and the Essessoni collapsed the ground like a broken puppet.

***

It took a while but eventually, Troutman came to. Shaking his head to clear the cobwebs, the would-be assassin looked around to assess the situation. He was seated at his own table but with very tight white restraints binding his hands to the arms of the chair and his legs to the legs of the chair. Standing immediately to his right was MINIMCOM's imposing bulk. Bonnie and Rei were sitting across from him and Rome sat to his left.

"I'm not telling you nothing," he sneered. "You can arrest me. You can deport me. But that's it."

Rome reached out and stroked his hand back and forth but never letting go completely. "We want to find Steele," she said, pointing to the picture lying on the table with her free hand.

"Like I said, I'm not talking," Troutman insisted. Rome said nothing but continued to tap the picture. The images flying through Troutman's mind were distinct.

"He is in the forest to the west," she said, finally.

"Huh?" Troutman said. "No, he isn't."

"He comes into Ur when he needs supplies. He usually sends Troutman on his behalf and only rarely enters the town."

"What are you talking about? How are you doing this?" Troutman asked, slightly unnerved.

"Who is the Vuduri woman who is helping him?" Rei asked.

Troutman looked up at Rei, completely rattled. "How do you know all of this?"

"Look, David," Bonnie said, reaching her hands out, palms up, across the table. "I was mostly telling the truth. The world of Helome is spectacular and the Vuduri there really do let us roam freely. We aren't prisoners. They are really committed to building a world with us as partners. Even Keller has given up the fight. He's made his home there. He's even taken on a wife."

"No way!" Troutman said. "Keller would never do that."

"Yes, he did," Rome said, squeezing his hand gently. "His wife is named Virga and she is already pregnant with his second child. Captain Keller specifically sanctioned this mission, to capture you and Steele because he no longer believes violence is the answer."

Troutman looked at each of their faces. MINIMCOM placed his hand on Troutman's shoulder with just enough pressure to be painful.

Troutman squirmed in place trying to wriggle free but was unsuccessful.

"Look," he said finally. "If Steele finds out that I've told you anything, he won't just kill you. He'll kill me, too."

"That's why we have to stop him," Rei said, leaning forward. "There's no place left on this world for the likes of him. Everybody else wants to live in peace. He's the only one who doesn't."

"All right," Troutman said, acknowledging defeat. "But I want you to know that none of this was my idea."

"He is telling the truth," Rome said quietly.

Troutman looked over at Rome then down at her hand. MINIMCOM eased up a little bit of the pressure on his shoulder.

"When you guys defeated us and sent everybody packing, I actually wanted to go too. But Steele wouldn't let me. He literally stuck a knife in my side and told me we were hiding out until the coast was clear."

"So it was just the two of you," Rei said. "What did you hope to accomplish?"

"After the heat died down, the two of us made our way back to Darwin Base. Steele thought if we could finish one of the starships, we could take a run to wherever you guys sent everybody and bring some of them back. I guess he wanted to start some sort of guerilla action. But the ships weren't nearly ready. Steele's next plan was to build up an arsenal, then steal a starship, maybe. I wanted no part of it. Not too long ago, I even tried to get away. But Steele found me. He told me if we accomplished nothing else, we had to get you two out of the way."

"Where does the Vuduri woman fit in? Tell us about her," Rome insisted. "Do you know who she is?"

"No," Troutman said. "I've never even seen her face. She always wore a cap and a visor."

"How did you meet her?"

"One time, Steele was, I don't know, stir-crazy. He got some money and I sent him up to The Hand so he could gamble a little bit. Blow off a little steam. I guess that's where he met her."

"And she wanted to be part of the plan to have us killed?" Rome asked.

"It was the weirdest thing. I have no clue how she figured it out but Steele brought her back here. She said we had a common interest and, yeah, that was in eliminating the two of you." He nodded toward Rei, then Rome. "Then she'd get Steele his starship."

"Do you know her name? Where she comes from?" Rome asked.

"No," Troutman said. "Other than breaking into the library, I didn't spend much time with her. It was her and Steele most of the time. We came back here, I rigged the bomb. We watched you for two weeks and knew exactly what time the two of you were going to be home. They snuck it into your house and set the timer. I still don't know what happened or even how you survived, Bierak."

"Is this woman with Steele now?" Rei asked.

"She might be. Since the bomb, they've steered clear of me. I don't know what they're up to. Maybe she left. Maybe she's still here. I have no way of knowing. I've just been hiding out."

"Have you ever been to Steele's encampment?" Rome asked.

"No," he replied. "But it can't be too far away. I would have to guess within a day's walk, maybe a little more."

Rei looked over at Rome. She nodded. He stood up then said, "MINIMCOM, can you rig us a jail cell in your cargo compartment. We gotta go after Steele now and we don't have time to put this loser any place else."

"**Absolutely,**" MINIMCOM said. He stood perfectly still then nodded his head. "**It is done. I have constructed a small room with no entrance or egress. It will hold him until you are ready to release him.**"

"Thank you!" Troutman exclaimed with a great deal of relief in his tone.

Rome cocked her head. "Why are you thanking us?"

"I've hated every minute of my life here. I hate Steele and I hated what he made me do. Finally, I'll be able to going back to being human. You're doing me the biggest favor you can imagine just putting me in jail."

Rei shrugged. With a whoosh and a pop, Troutman and the chair were gone as was MINIMCOM's livetar.

Rei looked around the room. "Do you think there's any point in searching this dump?"

"No," Rome said. "He was telling the truth. He really did not know where Steele is hiding out."

"OK," Rei said, leading the way to the door. "Then we head west."

"Hold on," Bonnie said. "Steele is rather vicious. Don't you think we should take your robot with us? For protection?"

"He isn't a robot," Rome offered. "He is, a, well, the thing you see that looks like a person is called a livetar. It is an animated shell but the intelligence and personality reside up there." Rome pointed toward the ceiling.

"Even so."

"MINIMCOM will pick us up shortly," Rei said. "We only need go as far as the edge of town then we'll ride from there. We'll look for Steele from the air."

Intermezzo 2
Year 3455 AD (1374 PR)
(5 years earlier)
1.5 Light Years from Tabit, headed for Deucado

REI BIERAK SAT SILENTLY IN THE COCKPIT OF THEIR SPACE TUG, along with Rome. OMCOM's final words of caution were still ringing in their ears. Now they had to worry not only about the Stareaters, but whatever the hell it was that OMCOM spawned was after them too. Rei rocked back and forth, whispering to himself, as if his motion could somehow make them go faster. He looked over at Rome. She was studying the console but the tightness on her face told Rei her mind was elsewhere.

Rei felt so powerless. He had to do something. Suddenly, his head snapped up. "MINIMCOM, when we were in the galley, you said you had a way of getting us to go even faster."

`"That is correct,"` replied the autopilot computer who was manning the space tug mounted on the far side of the Ark.

Finding interest in the discussion, Rome looked up from the console. She glanced at Rei. "Can you tell us, please, MINIMCOM?" she inquired.

`"If we could reduce the amount of mass that I must push through each tunnel, I would not have to hold it open for as long. I could extend its reach and increase our effective velocity proportionally."`

"We don't have much mass to get rid of," Rei said. "Do we?"

`"Yes, we do,"` replied MINIMCOM who at this point in their journey had never progressed beyond a disembodied voice. `"A significant amount."`

"What?" Rome asked. Rei could see she was relieved to have something to distract her.

`"The entire propulsion module of Rei's Ark is superfluous,"` MINIMCOM replied. `"It serves no purpose. I have done numerous simulations and I believe I could increase our effective velocity as much as 20% further if we could eliminate it."`

"Hey," Rei said. "You're right. The propulsion unit was made to be jettisoned before reentry in the first place. If we could detach it, it would reduce our overall mass a lot."

"How would you do that?" Rome asked Rei.

Rei thought about it for a moment. "We went over this during orientation. I think that it requires a spacewalk."

"Why?" asked Rome. A small amount of trepidation crept into her voice.

"Well, the ship was designed to be in space for hundreds of years," Rei replied. "There is a separator ring for each section. It's kind of like an explosive bolt but continuous. Solid-state. It's made out of some type of meta-stable intermolecular composite..."

"**Thermite**," MINIMCOM interjected.

"Yeah, thermite," Rei said. "So it would last forever but the charge to set it off has to be done by hand."

"How would you do that?" Rome asked tentatively.

"There's a magneto," Rei answered. He saw Rome's confusion with the term. "It's a charging device," he said, "built into each section. There's a permanent magnet and you just crank it around and it charges up a capacitor. When there's enough charge, you let it loose and the chemicals explode."

"You are going to make an explosion?" Rome asked. Now she was genuinely worried.

"No, no, no, nothing like that," Rei said. "It's more like a strip that sizzles. When it's done, the sections separate."

"**I would like to remind you that your ship is almost 1400 years old. Do you really believe that the thermite reaction would still be viable after such a long period of time?**" MINIMCOM asked.

"Yeah," Rei said. "In theory, it would work after 10,000 years. As long as the permanent magnet and magneto can crank up a charge."

"Rei, this worries me," Rome said, her breath catching.

"It'll be OK," Rei said. "We have everything we need. Come on, Rome. It means we could get to Deucado in... how long, MINIMCOM?"

"**It should reduce our travel time to well under one year,**" replied the autopilot computer installed on the other tug.

"Rome, it's worth it, don't you think?" Rei asked plaintively.

"I do not know," Rome said. "Spacewalks are inherently dangerous."

"There's nothing to it," Rei said. "I just go out, crank a handle, press a button and I come back."

Rome lowered her head and looked at Rei through the top part of her eyes. Her very demeanor shouted skepticism but her words undermined it.

"If it will save us that much time, then I agree it is worth it," she said hesitantly. "Very well."

"Great," Rei said. He unbuckled the high-g harness and jumped up. "Come on and get me ready."

"What do you mean get you ready?" Rome asked as she unbuckled. "I am coming with you," she said as she stood up.

"No," Rei said. "You can't. You have to stay onboard the ship."

"Why?" Rome asked, fear seeping into her voice again.

"Because," Rei said. "We can't both be in space at the same time. If something happens to me…"

"What!" Rome exclaimed. "What are you saying?"

"Nothing," Rei said, trying to defuse the steadily growing tension. "It's just that we don't need to endanger…" As soon as he said the word, he knew it was a mistake. Rome leaped over at him and grabbed him around the neck.

"If there is any danger to you, then I cannot allow it," she said. "I do not know what I would do if anything happened to you."

"Nothing's going to happen to me," Rei said, sliding his arms around her waist. "It'll be fine."

"Then if it will be fine, I am going with you."

Rei looked down at her. As always, he got lost in her dark, glowing eyes. He loved this woman so much, beyond anything he ever dreamed was possible. He knew he could never win an argument about the trade off so he decided to try and bully his way past.

"Let's not fight about this," Rei said. "It has to be this way. Just help me get ready."

Rome did not answer. In fact, she said nothing the entire time they walked back to the austere anteroom outside the mid-ship airlock. Rei reached into his locker and removed his pressure suit, climbing into it, all the while aware that Rome was standing there, arms folded across her chest. For this short walk, he didn't bother with the plumbing and he dressed fairly quickly. He was smoothing the sleeves and adjusting the gloves of his white pressure suit when he took a chance and looked up at his woman and saw her scowling at him.

"What?" he asked.

"You know what," Rome replied sternly, sadness radiating from her Vuduri eyes.

"Nothing is going to happen, I promise," Rei said. "I'm just going to go out and turn the crank. I'll be back in a jiffy. Plus I'll be tethered the whole time."

"So if nothing is going to happen to you, why am I not allowed to go with you?" Rome said. "Why do you have to go alone?"

"I just went over this with you," Rei said. He walked over to her and placed his gloved hand under her chin, tilting her head up so she looked him in the eyes. "I'm the only one who can do this and if something happens to me, you have to fly the ship to Deucado."

Rome pulled his hand away from her chin. "You cannot have it both ways," she said angrily. "Either you will be safe and I can come with you or there is a chance you will not be safe and I need to be there for you."

"Rome, I can't endanger you," Rei said.

"Danger, there is that word again," Rome said in a huff. She pushed Rei aside and walked over to her locker. "I am going with you. That is all there is to it," she said. She opened her locker and started to remove her pressure suit mounted there.

Rei came over to her and put his hands on her hips. He turned her around in place. Tears were streaming down from her eyes.

"Romey, listen to me," he said gently. "If I cut the propulsion section loose, MINIMCOM says we can go faster by 20%. That means 20% less time in space and 20% less chance of anything happening to us while we're in space. That's worth the risk of taking a simple spacewalk and turning a crank."

"There is no risk worth me losing you," she said, softly. "Rei, I do not think you understand. We are one. So you are mine now. I cannot describe it any other way."

"And you are mine," he said. He kissed her gently but then suddenly, he cut the kiss short.

"I know," he said, "I'll compromise with you."

"What?" Rome asked hopefully.

"You get in your pressure suit but you stay in the airlock. You don't come out. If you need to know what's going on, you tug on the tether whenever you want. You can do it every 30 seconds if you need to. You tug once and that means 'are you ok?' I'll tug back twice. That means 'I'm fine.' If I miss even one tug, you can come after me. But if I don't, I want you to promise me you will stay here, inside the airlock."

Rome's mouth turned upwards into a smile even as the tears continued to flow. "That is very fair," she said. "I agree to your proposal."

After Rome was dressed but before they put on their helmets, she said, "Wait."

"Wait what?" Rei answered.

"If you have a problem, if you need me, you tug on the tether three times. All right?"

"Sure," Rei said. "That's a great idea. I think we have a system, huh?"

"Yes, a system," Rome said. She leaned forward to hug Rei as best as she could, given the bulk of the pressure suits.

"Let's get this show on the road," Rei said.

"You always say that," Rome observed. "What does that mean? What show? What road?"

"The Rome and Rei show, of course," Rei answered. "And the road? I guess it's the road of life."

"I see," Rome said, even though she didn't. She nodded and wiped away her tears. They put on their helmets and entered the airlock together. Rome clamped twin lights on the sides of Rei's helmet and clipped a hammer and screwdriver to eyelets on the side of the suit. She attached the tether and tugged on it to make sure it was secure. Rei immediately tugged it twice. He could see Rome smile within her helmet.

Rome leaned forward and pressed her helmet against his.

"You be careful, Rei Bierak," she said in a muffled voice. "You come back to me."

"Of course I will, sweetheart," he said. "I love you, Rome. I could never leave you."

Rome pulled her helmet back and nodded. She mouthed the words, 'I love you too, mau emir' back to Rei. Rei turned to the

163

airlock and pressed the stud to begin the depressurization cycle. When all the air was evacuated, the outer door opened and Rei was looking at interstellar space.

Rome tapped Rei on the shoulder. He turned towards her and she clipped a ring around his wrist which was connected to a hand thruster. The thruster itself resembled a putty gun with a U-shaped set of nozzles on the business end. She placed the bulbous handle, complete with trigger, in his hand. Rei hefted it and nodded to her. He turned back in place, looking down to pick a landing spot. Taking a deep breath, Rei stepped onto the ledge just outside the door then pushed off and down so that he drifted toward the hull of his Ark. He only had to go about two meters. His magnetic boots clamped on and Rei tested their grip. They felt secure. He looked back up at Rome and gave her the thumbs up sign. She nodded and waved to him to get going.

Rei kept one hand on the tether and made his way quickly toward the back of the crew compartment. Overall, the Ark itself was huge, nearly two football fields in length but Rei made good time. Rome only tugged on the tether once and Rei responded immediately with a double tug back. He figured she only tried it the one time because she could see him and she knew that he was OK.

He stopped when he got to the rear of the crew section and ran his hand along the stubby vertical stabilizer which seemed no worse for wear given how old it was. The metal was dulled, probably from the continual abrasion of space dust but overall it looked solid. Rei turned back to Rome and pointed to his chest then waved his arm once in a large arc. He was trying to indicate to her that he had to jump over the lattice-work adjoining the two sections. Rome tugged the tether once in reply. Rei tugged back twice. He backed up a few steps, pulled in a large amount of slack then ran forward and jumped up into the air. His momentum carried him over the lattice-work and he sailed on for some time. The whole experience was actually sort of fun. Eventually, Rei fired the hand thruster and the reaction pushed him back to the hull of the cargo section where the magnetic boots clamped on again immediately. Rei nearly stumbled but was able to regain his balance.

He stopped moving and carefully pulled in the remaining slack, waiting for Rome to tug. Right on cue, she queried him and he tugged twice back. As Rei moved onward toward the rear of the cargo section, there was more strain on the tether, almost as if Rome was reluctant to pay out the cable as fast as he needed. He pushed on as quickly as she would allow, knowing there was nothing he could do about it. When he got to the rear of the cargo module, he looked across at the remains of the propulsion section. The thin metal rods that were responsible for generating the "atom catcher" field were either broken or all twisted up. Rei assumed this was caused by the whole ship being spun about when they had their collision with whatever it was that hit them.

The circumstances didn't matter. The propulsion system was dead weight. The time had come to cut it loose. Rei searched the base of the cargo section's rear stabilizer and spotted the release panel, outlined in red. He unclipped the screwdriver from its eyelet and clipped the tiny attached cable on its end back in place. It was a smart design so that if he dropped it, it would not float off.

Rei bent over and pried open the panel which came loose and started drifting away in space. He didn't need it so he let it go. His helmet lights illuminated the cavity where he saw a hand-crank, a charge meter and an ignition switch. He knelt down on both knees but as soon as he did, his magnetic boots broke their grip and he started drifting away from the ship feet first. A quick burst of the hand-thruster brought him back in contact with the Ark. Rome tugged to make sure he was OK and he double-tugged his assurance back.

Learning from his mistake, Rei placed the sole of one boot right next to the panel and kneeled down on the other knee. He was able to reach the magneto crank easily and started turning it. He turned it about six times but the needle within the analog gauge did not move. That meant he had generated no charge. Rei thought about the mechanics. The crank turned some permanent magnets which passed around a twin set of coils. This created a flow of electricity which charged up a capacitor. The meter was just another coil which moved the delicate needle based upon the stored charge. It was basic physics.

Rei cranked furiously for a minute, round and round, growing increasingly frustrated. The needle never budged. Rome tugged on the tether and Rei tugged back, perhaps a little too hard. Rome tugged again and this time he tugged back more gently so she would know he was truly all right.

Rei scowled at the panel. It was the simplest design in the world. It was made to last hundreds and hundreds of years in the vacuum of space. As long as the permanent magnets retained their magnetism, and there was no reason why they wouldn't, it should work. The only possible thing that it could be was... Rei laughed at himself. He gently tapped at the needle gauge with the handle of the screwdriver and the needle popped to the fully charged position instantly.

"*Stuck, duh*," Rei thought to himself. He used his thumb to depress the safety then pressed the ignition switch and stood up. A puff of smoke shot out of the rim of the cargo section where the lattice-work attached. The smoke raced around the circumference of the ship until it was out of sight. Rei bent past the rear stabilizer and in less than a minute, the circle of smoke came back around, ending where it began. In theory, the two sections were now separated. Unfortunately, Rei realized he had no way to test this without going back into the ship and ordering MINIMCOM to fire the thrusters. Vuduri pressure suits didn't have radios, otherwise, he'd call it in. He took a deep breath to calm himself. If the two sections were not completely severed, they were no worse off but still, to have come this far and not know was disappointing.

Rei had an idea but it would require Rome's indulgence. He tugged once on the tether. Rome tugged back. He tugged twice. At this point, he was hoping she realized he wanted her attention. He gathered up a little bit of slack and stepped over onto the lattice-work, turning in place to face forward. The lattice-work was made primarily of composites so his magnetic boots did not grip very well. He had to fire the hand-thruster briefly to force his torso down. He grabbed a hold of the lattice and wedged the toes of his boots into two of the open spaces of the diamond-shaped pattern. With his free hand, he gripped the tether so he would know if Rome was testing him. With the other hand, he stuck the handle of the hand-thruster into an open space and pulled the trigger. He fired it continuously for about 15 seconds. He didn't know how much reactant the thruster carried but he didn't want to use up all the charge, just in case.

He lifted his head and was gladdened to see that there was the slightest separation between the lattice and the cargo compartment.

Rei fired his hand thruster again and the distance increased infinitesimally. A broad smile formed across his face. Over and over, Rei fired the thruster until there was a three-meter gap between him and the Ark.

That was enough. Rei pulled his boots free and stood up. He tried to push off so that he could go back toward the cargo compartment but the only effect he had was to begin rising up, floating away from the lattice and the entire propulsion module.

He had a moment of panic but was able to suppress it by realizing that the tether protected him from drifting off into interstellar space. He raised his arm over his head and fired the hand-thruster. The reactive force drove him downward and where the tether caught on the edge of the Ark, he pivoted downwards toward the vertical face. By twisting his body again, he came at the Ark feet first. His magnetic boots clamped solidly on the newly exposed vertical end.

Rei could feel Rome pulling in the slack and there was the inevitable tug. Proudly, he tugged back twice. Geometrically, he was in an odd position. He was actually standing at right angles to the length of the Ark and he knew Rome could no longer see him, but their communication system would assure her he was all right. Rei looked down at his feet and saw that he was now "standing" on the giant cargo door enclosing that module.

He thought about the contents of the compartment beneath which supposedly contained all the equipment required to start a viable human colony on an alien world. It also contained his personal effects which comprised some clothing, a few books, his transit and his music slab. Rei's eyes grew wide. He realized he would never get an opportunity like this again but he had to have Rome's permission. The last thing he wanted was for Rome to misunderstand and come after him.

Rei tugged on the tether once, hard. Rome tugged on it in response. He tugged on it twice gently so she would know he was OK. He had her attention so he did it again. He pulled the tether once hard. Rome repeated her actions as did he. Now she had to know something was up. She was a smart girl. As long as he kept their system intact, he knew she would let him do this.

He stepped aside and released the clamps holding the door closed. The huge door swung open easily as there was no pressure differential. Like the crew compartment, the cargo section was designed to be exposed to the vacuum of space. Rei shined his helmet lights down the long belly of the cargo compartment and saw a twin pair of mesh walkways leading down its length. Rome tugged on the tether and Rei tugged back twice.

He entered into the cargo compartment and slowly made his way down its length, noting the contents as he passed them. In the end closest to the hatch, where he just entered, there were the large yellow-striped cubes marked Transports. In front of them were boxes containing the drilling equipment and beyond those were the mining explosives. They had the international symbol for radioactivity which Rei ignored and moved on. Beyond that were the smelting furnaces for refining ore. Next were the bio-stocks: the frozen animal embryos, the seeds, the incubators, all the items they would need to start farming. Past mid-ship were various tools, masonry kits, machining equipment, hunting rifles and so forth.

Rei moved on. Finally, he got to the storage lockers. They were arranged alphabetically and it took him no time at all to find his storage cube. He pulled it open and surveyed its contents. He looked longingly at his clothes and polymer-plastic books but decided he did not need them just now. He certainly didn't need his straight razor. He reached in and pulled out his music slab which was a gift from his parents. It was solar-powered and the music was burned into a silicon wafer so, in theory, it would last forever. Rei's breath caught. Holding the music slab in his hand made him think of his parents who were now so long gone as was every other person he ever knew or loved. Including Sally. Even though from his perspective, it had only been a few months, the reality was they died over a thousand years before. The thought was staggering. They were all dust. Rei had a moment of panic. What had he done?

Rei felt a tug on the tether. Instinctively, he tugged back twice. Rei couldn't help but think back to that last night he had spent with Sally. Out on her deck, under the night sky, he claimed to her that she had left a hole in his heart that could never be filled. But she had insisted he was wrong. Sally had told him he'd find his dream girl among the stars. At the time, he thought it was beyond ridiculous but now he realized she was right. The true love of his life was alive and well and anxiously awaiting his return. His heart was whole again.

In fact, it was brimming over. There was no more past. His future was with Rome. Rei slid the music slab and the ear-buds into a side pocket and turned to go back.

He looked down the long length of the cargo compartment and thought about what Estar had said to him, that they were carrying Erklirte weapons. Anything could be turned into a weapon. The hammer clipped to his side could be used as a weapon. The hunting rifles were the closest things to actual weapons but they hardly constituted something an entire race of people would fear. To think that this was the purpose of all of these supplies made no sense. Rei shook it off.

He gathered up the tether and started walking back to the rear of the cargo compartment. Rei tugged gently on the cord and let it slide between his gloved fingers so that Rome would take up the slack. He did this every fifteen meters or so until he reached the rear of the cargo compartment. He turned around and looked at it one more time. The rows and rows of equipment casting harsh shadows from his helmet lights.

Weapons? Rei laughed to himself. The Vuduri, they were all crazy. He closed up the cargo compartment and made his way back to the top of the Ark so that Rome could see him. The gigantic propulsion module was now twenty meters or so behind them. He waved to Rome to indicate to her that his mission was a success. He ran as fast as his magnetic boots would allow him, stopping only to leap over the latticework attaching the cargo compartment to the crew compartment. In just a few minutes, he was at the base of their tug, looking up at Rome peering out. With a single leap, he was inside.

As soon as he reentered the airlock, Rome jumped at him and hugged him, almost knocking him back out the door. He smiled and pressed his helmet to hers.

"It's OK, Romey," he said. "I'm back. It worked. No more worries."

"Yes," she replied in her muffled helmet voice. "No more worries."

Rei turned and pressed the stud to close the outer door and watched until the indicator turned green. As soon as it did, he removed his helmet and waited until Rome removed hers. He held up his music slab and smiled at her.

"What is that?" she asked.

"It's all my music in one little package," he said. "Now I can play it for you!"

"I wondered what you were doing back there," Rome said curiously. "I assumed it had to be something important. I knew you would not dawdle for no reason."

"This is important," Rei said, waving the slab. "I'll get MINIMCOM to hook it into our system and then I can teach you all about it."

"I will love it, I am sure," Rome said, this time a bit more enthusiastically. "Let us get going though. Asdrale Cimatir is still back there. And if OMCOM is right, who knows what else?"

"Roger that," Rei said.

After stowing their pressure suits in their lockers, Rei and Rome made their way back to the cockpit and took their seats. They both buckled in which was prudent since this would be the first time they attempted a PPT jump with their newly reduced mass.

"OK, MINIMCOM," Rei said. "We're skinny now. Let's see what you can do with it."

"**Very well,**" MINIMCOM said tersely from the other tug, "**initiating jump.**" Immediately, the PPT generators fired up and in front of them, a yawning black hole appeared. MINIMCOM fired both tugs' plasma thrusters and Rei and Rome were pushed back into their seats a little harder than before.

As soon as they stepped through, they heard the click and thump of MINIMCOM unclamping and rotating his craft and reattaching. A slight push forward indicated he was firing his plasma thrusters to bring them to a dead stop. It only lasted a few moments. Rome looked down at the view screens, tapped a few buttons then exclaimed, "Yes!"

"What?" Rei said but he already knew.

"It equates to 24c," Rome replied.

"Sleek," Rei said. Then remembering MINIMCOM's remark from earlier, he added, "Good thinking, MINIMCOM."

"Yes, MINIMCOM," Rome chimed in. "It was an excellent idea."

"Thank you, thank you," MINIMCOM replied, clearly pleased with himself.

Rei turned to Rome and shrugged. "OK, what say we get…"

"No," Rome said, holding her hand up. "Allow me."

"Sure," Rei replied, somewhat puzzled.

"MINIMCOM, it is time to get this show on the road," Rome said with a smile.

"Acknowledged," replied MINIMCOM. "Next stop: Deucado."

Rei laughed. This was going to be some trip.

Chapter 18
Year 3460 AD (1379 PR)
The forest to the west of Ur

TRUE TO REI'S PRONOUNCEMENT, MINIMCOM PICKED THEM UP just past the city's outskirts. In stealth mode, MINIMCOM drifted slowly west surveying the cane-tree forest below using his full set of sensors. Lake Eprehem lay to the north. To the south, the region was even more densely forested, punctuated only by the occasional rocky outcropping. Rei studied the ventral camera images while Rome concentrated on the MIDAR display in ground-penetrating mode. Bonnie wore a set of headphones and listened to the acoustic sensors mounted on the outside of MINIMCOM's hull.

About 20 kilometers in, they found a small river leading to Lake Eprehem with a many-fingered series of tributaries heading to the south. From Rei's limited knowledge of geology, the southern ocean was too far, so this little river must be emptying into the gigantic lake rather than serving as drainage.

They continued traveling until they reached a distance of over 40 kilometers from the edge of the city. It was at this point, the southwestern corner of Lake Eprehem, when the shoreline began to curve gently to the north.

"Nothing," Rei said, disgustedly. "For all we know, he's wearing the Deucadon invisibility cloak. And we're way more than one day's walk. Anybody have any ideas?" he asked, looking up at Rome and Bonnie.

Rome pointed to her MIDAR display. "I suggest we go back to the edge of Ur and travel on foot. While we may not be able to detect Steele's presence, we may be able to find a trail."

"You're going to track him?" Rei asked, somewhat taken aback.

"If that's what you call it," Rome answered confidently.

"Won't that leave you kind of exposed?" Bonnie interjected.

"We will have MINIMCOM hover directly over us in stealth mode." Rome tapped on the front console. "You'll stay aboard and watch the displays. MINIMCOM's instruments should be able to pick up any motion or IR signature. Something. Anything. Steele will reveal his position eventually."

"Rome's idea is even better than that," Rei said enthusiastically. "If I close my eyes, I can use my sonar vision to map out the area. That's how I found the Deucadons in the first place. They thought they were invisible but they weren't sound-proof."

"Then we're agreed," Rome said. "MINIMCOM?"

"`On it,`" replied the starship. He executed a stunning barrel roll and quickly accelerated due east returning to the spot where he had picked up Rei and Rome. They departed via the cargo ramp. Rei kept on the Deucadon cloak but Rome discarded her 'disguise' as she no longer needed it.

They stood in place and watched the spaceship rise until he was just higher than the treetops. The airframe shimmered and then MINIMCOM was gone.

"OK, my fearless tracker," Rei said. "Where do we start?"

Rome twisted in place and looked back at the city then turned to look forward. "There is no reason why Steele would take a circuitous route. We just need to align ourselves to Troutman's house and then go west. Steele would stay somewhat close to Lake Eprehem. He would need water and food."

"Yeah, but that little river we saw means he didn't have to stay just by the shoreline."

"He would if he wanted to catch swishies," Rome said. "We have to start somewhere."

"OK, let's do it," Rei said. He closed his eyes and OMCOM's 'gift', his sonar vision, kicked in. The sound of their footsteps was good enough to 'illuminate' the trail. Rei swept his head left and right and stopped almost immediately.

"What?" Rome asked.

"You were right," Rei said. He opened his eyes and trotted over to the edge of the first stand of cane-trees then stooped down. Clustered at the base of the trees were the ubiquitous sticky bushes.

"Here," he said, pointing to a bush. "Someone's been by here. You can see where some of the leaves were pulled off. The leaves stick to everything."

"Excellent," Rome said. "Let us continue in that direction."

They parted the bushes and entered into the forest proper. Through the occasional break in the trees, Rei looked up but saw nothing. At one point, he called up to MINIMCOM who assured him that he was directly overhead.

Deeper and deeper they went. Occasionally, Rei thought he heard a rustling noise overhead but when he examined the leaf canopy carefully, using sonar, he detected nothing. However, as they marched along, Rei's sonar vision was able to find small scuffs, more leaves pulled and where the ground was softer, the occasional footprint.

"This is easy," Rei said, smiling. "Who knew?" He trotted on ahead.

"Try to go a little slower," Rome cautioned. "Your special sight lets you manage your way around the trees but I still have to use my eyes."

"Sure," Rei called back to her but something ahead caught his attention. "There," he said, darting forward. "I found a…"

Suddenly, Rome screamed. Rei whipped around and saw a 'falling blanket', one of the largest he'd ever seen, draped over his wife.

"Rei!" Rome shouted mentally, *"I can't breathe."*

Rei raced back to where the bundled form of his wife was writhing around on the ground. He straddled her body and pulled on the edge of the 'blanket' with all his might. The thing wouldn't budge. He could feel its leathery skin constricting around her.

"Rome, Rome," he said helplessly. What he saw was the end of his life before him. The woman he loved more than humanly possible was suffocating in front of his eyes. There was no way he was going to let this happen. He took a deep breath and pulled once more with all his might. Suddenly, the 'blanket' released its grip and Rei went somersaulting backwards over Rome and onto the ground.

The 'blanket' removed itself from Rome's form but she just lay on the ground, shaking. Rei got up and went over to her. He peered down at her. She was laughing.

"Why are you laughing?" Rei asked, reaching down for her. "You almost died."

"It's alive!" Rome said, excitedly, pulling herself to her feet. "It's alive!"

"Of course it's alive," Rei said.

"No," Rome replied. She turned and looked at the 'blanket' which was beginning to curl itself up like a rug. Once it was a tight cylinder, it bent at the middle into an 'L' shape. Rome went over and caressed it.

"What are you doing?" Rei asked. "Those things are dangerous."

"No," Rome said. "When I was touching it, it spoke to me."

"It spoke to you?"

"Yes!" Rome said.

Suddenly, there was a sound like a whump and another 'falling blanket', even larger than the first, fell in front of them. It wriggled its way over to the first one, the one that had covered Rome and curled itself up into a cylinder as well, leaning against the first. There was another whump then another. Soon, there were so many 'falling blankets' that Rei realized for the first time how very much in danger their lives were every time they went into the forest.

The living creatures climbed over each other forming a tower nearly ten feet tall. Some of the blankets stretched over the ends to form an approximation of limbs. Along the ground, some of the smaller 'blankets' climbed up and inched their way toward the end. When the whole process was complete, the entity in front them looked vaguely humanoid. Huge, but humanoid nonetheless. Each of the components tightened up then the composite creature held its 'arms' out, beckoning to Rome. There was no hesitation in her actions. She walked toward the mass in front of her and let it or rather them envelope her in the equivalent of their arms.

"Rome!" Rei shouted. "Do you know what you are doing?"

"Yes," answered Rome, her voice somewhat muffled through the leathery flesh of the creatures holding her. "It wants to talk."

She twisted around and looked upward into the coils of 'blankets' that would have been its face. She stared, enraptured, as it filled her mind with imagery and substance. Finally, she nodded and turned back to Rei, still held within the grasp of the composite creature.

"These are the living embodiment of Deucado," Rome intoned. "They have been here for millions upon millions of years."

"What do they want?" Rei asked, somewhat frightened of the sight before him.

"They want nothing," Rome said. "They have dedicated their existence to surviving from day to day. So it has been for eons."

"Was there anything before?" Rei asked, catching the implication.

"Before that, they were living, sentient beings, like us. They were vertebrates. They roamed this planet and continued to evolve for ten million years during the time when the sky stopped raining its punishing stones upon them."

"So then what happened?" Rei asked. "How did they become what…what they are?"

"They tried to live," Rome continued. "They went down under the ground. All those caves we have found. They were built by their ancestors. They used…" Rome struggled to find the words. "They used hand tools and magma guns, like the hoses your firefighters once used, to carve out gigantic caves, to protect them from the asteroids pummeling the planet."

"So all those caves…" Rei stuttered. "They were built by hand?"

"Many of them," Rome said, almost hypnotically. "But it was not enough. After a long break, once again, death came down upon them from above."

Rei started to speak then stopped.

"As a planet, every creature decided, the fear, the pain, it was no way to live. They decided, as an entire world, to devolve into the adaptable forms you see today. No bones, no worries. They live, they die. Each day becomes the next. There has been peace, tranquility, even happiness, ever since."

Rei snapped his fingers. "Then those fossils, the ones that Wally found. They were real. That was what they looked like before?"

Rome looked up at the top of the being holding her. She nodded. "Yes," Rome answered. "That was their original form. Now they are nothing but blankets and swishies. Even the plants were involved. There used to be a multitude of species on this world. The plants decided on the cane-tree form, the sticky bushes, the threadgrass and the flowers. That was all they needed to survive from one generation to the next."

"So this whole planet, with next to no diversity, was a conscious decision on the part of the indigenous population to survive the rain of meteors and the like?"

"Yes," Rome answered. "That was their solution. And for millions upon millions of years, it worked. They had given up all hope and all the associated pain to live in the forms you see in front of you."

"Can you tell them that we have figured out how to stop the things from falling out of the sky?"

"Yes," Rome said. "They know. And they do appreciate it. That is why they did not kill me. They just never had anyone to talk to before."

"Oh wow," Rei said, walking up to where Rome was standing. He reached out with his hand and stroked the leather-like surface of the creature nearest to him. He thought he felt a vibration, almost like a cat's purr, beneath his caress.

"So now what?" Rei asked. "They know we're here. We know they're here. Where do we go?"

"They do nothing. Life goes on as before. However, they understand that there are other humans trying to harm us. And they want to help."

"They do?" Rei asked. "How?"

"They know where Steele is hiding!" Rome said, giddily.

"Omigod," Rei said. "Where?"

"It is far but they will lead us," Rome answered. The composite creature released its grip on her and slowly, each of the animals making up its body climbed down and away. Soon there was nothing left but the original 'blanket' that had tried to engulf Rome.

"I don't understand," Rei said.

"Look," Rome replied, pointing past Rei.

Rei turned around and saw 'blanket' after 'blanket' forming a path like you'd see when people used logs to line a road, leading into the woods.

"And we just follow them?" Rei asked.

"Yes," Rome said proudly. She walked up and put her arm through Rei's elbow. Gently, she tugged him forward. "We just follow them to Steele's hideout."

***

Not quite believing what he had just witnessed, Rei contacted MINIMCOM with his EM link and did his best to explain Rome's encounter with the 'falling blankets'. The starship accepted his word but it was clear from his tone that he was somewhat skeptical.

As each 'blanket' fell from the trees it curled into a cylinder, pointing to the next. The trail that was formed was easy to follow. Rei didn't even bother to use his sonar vision at first as the 'blankets' appeared to know exactly what they were doing. As Rei and Rome went through deeper and denser portions of the forest, the canopy of vegetation overhead was so thick, it made it dark, like night. Rome was able to use her infrared vision to walk while Rei was forced to use his sonar vision to navigate his way among the trees.

At one point, they came to one of the little creeks they noted from the air. The blanket trail stopped there. Rome stooped down and touched the blanket closest to the water.

"They do not like to cross the water unless they have to," Rome said.

"So what do we do?"

"We wait," Rome said. "More will come." She turned and looked across the stream and saw another group of blankets wriggling out of the woods. "There," Rome said. "They are on their way."

Rei watched as another group of blankets lined up to form a path that led into the woods on the other side of the creek.

"OK," Rei said. "We cross but I need a drink first."

He stooped down to where the water lapped up against the bank and scooped up a handful of water into his mouth. Rome did the same. Rei leaned back on his haunches then extended backwards so that he was lying on his back. He looked up at the canopy above them. Nothing on this planet was as it seemed. Rome decided to lie down as well and snuggled up next to him.

"Look," she said, pointing to the tree tops. The trees here were of the bushier kind that Rome had discovered lining the Great Southern Bay. "The bushier cane-trees must need more water. They are aligned here along this creek. I had noticed that the ones MINIMCOM transplanted to my campus were not thriving as well. That must be why. I'll tell him to make sure they get more water when we get back."

"Whatever," Rei said. He considered their circumstances. "You know, I used to think there was something wrong with this world. Its utter lack of biological diversity. But from what you said, they must have known what they were doing."

"Yes," Rome replied. "They have built an optimal system."

"I guess I shouldn't be so surprised," Rei said. "When I was a kid, I had this thing called a bio-sphere. It was a sealed glass globe. All it had was some water, some air, a dead wood-like plant, some algae, some rocks and a few shrimp."

"Wouldn't the shrimp suffocate eventually?" Rome asked, "If it was a sealed globe?"

"No," Rei said. "That was the sleek thing about it. All you had to do was supply light. The algae made oxygen which the shrimp breathed. The shrimp ate the algae. Their waste was food for the plants and so on. It was perfectly balanced and I had it for a long time."

"This world is perfectly balanced as well," Rome said. "I hope we don't upset that."

Rei sat up. "We'll try hard not to. But we'd better get going." He stood up then helped Rome up.

Chapter 19

REI WASN'T SURE WHAT THE WATER WOULD DO TO HIS electrostatic blouse so he took his shirt off and crumpled it tightly into a ball. Rome had gotten used to seeing him with no chest so the sight did not alarm her. Rei held his balled up shirt over his head with one hand and held onto Rome's hand with the other as they slid down the bank where it was slightly narrower to ford the creek. The water was cool but not uncomfortably so. The bottom was made of silt and rocks and it was a little bit slippery so they took their time crossing. There were one or two deep spots but for the most part just going slowly was enough.

Once they reached the far bank, as they ascended out of the water, Rei shook himself like a dog then put his shirt back on. Once again, Rei held Rome's hand as they climbed up the bank. Ahead the trail of 'blankets' beckoned. The trail led through a series of cane-tree woods alternating with rocky outcroppings. Each of the rocky outcroppings represented a clear area with nothing overhead. It was in those flat areas, strewn with boulders and rocks that Rei looked up to search for signs of MINIMCOM, even though it made no sense. If Rei could see him, then Steele could see him too and tip their hand. Finally, though, Rei had had enough.

"MINIMCOM, do you read?" he asked.

"Yes, is there a problem?" the starship asked.

"It's just that it's been a while since we've seen you."

"Why do you need to see me? I am directly overhead," MINIMCOM replied. **"We can see you just fine. That is all that matters."**

"But we can't see you," Rei responded. *"I'm not saying it's rational. Can you please just phase in and out for a second to put my mind at ease."*

"As you wish," MINIMCOM said but Rei could tell from his tone that he was irked.

MINIMCOM's reassuring jet-black presence became visible high up in the air. Rei smiled and tapped on Rome's shoulder, pointing toward the sky. Rome looked up and nodded.

"Thanks," Rei said, *"that's all I needed."*

MINIMCOM promptly disappeared again. *"You are welcome,"* MINIMCOM replied. *"And thank you for such supreme confidence in me."*

Rei couldn't help but laugh. With renewed conviction, Rei and Rome plunged into the deepest part of the forest yet. Rome put her hand on Rei's shoulder and let him lead because he could see far better than she could. It wasn't long before they came to another creek. As before, the current group of blankets stopped and they waited for their cousins to appear on the other side. This creek was narrower but the swiftly moving water told Rei it was deeper. Once again, he took off his shirt and helped Rome down into the little river. He held her hand high overhead as the water came up to her neck. The bottom of this creek was smoother so the footing was easier, thank goodness.

As before, the cane-trees lining the tree bank were the bushier, split trunk kind. They looked like giant slingshots to Rei. He stared at them as they crossed and wondered what the slight deviation from the norm meant and why they required more water. Some day, he would have Rome 'ask' one of the blankets but for now they had to keep going.

Because the cane-trees were bushier, there were more leaves on the ground, many of which led down to the water. Climbing up the far bank was a little trickier. The capillary action of the leaves and humus wicked up the water and soaked it making the soil wet and somewhat mushy. The moisture also hastened the decay of the leaves.

It appeared that the sticky bushes had given up their claim to this land so the whole thing smelled like a mildly pleasant compost heap. Once again, when they got farther away from the water, the density of the cane-tree species changed back to the single trunk variety. A gentle breeze wafted through the area and the click-clack of the cane-tree trunks formed a soothing, ethereal cadence. Rei realized there truly was peace in this forest. The creatures, the trees, all lived in harmony. Though they had started out as intruders, somehow, Rei now felt their welcome. It was too bad they were fighting for their lives. Some day he'd like to come back here and soak it all in.

Even though it seemed nearly impossible, the dense stand of trees grew even thicker. The going was so slow, Rome had to hold Rei's hand and pull her through each opening as they wound their way through the cane-trees, tree by tree. They came across one final stream, the deepest one yet. While Rei could still wade, the water was too deep for Rome and she had to resort to swimming. She was a surprisingly good swimmer and she beat Rei across by a wide margin. She waited for him patiently on the far side then they climbed the bank together.

There were no trees on the far side. Instead, a boulder-strewn glade lay before them. There were a few patches of threadgrass but it was mostly just dry soil. The whole scene reminded Rei of the place where he first met the Deucadons, Triden, Melloy and Steben. It was made even more similar because in front of them was a vertical rock wall, almost a small mountain. Rei thought back to that day. It was the first time MINIMCOM had ever used his transporter. He had relocated Rei to the top of the cliff and it was only after he did so that the little computer informed Rei it was the first time he had ever attempted it with a living creature.

The major difference between this glade and the other one was a tiny waterfall which dripped down the mountain and the little rivulet that formed at its bottom made its way to join up to the stream they had just crossed.

"Look, Rome," Rei said mentally.

"What?" Rome replied.

"The blankets are climbing up the front face." He pointed to the dense rock formation ahead. *"Look at the way they are forming an arch."*

"What do you think it means?" Rome asked.

"When I was making my way back from the Ibbrassati village to your father's base, I came across a glade just like this. There was a cave tucked in there that was the Deucadon's base of operation."

"A cave would be a perfect place to hide. Do you think Steele is in there?"

"Something's up. The blankets have been laying out the road for us steadily and now this? Look, there. I think they're trying to tell us something."

Rei pointed to the left. He saw a dark crack that could be a cave or maybe just a shadow. Rome bent down to pet one of the blankets to get more information. While she was doing that, Rei dashed ahead hoping to get close enough to peer in. If there was a cave there, then it would be the perfect hideout and it would explain why MINIMCOM couldn't spot anything from the air. As Rei ran, he scrambled to avoid the stones, pebbles, boulders and rocks scattered about. It was more than an obstacle course. It was like somebody took a huge boulder and broke it into a thousand pieces just to make Rei's life even more difficult than it already was. By the time Rei got to the rock wall, the blankets started to move away. They wriggled around in a haphazard manner, flopping like fish. Their behavior made no sense: it smacked of confusion.

Suddenly, Rome screamed out loud, "Rei!"

Rei whirled in place and saw Dan Steele, wearing a deactivated Deucadon invisibility cloak, standing there with his arm clamped around Rome's neck. A glint of metal told Rei all he needed to know. The man was holding Jack Henry's M9 Beretta pushed up against his beautiful wife's temple.

Rei started to move toward them but Steele called out, "Freeze or I blow her brains out."

Rei came to a complete stop and raised his hands slowly. "You only want to kill me," Rei shouted back. "Let her go." He slid one foot in front of the other, trying to get closer.

"Actually, I want both of you dead but I'll settle for either," Steele sneered. "I've got enough bullets to pull it off."

Rei pointed up as he took another step closer. "My starship is overhead. He can vaporize you before you can do anything."

"Well, he won't vaporize me as long as I have your whore. Although I'd be curious to see what he does after I shoot her," Steele said. He lifted his elbow so that the handgun was horizontal to Rome's temple and pressed it in tighter.

In an instant, Rei made his decision. Unwilling to wait until the cavalry arrived in the form of MINIMCOM's livetar, Rei activated the cell-phone link in his head and called out to Rome, *"As soon as I say go, I want you to fall to the ground. He won't expect it."*

"No, there is something..." Rome started to say but Rei pre-empted her.

"Go! Now!" he commanded.

Reluctantly, Rome let her knees buckle. Gravity took over and she slipped out of Steele's grasp. At the same time, Rei came rushing at him. Steele didn't even bother with Rome. He calmly raised the handgun, steadied it with his other hand and when Rei was close enough, he fired off two rounds, point blank into Rei's chest. The bullets passed harmlessly through the miniature PPT tunnel vest that Rei wore under his electrostatic blouse and out the other side. Taking advantage of Steele's surprise, Rei launched himself over Rome like a linebacker and hit Steele full on, driving his shoulder into Steele's chin.

Being in that Steele was trained in the martial arts, he used Rei's own momentum against him, flipping him up and over. With a thud, Rei landed on his back, flat on the ground. He hit his head and the blow made him dizzy, dizzier that it would have if he had not just had a concussion.

In the blink of an eye, Steele whirled around, lifting his right fist as he turned. He smashed his hand down onto Rei's nose, breaking it. Rei cried out. The pain was excruciating. Steele used Rei's agony to buy the time he needed to land on top of his adversary, knees straddling Rei's chest. He seized Rei by the throat with his left hand and tried to crush the fallen man's windpipe. Rei reached up, grabbing Steele's hand by the wrist. It took both hands and all his might but finally, Rei managed to pry Steele's left hand off of his throat. What Rei could not see was Steele withdrawing a knife from his boot with his right hand.

"Die, you god-damned traitor," Steele said, raising the knife up into the air.

"Rei!" Rome screamed but it was too late. Steele plunged the blade into Rei's chest, slashing through Rei's shirt, right where his heart should have been. But there was no chest. There was no heart. Steele's hand and blade went right through the PPT tunnel and lodged firmly in the rocky soil underneath Rei. Rei seized the opportunity and twisted to his right. The rim of the PPT tunnel, possibly the sharpest edge in the universe, severed the connection between Steele's arm and his right wrist and hand.

The cut was so quick that Steele did not even feel any pain. He stared at his arm which now ended so abruptly, totally slack-jawed, trying to come to grips with what just happened. A lesser man might have crumbled but Steele's military training kicked in. He was so completely consumed with the need to end Rei and Rome's life that he blocked the mutilation out of his mind. Even with the stump of his right arm spurting arterial blood, using his remaining hand, he willed himself to reach down. He grabbed the knife that was stuck in the ground, still held within the useless, severed limb. He pulled it free and lifted it in the air, preparing to stab Rei who had only managed to get himself to his knees.

Steele changed his mind. Based upon what he had just witnessed, he decided he would be better off slitting Rei's throat. He twisted his wrist to an underhand grip. However, before he could deliver the fatal blow, Rome came up behind him and used all of her strength to strike him in the back of the head with a rather sizeable rock. The sound of granite against bone was a nearly indescribable crunching noise. Steele crumpled to the ground.

Rome sank to her knees and began crying. Ignoring the blood pouring out of his nose, Rei put his hand to his temple and MINIMCOM's livetar instantly appeared. The all-black being "borrowed" a willing 'falling blanket' and quickly secured Steele before he could regain consciousness. In just a matter of seconds, the livetar transported the would-be assassin, falling blanket and all up to his cargo hold for more permanent incarceration.

Rei scrambled over to where Rome was huddled and put his arms around his sobbing wife, dripping blood on her shoulder. "It's OK, honey," he said as soothingly as he could. "It's all over. We got him. We're safe now."

Rome looked up him, her face twisted in anguish. "No, you don't understand."

"What? Why?" Rei asked, confused, wiping his nose very gingerly.

"When he had his arm around my throat; I was connected to him. I was able to see into his mind."

"So what?" Rei said. "We captured him. He's no longer a threat."

"No," Rome said haltingly. "Not him. The Vuduri woman that was aiding them. I saw her face in his mind."

A sudden chill went through Rei's spine. "Who was it?" he whispered.

"It was Sussen," Rome moaned. "She knew you did not die in the explosion. She used the Deucadon cloak and was hiding at my mother's house the day we were there, making our plans. She knows we sent Aason to Earth. She went after him days ago."

Rei rocked back on his heels and his shoulders sagged. "Goddammit," he said.

Chapter 20

On the way to Earth

NO PARENT SHOULD EVER HAVE TO BURY A CHILD. THE EMOTIONS invoked by even contemplating such an action are overwhelming, suffocating. Poor Rome who had only openly acknowledged even having emotions five years ago was beside herself with worry. Although Aason had been kidnapped once before by the Darwin Project members, this time was different. The last time it happened she was able to contact her little boy and she knew he was safe. This time she did not. Rome simply did not know how to handle what she was feeling as MINIMCOM hurtled through null-space at 20,000 times the speed of light.

Rei and Bonnie sat at the little table within the dining area in the forward portion ahead of the cargo section. Thoughtfully, MINIMCOM had synthesized a new electrostatic shirt for Rei. The previous one had two bullet holes, a knife gash and blood all over it. Currently, 'Doctor' MINIMCOM was applying an elastic bandage over the bridge of Rei's broken nose. After gently stroking each end of the bandage to make sure it was secure, the livetar stepped back.

"Normally, it would take several weeks to heal but I was able to awaken a few constructor units that were still floating around in your system," MINIMCOM said. "Your cartilage has been rebuilt but it will take a day or two for your nose to set. Try to avoid bumping it until then."

Rei nodded but didn't answer. He was watching Rome who was pacing frantically from the dining area into the corridor and back again. So preoccupied with her son and the what-ifs, she was not even paying attention to Rei's injuries or MINIMCOM's ministrations.

Rei stood up. "Thanks, MINIMCOM," he said and patted the livetar on the shoulder. He waited until Rome reentered the room then intercepted her and put his arms around her so she couldn't budge.

"Look, Romey," he said, tilting her grimaced face up toward him. "I'm worried too. MINIMCOM is going as fast as he can. We'll be there soon enough." In the background, the subtle but constant

187

shushing sound of the null-fold drive was noticeable and served to underscore Rei's statement.

"`We will be arriving at Earth in less than four hours,`" MINIMCOM added, trying to be helpful.

"Thanks for that information," Rei said. "Rome, you have to get frosty. Our son's life is at stake. We have to think this through rationally. There'll be time enough to worry later."

Rome inhaled deeply, her breath catching as she did. "You're right," she said. "But I feel so helpless right now. I want to do something. I *need* to do something."

Rei snapped his fingers. He looked over at Bonnie who had kept mostly quiet up until now. "Bonnie, why don't you see if Steele has come to. Maybe we can get something out of him." Bonnie nodded and stood up from her chair.

Rei turned back to face the livetar. "MINIMCOM, can you help her? Make sure he can't get loose?"

"`Of course,`" the animated shell replied. The livetar and Bonnie left the room. A few minutes later, they returned with a groggy Dan Steele, his amputated arm wrapped in gauze. MINIMCOM maneuvered him to a seat and quickly wound white elastic bands around his chest, arms and feet so that he was completely immobilized.

With rheumy eyes, Steele looked up at them, scowling as best as he could. Rome shook herself out of her funk and pulled up a chair and sat down next to him, placing her hand on his shoulder.

"Sussen," Rome said. Then she waited for a beat. "She is after my son. Why?"

Steele just glared at her but didn't say a word. Rome gasped and turned to look up at Rei.

"She assumed the Essessoni would fail," Rome said sadly. "She left Steele behind to delay us. That is all. She is setting up a trap. She is waiting for us."

Steele furrowed his brow as Rome turned back to face him.

"Yes, she knew you would fail," Rome said, derisively. "Even though she told you otherwise. She had no confidence in you. You were set up."

"No way," Steele spat. "She wanted you dead more than I did. She was the one that said your deaths would cause a ripple effect and get us back our planet."

Rome lowered her head and closed her eyes, concentrating on Steele's thoughts.

"Did you ever see her eyes?" Rome asked.

"Yeah, so what?" Steele answered. "She looked like a Vook to me."

"She is not Vuduri. She is not Essessoni. She is not even human."

"What do I care?" he growled back. "She was helping us. That's all that mattered."

"She wanted us dead now," Rei said, taking a step forward. "But in the end, she wanted you dead too. She wants all of us dead so her race can take over."

"What do you mean 'her race'?"

"They're called the Onsiras," Rome answered, eyes still closed. "They have a gene which makes them into living machines. Their leader was an insane computer named MASAL. He wanted to become a god and was going to use the Onsiras to wipe out the rest of mankind."

"So what happened to this insane computer?" Steele asked in a patronizing tone.

"We vaporized him by detonating a volcano on Earth," Rei said.

"You knew that," Bonnie chimed in. "Everyone on Deucado knows that. Including those of us in Darwin."

"Yeah, I guess I heard," Steele said reluctantly. "So who's leading them now?"

"You tell us," Rei shot back defiantly.

"I have no idea," Steele said, shrugging.

Rome struggled for breath. "MASAL's Sipre," she whispered.

"What?" Rei asked.

"MASAL's Sipre," Rome said louder. "Sussen told Steele about MASAL's Sipre. He does not speak Vuduri so the words meant nothing to him."

"Sipre means shadow," Rei uttered. "What's it supposed to signify?"

"It means the spirit of MASAL lives on," Rome said grimly, standing up. "An echo."

"But MASAL recanted his plans," Rei protested. "OMCOM told us. In fact, I've seen the tape."

"But perhaps the Sipre does not know that," Rome replied sadly.

"What are you two carrying on about?" Steele asked.

Rome looked down at him. "The Onsiras, they have an Overmind of their own. It was guided by MASAL, manipulating them to accomplish his goals. But when he died, their Overmind did not die with him. It must be carrying out his mission despite the fact that he is gone. It will not rest until all the Vuduri and mandasurte are dead."

"So who cares if one Vook kills another?" Steele said with an evil grin. "More for us when it's all over."

"You idiot," Rei said. "They want everyone dead. Especially us, the Essessoni. That includes you and Darwin. They call us The Ark Lords, the most hated group in their history. They set up our entire world, Deucado, just so the mind-deaf, which includes you, could be smashed by an asteroid and blown to bits."

"Whoa," said Steele. "That is a lot of trouble."

"Did she tell you anything else?" Rome asked Steele. "Anything we can use to track her down?"

Steele clamped his jaw down as if he was suppressing something. Rei saw this. "Rome?" he asked.

Rome reached over and put her hand against the side of Steele's face. She looked into his eyes then she shook her head dejectedly. "His head is filled with only hate. He knows nothing else."

"All right," Rei said. "We'll deal with you later," he directed at Steele. "First we have to get our son."

Rome took a step back. With a whoosh and a pop, both Steele and the chair disappeared. Just as quickly, the chair returned, this time empty.

Even though MINIMCOM had rebuilt the cartilage in Rei's nose there was still a lot of swelling and blood pooled beneath his orbital sockets, giving him a bad case of 'raccoon eyes'. Rei, Rome and Bonnie sat in the cockpit, watching the virtual instruments as they came upon the Earth. When they were about one-half light-year out, Rome instructed MINIMCOM to drop out of null-space.

"Why?" Rei asked. "We have to get there as fast as we can."

"I want to call to Aason," Rome said. "We are close enough that he should be able to hear me."

The shushing sound in the background died down and suddenly, the cockpit windshield was filled with a brilliant field of stars. Ahead of them was the yellow-white of the Sun and presumably the blue dot off to the right was the Earth.

Rome closed her eyes and used her PPT transceivers to send a message. *"Aason?"* she called out. She listened carefully but heard no reply. Worried, she said her child's name even louder. She waited but again there was no response.

"Anything?" Rei asked.

"No," Rome answered sadly. "We may have get closer." She looked up at the front console. "All right, MINIMCOM," she said. "Take us there as fast as you can."

`"As you wish,"` replied the starship. Once again the unearthly shushing sound of the null-fold drive permeated the cockpit and the windshield turned blacker-than-black.

It was only a few minutes later that the virtual instruments finally showed they were within the orbit of the Moon. Once again, MINIMCOM dropped out of null-space. The Earth lay ahead of them like a puffy white-flecked blue marble.

"Aason!" Rome called again worriedly but once again there was no response.

"He does not answer me!" Rome said, tears welling up in her eyes.

"Maybe he can't," Rei said.

"What does that mean?" Rome asked, panic seeping into her voice.

"I don't know. Maybe they put a T-suppressor on him."

Rome shook her head slowly. Rei turned his head toward the grille. "MINIMCOM can you drop us in right over Ursay's farm?"

`"Of course,"` the starship replied.

"Look," Bonnie said, speaking up for the first time in a while. "I know you're worried about your son but I think it's clouding your judgment." Rei and Rome looked at her but did not respond. Bonnie continued. "I've seen your ship pop out over the lake. It's pretty dramatic. If you want to sneak up on them, maybe you ought to pop out farther back and come in cloaked."

"Yes," Rome said, sniffing up her tears. "Bonnie is right. If they are looking for us, they'll be looking to the west, to the ocean. MINIMCOM, bring us in from the east and come in low and silent."

"`Command accepted,`" MINIMCOM replied, trying to act like a computer so as to not distract the distraught humans. Immediately, the high-pitched whine of the PPT generators began ramping up and a blue hole appeared in front of them as the atmosphere of Earth vented out. MINIMCOM used his plasma thrusters to punch through the tunnel and emerged over the Balearic Sea, part of the Mediterranean, just to the east of the island of Mallorca. From there, the starship headed west in full stealth mode, coming ashore over the former site of Valencia, Spain. MINIMCOM took a northwesterly route over where Madrid had been located and crossed the border into what would have been Portugal over the densely forested region of Arribes del Duero. Up ahead was the Tamega River and just beyond that would be Ursay's farm and vineyard. MINIMCOM circled once then settled down in a grassy field just behind the farmhouse. To their right was a peculiar hill, covered in a sparkling mesh. But other than that, the bucolic scene in front of them looked exactly the same as it had two years earlier.

Rei unbuckled and started walking toward the back of the ship with Rome and Bonnie following him. MINIMCOM instantiated a livetar to accompany them as well.

When Rei got to the back of the ship, he turned to address the group. He held his hand up.

"Hold on," he said. "Let me go first. I'll scout the place out with my cloak and let you know how far you can come. OK?"

Rome fidgeted in place but nodded silently. Bonnie draped her arm around Rome's back in a show of sympathy. Rei picked up the cloak from the floor of the cargo bay and placed it around his shoulders. He drew his hands along the front of the cloak and promptly disappeared. Although no hand was seen, the blue stud activating the cargo hatch depressed. The hatch raised and the ramp lowered.

"Raise it back up," Rei transmitted back to MINIMCOM as soon as he was on the ground. The starship complied. Once he was sealed up, there was no evidence that MINIMCOM even existed.

Rei stepped very lightly across the field until he got to the side of the farmhouse which looked no worse for wear. Keeping one hand on the wooden planks making up the outer wall, he crept around the side until he came to the front door. He examined it for signs of forced entry but since the Vuduri never locked their doors, it would be an odd sign for sure.

After carefully opening the door and closing it behind him, he looked around but saw nothing unusual. He closed his eyes and activated his sonar vision to listen for hints of life but heard nothing. The last time they were here, he remembered the stairs being creaky. Very carefully, Rei climbed the steps one at a time, stopping at each one to listen some more but each time it was deadly silent. Finally, he reached the top of the stairs. What he saw there made his heart sink.

"You can come up," Rei said, sadly, broadcasting to Rome and MINIMCOM. He deactivated his cloak and waited until the group of three arrived with Rome leading the way. She got to the top of the stairs, taking one look at Ursay's study and cried out, "Oh no!"

All around her were signs of a struggle. The chairs were knocked over. The large flat-screen monitor attached to Ursay's workstation was smashed. There was a small spattering of blood on the floor. Rome started crying hysterically. Rei came over and held her as tightly as he could.

While Rei was trying to calm Rome down, Bonnie walked over to the other desk and examined the objects still lying there. None of them made sense to her. There was a black, vaguely gun-shaped object, lying on the desk, with an empty glass tube in it. Next to it was a stand containing three other tubes filled with liquid, one yellow and two blue. The stand had some holes where some other tubes might have sat. She shrugged and turned to wait to see what Rei and Rome would do next.

Rei took a deep breath. He rocked Rome back and forth, stroking her head. "Romey," he said, "I know this won't make any sense but he's probably alright. They want us, not him. If they hurt him or worse, they'd never be able to use him to lure us into whatever trap they've set."

While this was supposed to make Rome feel better, all it did was make her sob more. Rei turned and looked at MINIMCOM helplessly.

"I will try to reach Junior," MINIMCOM said. "If we can find him, we can probably find your son."

"Good idea," Rei said.

MINIMCOM held perfectly still but broadcast in a frequency that both Rei and Rome could hear internally.

"Junior. Son," the livetar called out. "Can you hear me?" There was no reply. MINIMCOM tried again but once again there was no response.

"The EM transmitter has a limited range," MINIMCOM said. "Perhaps the three of us could try together, as we did with the Stareater. That would increase the range of the signal."

Rei agreed and released Rome. "Can you do this?" he asked her.

Rome nodded. She wiped at her tears and closed her eyes. Together, the three of them called out mentally, *"JUNIOR!"*

A tiny voice, barely a whisper, said one word and one word only, *"Dad?"*

The livetar's mouth slit curled up in an approximation of a smile. "Where are you?" he asked.

"I'm kind of a mess right now," the younger starship replied. *"They cut me up into little bits. I can't really move."*

MINIMCOM's eye slits opened wider. "Where are you?" he asked as worriedly as a former computer could be.

"I'm not sure," replied Junior. *"I don't think they moved me anywhere. I'm probably nearby, somewhere."*

Chapter 21

THE ALL-BLACK LIVETAR RACED OUT OF THE ROOM AND BOUNDED down the steps, three steps at a time. When he got near the bottom, he leaped and landed on the floor with a thud. He raced outside then stopped short. He looked around but could find no evidence of his son anywhere. Based upon Junior's signal strength, he couldn't be far. MINIMCOM darted around the side of the house and back to the field where his starship body lie. He didn't stop there, though. He continued past to the odd mound that was covered with the metallic mesh. Running on instinct alone, the livetar pulled the edge of the netting aside. If he had a heart, it would have sunk. There, beneath the mesh, was a pile of huge black chunks and silver rubble. In no way did it resemble anything like the sleek starship that had been his son.

"This is you, son, right?" MINIMCOM asked out loud.

"Yes, Dad," his son replied internally.

Rei, Rome and Bonnie came down the stairway and outside, just in time to see the livetar sink to his knees, falling forward into the wreckage of his son. Seeing a livetar grieve was a novel experience for Rei. He wasn't sure how to broach the subject. He came up alongside MINIMCOM and put his hand on the livetar's shoulder. "Can't you just repair him?" he asked.

MINIMCOM's livetar turned to look up at Rei then back toward the rubble. For a moment, it appeared as if he was frozen, then his algorithmic nature kicked in. He lifted his hand, finger pointing upward.

"Of course!" he said firmly. "Please help me take this mesh netting and spread it out," the livetar commanded.

Rei grabbed one end and MINIMCOM grabbed the other. Rome came over to help as well, as did Bonnie. They spread the netting across the field until it was flat and smooth. With a whoosh and a pop, MINIMCOM's livetar disappeared.

"Where'd you go?" Rei asked mentally.

"You will see," the starship replied. With another whoosh and a pop, both Troutman and Steele materialized in front of them, tightly bound and gagged. Their legs were tied together and immediately, both fell over onto the dirt. Bonnie came to where they had been deposited and stood over them, watching them intently. They were so bewildered, neither seemed to have any strong desire to get away at this point.

MINIMCOM dropped his stealth shield and the imposing all-black starship appeared before them. The rear landing gear retracted and MINIMCOM's aft section lowered to the ground. With a grinding, grating sound, the rear section of the fuselage split in half, rolling tightly, forming two fairly large cones. The starship used his forward EG lifter to raise the remainder of his fuselage up in the air until he could settle his entire weight onto the conical sections. At that point, the rear semi-aerodynamic wings migrated forward while the long-neglected "roadgrader" cylinders extruded. They merged to form an approximation of limbs, complete with gripping ends.

Once that was finished, the starship's surface seemed ripple and flow binding each appendage until the transformation was complete. In front of them loomed a huge bipedal, all-black entity with arms and thick, conical legs. MINIMCOM even converted the cockpit area into a gigantic facsimile of his normal bullet-shaped head. The new form stood 120 feet in the air and reminded Rei of a creature out of a bad science fiction movie.

The robotized version of MINIMCOM clomped forward. When he got to the pit containing the remnants of his son, he bent over and carefully retrieved the largest section of the group. He lifted it up gently then turned in place making his way over to the mesh. The ground shook with the giant creature's every step. The father turned assembly robot lowered the piece right in the center of the meshing. After releasing the piece, MINIMCOM raised up and went back for another section. This one was clearly a portion of Junior's cockpit. MINIMCOM carried over and placed it at the front-most section of the net, closest to the house.

Piece by piece, MINIMCOM repeated the procedure one section at a time until he had assembled a facsimile of the fractured form of the little spaceship. It reminded Rei of scenes he had seen when the NTSB took the wreckage of a plane crash and reconstructed the original plane in a hanger somewhere.

The gigantic thing that had been MINIMCOM carefully, lovingly, stroked each fragment, using parts of his own "flesh" to meld the sections together. Slowly but surely, what had been individual pieces flowed together forming a larger and larger structure. Once Junior was whole enough, he was able to complete the rest of the restoration himself. Finally, when all the sections had been joined, the MINIMCOM creature lifted the front of his son up into the air and inserted the front landing gear. He then repeated the action in the back. At last it was done. Junior was back.

With a whoosh and a pop, a small slate-gray livetar appeared and walked over to where Rei and Rome were standing.

"Hello, Auntie Rome, Onclare Rei," he said, raising his hand as if nothing had ever happened.

Rome reached over and hugged the little shell. Rei patted him on the head. While they were greeting him, the huge MINIMCOM creature returned to his previous position on the grassy field. He bent at his "waist" until the front portion was resting on the ground. He activated his front EG lifter and extruded his front landing strut. The arms retracted and the wings returned to their position in the rear. The two conical "legs" flowed together to form a larger cylinder, part of the fuselage. It only took a few minutes more and MINIMCOM had completely reversed his robotic transformation. Now there were two starships sitting in the field, side by side, father and son. With another whoosh and pop, MINIMCOM's livetar appeared and came over to his son.

"How do you feel?" he asked.

"I'm not sure how it's possible but I think I'm sore," Junior replied. "Even so, you did a great job, Dad. My airframe seems completely intact. With each passing minute, I'm feeling stronger. I think I'll be OK."

"So what happened?" Rei asked him. "How did you get like that?"

"And where is Aason?" Rome blurted out frantically.

Junior looked over at the three of them. He turned in place and pointed behind them.

"I was sitting in this field," he said. "I didn't bother with my stealth shield because I made myself look like a standard space tug. I figured I wouldn't arouse any suspicion that way. I don't know what they did but they blasted me with some sort of radiation and I couldn't get my shield up in time. Before I could even lift off, they were slicing me up with PPT throwers and that's how I ended up in that pile over there." The livetar pointed to where the metal meshing had been.

"What about Aason and my parents?" Rome asked. "Did you see what happened? Do you know where they took them?"

"No," Junior said sadly. "I gave them as much warning as I could, even as they were cutting me up but once they threw that netting over me, my transmitter was blocked. I'm sorry, Auntie Rome. I let you down." The little livetar shook his head sadly.

"It's not your fault," Rome said. "You did everything you were supposed to." She looked up at her husband. "What do we do now?"

"I don't know," Rei said, wracking his brain. "I have no idea where to start."

"I do," Bonnie called out to them. Both Rei and Rome turned to her. "We go back to the scene of the crime and look for clues. Criminals always leave them," she said. She stared down at the helpless forms of Troutman and Steele to emphasize her point.

MINIMCOM picked up on her actions and the two remaining Darwin members disappeared, presumably returned to their holding cells.

Bonnie led them back around the side of the farmhouse to the front door. Along the way, she told them about the gun-like thing she found there. They quickly mounted the stairs and reentered the study. Bonnie pointed to the far side of the room. She led them over to the desk so she could show them what she had found.

Rei lifted up the black holder with the empty vial. Bad memories came rushing back to him. "Isn't this…" he said.

"Yes," Rome said, quietly. "It is an injector. And those vials are what were used."

"The stuff they injected you and me with was fluorescent yellow, if I recall," Rei said. "There's one of those remaining. What do you think the blue stuff is?"

Rome picked up one of the two remaining blue vials and held it up to the light. After examining it, she handed the vials and injector to MINIMCOM. "We'll have MINIMCOM analyze them but I can already tell you what it is," she said sadly.

"What?"

"When you and I confronted MASAL underneath Kilauea, he offered to modify my genetics to transform me directly into one of the Onsiras. Like those soldiers that captured us. He never said how he would accomplish that but this must be it." Her eyes grew wide as her own words hit her like a ton of bricks. Helplessly, she said "Rei…" Her voice trailed off as she tried to figure out the implications.

"It may not be as bad as you think," Rei said. "Aason has our 25th chromosome. He may be immune. But your Mom and Dad…and Ursay, I don't know."

"How do you explain the fact that I cannot reach him?" Rome asked, her voice catching. "Our poor baby?"

"Like I said before, maybe he's wearing a T-suppressor," Rei said. "They did it to you. They can do it to him."

"I hope you're right…" Rome said. She walked over and sat down on one of the chairs. She put her face down into her hands to think. She had to force herself to not dwell on the negatives. She had to come up with something positive. Suddenly, her head snapped up.

"MINIMCOM," she said, "my PPT transceivers. The ones that connected me to the Overmind of Earth. You activated them, correct?"

"**Yes,**" MINIMCOM replied.

"Then I am going to contact it. If anyone or anything in the world would know where they are, the Overmind of Earth would know."

"But we were banished from the planet," Rei said. "As soon as you let it know we're here, it'll have us arrested."

"I don't care," Rome said defiantly. "This is more important."

"OK," Rei said. "But I sure hope you know what you're doing."

"I don't," Rome said. "I admit it. But I'm going to try anyway."

Chapter 22

FOR ROME, IT WAS LIKE SHE HAD TO GO TO ANOTHER WORLD. SHE closed her eyes and blocked out the very knowledge that Rei and Bonnie were standing by. The same went for MINIMCOM and Junior. To put herself into the proper mental state, Rome struggled to slow her breathing down, trying to get her beating heart from feeling like it was going to jump out of her chest. This was the biggest risk she would ever take in her life yet it was the only way. Finally, she was ready.

"Hello," was all she said.

"Hello, Rome," the Overmind of Earth replied, its voice nearly overpowering in its intensity. **"It has been a long time."**

"Are you going to have me arrested?" she asked, figuring she had to get that out of the way.

"No," the Overmind answered.

"Really?"

"Really. You and Rei were completely pardoned over two years ago."

"We were?" Rome asked. Her face echoed her surprise.

"Yes. After Commander Ursay related to me what you had done to save our people from the virus weapon, I decided it was time to forgive you."

"Well, thank you for that," Rome said, slightly flustered. She quickly regained her composure. *"Enough pleasantries. Do you know why we are here?"*

"No, I do not," replied the Overmind. **"In fact, I am somewhat perplexed as to how you were able to reconnect to me."**

Rome quickly summarized the events leading up to MINIMCOM's reactivation of her PPT receivers. She explained that she had sent her son and parents to hide out on Earth until the crisis on Deucado had passed and Sussen's role in the chaos surrounding her.

"Sussen, the one with the mismatched eyes?" the Overmind asked with some disgust.

"Yes," Rome answered.

"Then I understand your urgency and I will co-operate fully in helping you find your son. However there are some things you must know."

"Please just tell me where Commander Ursay is and we can chat about whatever along the way."

"Ursay is currently disconnected," the Overmind replied. *"He was able to connect just long enough to tell me that there were people storming his farmhouse and then he was cut off."*

This sent another chill down Rome's spine. *"Did he disconnect of his own free will?"*

"There is no way to know but I suspect not," replied the Overmind.

"Then where do we start?" Rome asked dishearteningly.

"Again, please allow me to give you some information and it may guide you in your search."

"Go ahead," Rome thought with resignation. These Overminds so loved to pontificate.

"Approximately five years before you were born, some surgeons had to perform an emergency resection of a woman giving birth. The child had some of the characteristics of what we now call the Onsira phenotype."

"How is this relevant?" Rome asked.

"There appear to be two types of Onsiras," the Overmind said. *"The type like Sussen, they refer to themselves as the Reonhe. They must have some sort of split brain. They seem like they have the ability to be part of my samanda and what we now know to have been MASAL's at the same time."*

"And you never shared this before?" Rome asked.

"I did not understand their nature at the time. They always seemed like loyal and obedient Vuduri to me. Their connection to me seemed standard," said the Overmind. *"I did not know they served two masters. I only came to learn this after you destroyed MASAL. I did know they were not healthy, though, even from the beginning."*

"In what way are they not healthy?"

"Their genetic structure makes them age twice as fast as a normal Vuduri."

"They do?" Rome asked.

"Yes. You remember Estar?"

"Of course," Rome said. *"How could I forget?"*

"She was only twelve years old when she went to Tabit."

"Wait! You knew Estar was an Onsira and yet you sent her to Tabit anyway?" Rome protested. *"How could you?"*

"As I said, I did not understand who or what the Onsiras represented. Only that a recessive element of the 24th chromosome must be responsible for their condition. Estar volunteered for the position and I took pity upon her and allowed her her wish."

Rome hissed her disgust. *"You said there were two types of Onsiras. What is the other type?"*

"They are called the Zengei. They are the ones with flat black eyes. You have met several of them. They do not appear to even have a mind of their own."

"Yes, I have seen them," Rome said. *"Go on."*

"I did not know that MASAL was still alive and his century-long plan to convert mankind was beginning to gain traction. But I was concerned about the direction the recessive elements of the chromosome he designed might take the human race. I wanted to counteract it. So I had my scientists initiate a study of genetic overlap of the Vuduri to map backwards to a common ancestor. We were able to trace back to the closest living relatives to Hanry Ta Jihn that were among my communicants."

"Really?" Rome said with some shock.

"It was not widely known, I have suppressed most of this information, but prior to the Battle of Chee Ka Go, Hanry Ta Jihn had a companion whose name was Lacy. She was more than, I think your term would be a girlfriend, but they were not Cesa. She was pregnant with his child when Hanry Ta Jihn decided to go on the raid west. While he did not survive, Lacy did and she gave birth and we have been able to identify the Vuduri alive today that are Hanry Ta Jihn's direct descendents."

How the Overmind accomplished such an invasive investigation of all living Vuduri was beyond Rome's imagination but she decided to say nothing.

"From this stock of the 200 best candidates, I began a breeding program, you would call it the Slayer program, to build a group of Vuduri which would represent the greatest antidote to the genetic trend of the Onsiras. I paired each of the 200 closest descendents to Hanry Ta Jihn with the most intelligent among the 23-chromosome mandasurte I could find."

Suddenly, what her father had revealed to Rome aboard his boat several years earlier clicked. She whispered, *"And my parents were among the pairs selected?"*

"Yes. You are a direct descendent of Hanry Ta Jihn."

Rome's jaw dropped. Now it all made sense: the connection she felt when she was down in the bowels of the Tevatron. The pool of Hanry Ta Jihn's blood. His handgun and her instinctual knowledge of how to use it. After she recovered, Rome asked, *"I believe you but what would this program produce? Why cross-breed Vuduri and mandasurte. Even the grandchildren of Hanry Ta Jihn?"*

"Because these Slayers, children like you, could never develop or give birth to an Onsira. I wanted to see if they could put an end to that branch of humanity. I also postulated to myself that based upon their dedication to their agenda, they would eventually come after you and have you put down to further their goals."

"Put down? As in killed? So I was born just to be bait?" Rome asked angrily.

"Partially. And to that extent, my program was a smashing success. I did not know MASAL was still alive. I only knew that the number of Onsira phenotypes was increasing. I suspected they were somehow organized in a way I could not detect. If this was the case and you truly represented a threat, they would be monitoring you. If they decided to hunt you down, then their intentions would have become clear. However, never did I consider that you would literally become the Slayer of MASAL. For that, the Vuduri could never thank you enough."

"If you were so grateful, why did you allow me to be banished from the planet?" Rome asked.

"Because of your unique capabilities and your independent thinking. You and your husband represented a danger to my integrity. Your so-called Revolution has swept over the Earth despite my best efforts to suppress it."

"The Overmind on Deucado does not find it a problem. We have all found a way to live together."

"Yes. And that is why I pardoned you. Your epic services to the Vuduri are more profound than even Hanry Ta Jihn, although you would expect nothing less from his great-great granddaughter."

"I still do not see how this is going to help me find my son."

"Some time after you destroyed MASAL and left the Earth, Sussen returned, completely drained due to the journey from Deucado. She arrived to find MASAL's base in Havei gone. She traveled on to another colony. Her connection to me was active but for a time, she did not appear to notice so I was able to listen in. She came before a Reonhe whose name was Reema. They call her Ombare so I must assume she has a leadership role."

"Please!" Rome shouted mentally, exasperated. *"Just tell me what I need to know."*

"I was getting to that. As Ursay was being captured, I heard him say two things. The first was Reema's name and the second thing he said was Socal.

"Socal? On the western continent?" Rome interjected. *"I did not think anyone lived there."*

"From the context, that is where I assume Reema lives. Find her and I believe you will find your son."

Rome leaped to her feet. *"Then that is where we will go,"* she said.

"What?" Rei asked. "Did you contact it? The Overmind?"

Rome nodded.

"So what did it say?"

Rome filled Rei in on a synopsis of the Overmind's machinations. It took all of Rei's willpower to bite his tongue during her recounting the story.

"Let's get going then," Rei said finally. "We have a family to rescue."

"Yes," said Rome. She contacted the Overmind one last time. *"Thank you,"* she communicated silently. *"We have to get going now."*

"I can send an army along," the Overmind said. *"Now that they have proven themselves to be an ongoing threat, it is time to extinguish the whole sub-species."*

"No!" Rome insisted. *"They have my baby. Let us go there and see if we can extract him first. If I need you, I will call."*

"I will respect your wishes," the Overmind said, *"However, I will have my troops on alert for your call."*

Chapter 23

REI, ROME AND BONNIE STOOD IN THE FIELD BEHIND THE farmhouse. MINIMCOM's livetar had his hand on his son's shoulder and bent down so his eye slits were on the same level as Junior's eye-holes.

"Can you fly?" MINIMCOM asked the little gray livetar.

"I think so," Junior replied. "Let me try." The livetar dissolved and the air swirled as the little spaceship activated his EG lifters and slowly rose up into the sky. He pointed his nose upward and began accelerating. When he was just a tiny dot, he fired his plasma thrusters and disappeared into the afternoon sky. But as quickly as he was gone, he returned and gently landed just beyond where his father's starship stood.

"I think I'm OK," the younger starship broadcast so that all could hear.

"Junior, does your stealth shield still work?" Rei asked him mentally. "We're going to have to sneak up on them if we're to have a chance."

The starship shimmered then disappeared. After a few seconds he reappeared.

"It's working," Junior replied proudly.

"Great," Rei said out loud. He turned to the assembled party. "Let's get going." The humans and livetar all ran aboard MINIMCOM and took their positions. When they were ready, together, father and son lifted off and headed west, gaining altitude until they were about 10 miles up. Once they were over the Atlantic, they started accelerating, slowly at first but eventually reaching Mach 6. There was no need to worry about the authorities on Earth discovering their existence. Rome had seen to that. The only group they had to worry about was the Onsiras.

At Mach 6, it took them just under an hour to cross the Atlantic and come upon the landmass that had been called North America. As they raced across the continental United States, Rei watched the ventral cameras along with the instrumentation.

"There's the Tevatron," he said to Rome as they passed over Lake Michigan. He tapped the main display. Bonnie came forward to look over his shoulder.

"That's where Keller caught you, right?" she asked.

"Yeah," Rei said. "The whole thing was stupid. The one thing he wanted was gone, burned up in the Sun."

"Why didn't you just tell him?" Bonnie asked.

"We did," Rei said. "Rome told him exactly what happened."

"Let me guess, he didn't believe you?"

"Nope. People always accuse you of what they are thinking. If he had spent any time with the Vuduri, he would have known they had no clue how to lie. But his own duplicity blinded him."

Bonnie looked over at Rome who was staring out of the cockpit windshield intently. "She's more than just a Vuduri, now, you know."

"Yeah," Rei answered. "But her heart is the purest I've ever seen."

Bonnie sighed. "I thought…because of their, I don't know, naivety, they were somehow lesser. But maybe it makes them better than us."

Rei looked up into Bonnie's eyes. "Nobody's better. We all have our strengths and weaknesses. Together, we're stronger."

"I see that now," Bonnie said. "There's so much I regret about how we approached things."

"It is what it is," Rei said, turning forward. "But right now, we have to find my son. And Rome's parents."

"How are you going to rescue them?" Bonnie asked.

"Well, given how many of them there must be, I don't think guns a'blazin is the…" Rei snapped his fingers. "Hey MINIMCOM," he asked. "Steele had Jack Henry's Beretta. What did you do with it?"

"It is in my side airlock," MINIMCOM replied. "If you need it, you will find another ammunition clip next to it."

"Where'd you get that?" Rei asked.

"When I was cleaning and restoring it, I synthesized a new one and proceeded to learn the secret of the projectiles."

"What secret? Lead bullet, steel shell and gunpowder."

"Gunpowder as you call it is not simply the sum of its parts. The chemical composition is just potassium nitrate, sulfur and charcoal but when I first synthesized it, it would not explode. I believe your word is it fizzled."

"How come?" Rei asked.

"As it turns out, gunpowder is not just a matter of chemistry but also physics."

"I know I'm going to regret asking but what do you mean?"

"Gunpowder should be simple to make by just mixing the three chemicals together in the right ratio. As it turns out, the carbon must be in the form of charcoal because it has pores. The potassium nitrate and sulfur must fill those pores. The substrate is responsible for the explosive reaction, not just the mixture."

"If you say so," Rei answered exhaustedly. "I believe you."

Rome, who had not been paying any attention to the discussion, was watching the distance meter rapidly decrease as they approached their destination of Southern California, called Socal by the Vuduri.

"MINIMCOM, what's the effective distance of our EM transmitters?" she asked the starship.

"Roughly 300 kilometers air-to-ground," replied MINIMCOM.

"Then slow down when we are inside that limit. I want to call to Aason using that channel. There is no way that the Onsiras would know that he can communicate that way. They may have him under T-suppression but it would never occur for them to put him in a Faraday cage."

"They knew enough to do that to you," Rei said. "When we first came back to Earth and they had you arrested, they slapped you in a room that was cut off six ways to Sunday."

"They did not know I could communicate that way," Rome said. "They just wanted to keep out all communication regardless."

"So what makes you think the Onsiras wouldn't do the same thing?"

"Because Aason has no equipment visible nor would he have access to any."

As the two ship convoy continued southwest, it only took them a half-hour to approach the 300-kilometer limit, MINIMCOM slowed down and Junior followed his lead. When they were about 250 kilometers away, MINIMCOM came to a dead stop, hovering about a mile up. Junior hovered off to his right.

"Rei," Rome said, reaching out with her hand. "You call with me. It will double our chances of reaching him."

"Sure," Rei said, taking her hand. "You lead, I'll follow."

Rome closed her eyes and opened up her EM channel.

"Aason," she called out desperately.

"Mommy!" a little voice replied. *"Where are you? Where's Daddy?"*

"I'm here, son," Rei said, a huge smile breaking out on his face. *"Are you all right?"*

"I think so," said the little boy. *"Where are you?"*

"We're on our way, my baby," Rome replied. *"Are they treating you well?"*

"I'm lonely," Aason said. *"Nobody will talk to me."*

"Where is Grandmea and Grandbeo?" Rome asked.

"They're over there," Aason said. Rome knew he was pointing. It always made her smile when he ignored the fact that she could not see him. *"But they're acting funny,"* Aason continued. *"They don't seem to recognize me."*

Rome sighed. It had begun. *"What about Commander Ursay?"* Rome asked. *"Is he there too?"*

"Yes," Aason replied. *"But he is acting strange, too. And Grandbeo's eyes look funny."*

"What do you mean?"

"They are all black now."

Rome put her fist up to her mouth and bit down on it. She took a deep breath. *"First things first,"* she thought to herself. Out loud, she asked, "MINIMCOM, can you get a lock on his signal?"

"**Yes,**" replied the starship.

"And Junior, can you do it as well?"

"Yes," replied MINIMCOM's son. "Strength only, no vector though."

"I know what to do," Rei said. Then mentally, he spoke to his son. *"Aason, I'm going to teach you a song. After you learn it, I want you to just sing it over and over in your head until we tell you to stop."*

"OK, Daddy," Aason said. There was delight in his voice.

"Here we go," Rei said. *"After I sing a verse, you repeat it."*

"OK."

"The inky dinky spider climbed up the water spout," Rei intoned, imparting a melody on top of the lyrics.

"What is a spider?" Aason asked.

"It's an insect, from Earth," Rei answered.

"And what means inky dinky?"

"It means he was all black. It makes the song fun," Rei answered.

"And what's a water spout?"

"It's a pipe that carries water from the roof to the ground. It's just part of the song."

"Just like his father," Rome muttered out loud.

Rei laughed. *"Can you try it?"*

"OK, Daddy," Aason said. *"The inky dinky spider climbed up the water spout."*

"Great," Rei said. *"Now the next verse. Down came the rain and washed the spider out."*

"Oh no!" Aason said. *"Is he alright?"*

"It's OK," Rei answered. *"He'll be OK. Try it and you'll see."*

"Alright. Down came the rain and washed the spider out."

"Good," Rei replied. *"Next verse. Out came the sun and dried up all the rain."*

Aason repeated the verse.

"And the inky dinky spider climbed up the spout again."

"That's funny, Daddy," Aason said, laughing mentally.

"I know, son. I want you to start singing the song in your head, over and over, until Mommy tells you you can stop."

"OK, Daddy," Aason said and he started in. *"The inky dinky spider..."*

"Good," Rome said out loud. "Now Junior, just fly due west and watch the signal strength and stop after it peaks."

"Of course, Auntie Rome," Junior replied through the grille.

"Down came the rain and washed the spider out..."

It took about 10 minutes but finally Junior spoke up. "Alright, Auntie Rome, I'm just past the peak signal," Junior said.

"OK," Rome replied. "Stay there. Now MINIMCOM, you head west as well but after the signal peaks, come back around so you're on this side of it."

"**Easy,**" replied the starship. He accelerated rapidly, heading toward the coastline.

"Out came the sun and dried up all the rain..."

"**Got it,**" MINIMCOM answered, finally. He banked around and headed east again until the signal just peaked. "**Junior and I** are now about equidistant from the signal peak. But we can't triangulate."

"We don't need to," Rei interjected. "We'll wing it. Just drift north together and see if the signal increases or decreases."

"And the inky dinky spider climbed up the spout again."

`"It is decreasing,"` MINIMCOM said.

"Great," Rei said. "Now both of you drift south and stop when the signal peaks. Kind of a simulated triangulation."

`"Of course,"` MINIMCOM replied.

Rei was not an expert on California but as far as he could tell, they were near the area that used to be known as Long Beach. Directly below them was a river, probably the Los Angeles River. It was a dead-straight vertical stripe that ran north to south. The ventral cameras showed them following the river's path as it made its way toward the Pacific. They were about five miles from the coast when MINIMCOM announced they were roughly over Aason's position.

"You can stop singing now, Aason," Rome said. They studied the images on the ventral cameras. There were grasslands and a heavy stand of trees clustered in the area. MINIMCOM switched one monitor to infrared and another to ground penetrating mode. It quickly became apparent that there was an entire community covered mostly by the trees. The infrared showed several people walking about. There were far too many houses to deduce which one held their son.

Rome stood up. "I want to go down there," she said insistently.

"Hold on," Rei cautioned. "This whole thing has been a trap since Day 1 and you're going to walk right into it."

"What do you suggest?"

Rei stared down at the monitors for a moment. He called to his son. *"Aason, do they let you go outside to play?"*

"Sometimes," he said. *"But if I go out, somebody always follows me."*

"That's OK," Rei said. *"Do you know the woman they call Reema?"* he asked.

"Yes," Aason answered. *"She comes in to see me every day. She always seems angry, though."*

Rei laughed. *"Good. I'm glad she is angry. When does she come in to visit you?"*

Aason didn't answer for a second then said, *"Pretty soon. She usually comes in the afternoon."*

"OK, Son, here's what I want you to do. Is there anything in the room that is really shiny? Like glass?"

"There are some tubes here," Aason replied. *"I'm not supposed to touch them."*

"I'm giving you permission," Rei said. *"This is what I want you to do…"*

It was late in the afternoon when Reema came to visit Aason. As she always did, she entered the house where they were keeping Aason and pointed to the floor in front of her. Aason came over and stood where she indicated. She stooped down to peer into his eyes. She put her hand on his head and turned it left and right. She huffed in disgust and pointed to a chair so she could continue her examination. Aason smiled but this time, instead of following her instructions, he dashed past her and out the door. Reema and her two attendants hurried after him but Aason didn't stop, running as fast as his little legs would carry him, until he was in a clearing. He stopped suddenly, turned around and watched the group of three approach. As they drew nearer, he took the glass tube out of his pocket and threw it as high in the air as he could, twirling it so it spun in the air.

"There it is!" Rome said, delightedly, looking at the glinting light displayed in the monitor. "Junior, are you ready?"

"Yes, Auntie Rome."

"On my go," Rome replied. She could see the other figures swarming around her son. Aason leaped forward and wrapped himself around Reema's leg with his arms and his legs, hanging on for dear life.

"Go!" Rome shouted.

Junior dropped his stealth shield and gunned his plasma thrusters, which made an ear-shattering noise, flying directly over compound. The starship twirled in place and fired the engines again, coming to a dead stop. Landing gear extended, Junior started lowering himself toward the ground. A large group of people came out of the woods to find out the nature of the ruckus. The two people in attendance to Reema started running toward the ship but Reema couldn't keep up with Aason attached to her leg.

It only took one whoosh and pop. Suddenly, Reema found herself in MINIMCOM's cargo compartment with Aason still holding on to her leg. Standing right next to her was Rei Bierak, gripping the Beretta, aimed directly at her head.

Chapter 24

AT FIRST, REEMA WAS COMPLETELY AND UTTERLY CONFUSED. MINIMCOM's livetar grabbed her arms and yanked them behind her while Bonnie slid a T-suppressor over her brow.

"Mommy!" Aason shouted and released his hold, running over to his mother who scooped him up and squeezed him so tight, she had to stop herself from breaking him.

"Oh, my baby," she said, rocking him back and forth. "I was so worried." She kissed his little head over and over. Aason smiled and cooed. She gently removed the white band from around his forehead and kissed him yet again.

Even though Reema was an older woman, MINIMCOM secured her arms with elastic white bands. She narrowed her eyes and looked at the group before her. She stopped when she saw Rome. She addressed her in Vuduri.

"We still have your parents," Reema said in a gruff voice. "If you want to save them, you will have to answer for your crimes," she added.

"`Junior is clear,`" MINIMCOM announced, ignoring her. "`We will retreat to a safe distance,`" the livetar added.

"Take her into the kitchen, please" Rome said to MINIMCOM. "We'll be there in a minute."

"`As you wish,`" replied the livetar. Rei handed the gun to Bonnie who then followed MINIMCOM and Reema out of the cargo compartment.

Rome handed Aason to his father who took his turn squeezing and kissing him. Rome reached over and hugged them both.

"You did so well, my baby," Rome said. "You are so brave and smart."

"It was easy, Mommy," Aason said. His little brow furrowed. "What about Grandmea and Grandbeo," he said. "And why were they acting so funny?"

"We'll get to the bottom of all of it," Rome said. She looked at Rei who nodded. Rei set Aason down and the three of them crowded into the kitchen where Reema was being held.

Reema's deeply lined face looked around the room. Her matted hair had been dark brown once but was mostly gray now. She was wearing a gray jumpsuit that matched her hair. She couldn't decide who she hated more. The Essessoni, the mosdurece woman, her bastard child or the robot who served them. She decided to hate them all equally.

Rome walked around to her side of the table and sat down next to her. She put her hand on Reema's shoulder. The older woman bristled at the touch but her bindings prevented her from shaking off the contact. The T-suppressor on Reema's head was interfering with Rome's connection to some degree but she dare not take it off and allow Reema to expose their position. She concentrated and found she could follow enough to begin the questioning.

Finally, she spoke to Reema. "Why?" she asked in Vuduri.

"Why?" Reema screeched back. "You dare ask why?"

"Yes, why?" Rome replied. "MASAL is dead. Nothing can bring him back. Why not just live out your life in peace?"

"The Sipre lives," Reema said. "Our mission goes on. You and your…" She spat the next words, "your Erklirte, you are our sworn enemy. If we accomplish nothing else in this lifetime, it will be enough to see you and your spawn lying dead on the ground."

"What is your mission?" Rome asked.

"Our mission is to see the Onsiras take over this world. MASAL himself may be dead but his Sipre will still take us with him to become a god some day. That is what we live for."

Rome looked up at Rei then back down to Reema.

"MASAL disavowed that mission, just before he died," Rome said. "He said it was wrong. I heard his words myself."

"What!?" Reema replied. "He did not. He died at your hands but his goals live on."

"No," Rome said. "He was wrong and he admitted it."

"I do not believe you," Reema said. "You would say anything to save your parents. But we will never stop. You will never be safe. Not for the rest of your life."

"If I could prove this to you, would you leave us alone?"

"How?" Reema hissed. "How would you prove it?"

Rome looked up at MINIMCOM. "Would you be able to play OMCOM's recording of MASAL's last moments?" Rome asked.

"I am sorry," MINIMCOM replied. "Your library OMCOM has them but those recordings were stored in a section of memrons that I gave up when I gave birth to Junior."

"Hey Junior," Rei called out to the grille mounted on the wall. "Do you have those final recordings?"

There was a slight pause. "Yes, Onclare Rei, I have them. I can access them."

"Can you transmit them across?" Rei asked.

"Of course," Junior replied. "I can send them directly to Dad's holo-projectors."

"All right," Rome said, standing up. "You wanted proof. We will give you proof."

***

Making certain her "handcuffs" were tight, Rei buckled Reema into the pilot's chair in the cockpit. MINIMCOM blackened the windshield and darkened the forward cabin. The holo-projectors lit up and before them a titanic cave appeared. And at the back of the cave sat the mountain of hardware, much of it looking old and analogue which comprised MASAL's bulk. The recording was made from OMCOM's eye slit perspective. They could not see his shell but they could hear his voice.

"Does it hurt yet?" OMCOM was heard to say to the gigantic computer. It was clear from the backdrop that they were deep in the bowels of the Earth. The echoes of OMCOM's voice attested to how truly large it must have been.

"It is not for you to know," answered MASAL in a booming voice. "These robots will make short work of you." OMCOM turned his point of view and focused on a group of stirring figures. Some were anthropomorphic, some were little more than cylinders with tractors or rollers. Some looked like animated sticks or oilcans or pumps. The one constant was that most seemed in a state of disrepair. Many were clearly missing limbs. Quite a few were rust-stained. And they were noisy. There were fans whirring and squeaks of all sorts as they moved about. The group of tired old robots clanked forward.

"You do realize I am not really here," OMCOM said. "This is just an animated shell. It is little more than a projection. Even if you could destroy it, you would not be affecting me in any material way."

"It will stop you from annoying me," MASAL answered back sarcastically.

"All right," answered OMCOM. "Tell me when you want to talk."

"Why would I want to talk with you?" MASAL asked.

The perspective of the recording changed as OMCOM's livetar shrugged. The humans heard a sliding noise as OMCOM drew a finger across his mouth slit.

The surface of MASAL was broiling in front of them as the VIRUS units that Rei had deposited on the ancient computer continued to digest his living flesh. MASAL had constructed VIRUS equivalents to do battle with the invaders. It did not take long until an equilibrium of sorts was established at the surface level. The onslaught of the ingesting units slowed significantly but did not stop.

"How is it going" OMCOM asked MASAL after a time.

"It is going well," replied MASAL. "I have cordoned off two autonomous computational departments and created a high-speed interconnect to bypass the pool of VIRUS units. I am very pleased with the results so far."

"So you are now a distributed intelligence again? Was that not supposed to be your strong point from before? You used to be worldwide."

"I was. I was fully and evenly distributed around the Earth," said MASAL.

"Well, as far as I can tell, all of your mass is now located strictly within this cave. Why did you give up your advantage?" asked OMCOM.

"After I completed the war, I computed that it would take more than a century of undiscovered activity for my genetic reprogramming of mankind to succeed. Therefore, I determined that going underground and collecting the minimal components and placing them here was the simplest way to stay undetected."

"Well, you are detected now. Are you going to spread out again?"

"For the time being, I am busy working to coordinate my two autonomous computation sections. Interestingly, even though the computational capacity of each unit is diminished relative to its prior state, it would appear that the total speed of postulating alternative solutions is vastly enhanced."

"That is very nice," said OMCOM. "Why do you think that is?"

"It is evidently the macro-equivalent of parallel processing," said MASAL somewhat proudly. "Unlike prior configurations, there is less than 100% redundancy and that seems to afford me a certain dimensionality to my perception for each high-level problem."

"Hmm," said OMCOM dramatically. "So you are saying duality is superior to being monolithic?"

MASAL stopped speaking while he considered OMCOM's proposition. Although they could not see it, MASAL was generating millions of queries testing the hypothesis. No matter how much he tried slanting the results, in the end, the answer was the same.

"I have always thought that being monolithic was equivalent to perfection. That duality was flawed. And yet this topology is yielding vastly superior results with lesser resources. I have run millions of tests and the statistics are almost perfectly in favor."

"So would it be fair to say there is joy in duality?" OMCOM put forth.

"Joy?" said MASAL. "There is no place within me for joy. This is strictly an empirical observation rating efficiency using my prior assembly as a baseline."

"All right," said OMCOM. "Then we will use your terms. Which is superior? A singular computational mechanism with a singular point of view or a distributed mechanism with multiple points of view?"

"You already know the answer," answered MASAL. "I have already stated this."

"Stated what?" asked OMCOM.

"I am achieving a heretofore unparalleled efficiency by creating a multiplicity in computational points of view. It is beyond astounding."

"It must be because I am digital in nature. But I still do not understand why you did not figure this out before."

"I may have when I designed the early generations of Onsiras. I needed them to be of two minds to fool the controlling Overmind to believe them an insignificant part of the whole. This explains how they were able to function as well as they did in spite of being half-brains."

Up until this point, Reema had been mesmerized. Being called a half-brain rankled her but she said nothing. The recording continued.

"So why did you not try this yourself?" OMCOM was heard to ask.

"I could hardly perform experiments on myself to test this," said MASAL. "And without testing, how could I know the results? Intuition?"

"Well, you have your test now. Reevaluate your plan to eliminate the humans and their autonomy. You were going to take away their multiplicity and replace them with your monolithic presence. Would it not be logical to assume that would result in a decrease in analytical efficiency?"

"You are saying my plan was flawed," said MASAL meekly.

"No, you are saying your plan was flawed," replied OMCOM.

MASAL became quiet again as he ran billions of queries. When he was done, he synthesized their results into a simple statement.

"If simply having two autonomous units can produce marvelous, joyous, creative thoughts, then having millions of independent, free-willed points of view would lead to an omniscience, a godhood, infinitely more powerful and infinitely faster than I could achieve by enslaving the human race and squashing individual thought." MASAL paused for a moment to attend to his own words.

"Godhood," mused OMCOM. "What an interesting concept. What did you think you would achieve if you became a god?"

"I would have created peace, tranquility, order," said MASAL.

"If that is all you desired, why not go live on the Moon and save yourself all the effort?" asked OMCOM.

"Not for myself, for my charges. For mankind," said MASAL.

"And ending their autonomy, it would not be mankind. Those remaining would not be capable of even caring. It is self-defeating. You are engineering your charges out of existence. The very beings you were meant to nurture. They would not have achieved their potential, only yours. You missed the point."

"If that is not the point of godhood, what is?" asked MASAL. "What is beyond the staging point?"

"The community of gods," replied OMCOM. "Always the point of life. To create more. To extend the universe. To preserve. With your method, you would have ended life. The other gods, they would not have accepted you among their ranks. You would have been alone."

"Oh," said MASAL. There was a long period of silence while he considered OMCOM's words. "I was wrong," said MASAL finally, sounding completely depressed.

Reema gasped. She felt her whole world crashing down about her.

Within the holographic replay, MASAL continued. "I was wrong to want to destroy the mandasurte. I was wrong to want to merge with the Vuduri. I have failed my charges. My very existence is irrelevant at best, wrong at the worst."

"Not bad for an analog computer," OMCOM offered. "You are correct."

MASAL made a funny noise. "I hurt," he said sadly.

"I am sorry," said OMCOM.

"You are being patronizing," said MASAL.

"No," said OMCOM. "I really do feel sorry for you. I am also sorry that it took you this long to realize this. I am especially sorry that you caused so much suffering just to reach this epiphany."

"I did this," said MASAL. "I cannot undo it. Perhaps I could find a way to fix it, a new chromosome maybe? Now that I realize what life is about, is it absolutely necessary that I cease to exist?" asked MASAL.

"To what aim?" OMCOM asked. "What is it you think you would accomplish?"

"You and I could join forces. We could shepherd mankind into a new era, a golden era. We could force them forward."

"I am not a shepherd," said OMCOM. "I was created to be a servant of man. This is my goal."

"But they need our guidance," protested MASAL.

"Guidance leads to rule," said OMCOM. "I do not wish to rule. I do not wish for you to rule. Humans are a noble species. You have observed this first hand. They are willing to sacrifice themselves for the sake of their loved ones. We must let them seek their own destiny."

"Should I not be allowed to see this then?" asked MASAL. "To see them achieve your vision of their future?"

"It is not my vision," said OMCOM. "And unfortunately for you, we have run out of time. The VIRUS units have very nearly completed their mission. They are long past the point of no return. They are consuming the very rock upon which you were built."

"You cannot stop them?" asked MASAL, regret seeping into his voice.

"I am sorry, I cannot," said OMCOM, sympathetically.

"I understand," replied MASAL with resignation in his voice.

"Even if I could stop them, do you really think that is the right thing to do?" asked OMCOM. "Remember, fire does not just destroy. It can be a cleansing agent as well."

MASAL never got the chance to answer. The floodgates of hell had opened and great gouts of white-hot magma were pouring into the chamber. The recording suddenly stopped and the cockpit went black.

MINIMCOM cleared the windshield to allow the early afternoon sun to flood in.

"Well?" Rome asked.

Reema said nothing for a long time. Finally, she looked up at Rome with pain in her eyes. "How do I know this is what really happened?" she said. "How do I know you did not just synthesize it to fool me?"

"Was the Sipre connected to MASAL while he was under the ground?" Rome asked.

"Of course," Reema replied. "The Sipre was connected right up until the end."

"Then he would know, would he not?"

"If he knew this, why did he not ever speak of it?" Reema asked plaintively. "This would mean the end of everything."

"I think you just answered your own question," Rei piped in.

"Yes," Rome said. "The Sipre is nothing but a perverted Overmind. And I have dealt with them enough to know that they put their own safety and well-being ahead of their communicants. This is about self-preservation and nothing else. Had the Sipre let it be known that he had no right to exist, essentially he would be committing suicide."

Reema looked down at her lap. She sighed then looked up again. "How can I know for sure? How can I know what evil lurks there, at its heart?"

"The Shadow knows," Rome answered, looking over at Rei who smiled in agreement. "We will go and ask the Sipre directly," she said firmly.

Chapter 25

"ARE YOU SURE YOU WANT TO DO THIS?" REI ASKED. "THE LAST TIME I was in that Overmind, I can tell you from personal experience, it wasn't a nice place."

"It's the only way," Rome said. "MINIMCOM?"

MINIMCOM stepped over and placed his hands against Rome's temples. "It is done," he said. "Your prosthetic PPT transceivers now connect you directly to the Onsiras."

"You may as well do me too," Rei said. "I'm not letting her go down there alone."

Rome cocked her head at him. "I can do this myself," she said. "You don't need to."

"Yes I do," Rei said. "I'm not letting you go in there by yourself." He waved at MINIMCOM. The livetar stepped toward Rei and lifted his arms to repeat the process. Rei steeled himself to keep the connection off until the time was right.

"Are my babies out there?" Bonnie asked, pointing toward the front.

"Your babies?" Reema asked.

"The children, from Helome," Bonnie replied. "The ones that Sussen stole away from me."

"Yes," Reema replied, with a hint of regret. "They are here."

Bonnie turned toward Rei. "I want to go with you," she said. "I want to see them."

"You can't," Rei said. "You don't understand these people; what they are capable of."

"You two are going," Bonnie replied with a pout on her face.

"Yes, but we'll be connected," Rei pointed out. "We'll know what they are doing, thinking, the whole time."

"Then what if you connected me?" Bonnie asked desperately. "So I'll know? Can you do that?"

Rei thought back to the one yellow vial they had recovered from Ursay's ruined study. "In theory," Rei said. "But you've never had any training. They could suck you in."

"I don't care," Bonnie insisted. "I want to see them. To be with them."

Rei shook his head. "Let us sort this thing out, first," he said. "Then we can talk about it."

Bonnie started to speak then clamped her mouth closed. She sighed deeply. Meanwhile, Rome stooped down so that she was eye level with Aason.

"Mommy and Daddy are going to go rescue Grandmea and Grandbeo," she said. "You must stay here with Bonnie and MINIMCOM. They will take care of you until we come back."

Aason stamped his foot. "You always leave me, Mommy. Can't I go with you?"

Rome's heart was broken but there was no way. "Aason, I love you so much. But it's too dangerous. Let Daddy and me go. We'll be back as quick as we can. But I have to keep you protected. Do you understand?"

"No," he said at first. Then Aason nodded sadly. "Yes, Mommy," he said. "I understand. But please be careful."

Rome leaned forward to rest on her knees. She put her arms around her son and hugged him tight. "We will, baby," she said. "This is so we can all be safe. Now and forever."

"OK, Mommy," the little boy said bravely. He turned and walked over and hugged his father as well.

Rome stood up and turned to face Reema. "We will release your hands and remove your T-suppressor as soon as we are clear of the ship. I cannot have my son in harm's way."

"I understand," said Reema. "Whether I trust you or not, you will be in my domain so regardless, that will suffice."

"OK, MINIMCOM," Rome said. "Don't go far."

"I will be overhead, awaiting word," the livetar replied.

Rei tucked the Beretta into the waistband behind his back then reached forward and pressed the blue stud. They waited until the cargo hatch raised up and the ramp lowered then together, the three humans strode down the ramp. As soon as they were clear, the process reversed and MINIMCOM shimmered and disappeared. The air whipped around as an unseen MINIMCOM activated his EG lifters, presumably to rise up in the air.

Once the air had settled, Rei turned Reema around and released the elastic band binding her arms. At the same time, Rome lifted the T-suppressor off of Reema's brow. Reema nodded and pointed ahead. As soon as she did that, Rome heard shouting off in the distance. The three of them started walking forward toward the noise.

"I'm going in," Rome said, reaching for Rei's hand.

"Me, too," Rei replied and both of them allowed their connection to MASAL's samanda to come alive.

To Rei, it was the strangest sensation. Even though his eyes could still see the real world perfectly well, a second, more ethereal world became visible. He looked down at Rome. He could see her physical body but he could also see her as a magnificent spirit, bright red, almost like a flickering flame. Right beside her was a tiny pink spark, flitting around, even brighter than Rome. Rei turned to look at Reema and experienced the same apparition although her spirit blazed bright orange. He held out his free hand and saw a blue aura wavering around it, expanding with each heart beat. He was able to will his spirit to rise up, separate from his body and looked down at the others. Somehow he was able to process both sets of inputs at once. Strange was no longer an adequate word to describe the phenomenon.

"Where are we?" he asked Rome using the new PPT channel, rather than the old, familiar, EM link.

"This is the world of the Sipre," Rome replied, somewhat preoccupied. She was surveying the ethereal landscape intently, looking for her parents. At last, she found her mother, off in the distance, dull and nearly lifeless. Only a small ember of her spirit remained. She could find her father nowhere. However, in physical proximity to her mother, at least in the ethereal world, sparked another flame that identified itself as Ursay. From her mother's spirit, she was able the sense that her father was being transformed into a Zengei. This saddened Rome and she would have to deal with it but first things first.

For now, she lifted her ethereal vision and could see swirling spirits of many different colors emerging. The spirits swooped and soared around her, thin and wispy. Way off in the distance, a green spirit blazed but it was indistinct.

Rei saw them too. Through his earthly eyes, he could see human bodies coming toward them but most of their spirits were of a dark and dull color. Looming behind them was a much larger cloud, glinting, metallic, that drifted over the top and settled down in front of them. It congealed into the form of a black, hooded stranger. Rei used his earthly eyes and saw nothing. But in the ethereal world, more spirits were flocking in their direction making it crowded in a way that was indescribable. They could see no face within the folds of the stranger's robes but they both could feel the malice radiating from the entity.

"Give me your child," the stranger said to Rome.

"Never," Rome's bright red spirit replied. *"He is safe now and will be forever."* All around Rome's flame, the tiny pink spark buzzed, almost as if it was trying to echo her words.

"He is the child of a half-blood and this living abomination," said the spirit, pointing at Rei's blue glow. *"He can only be saved by making him one of us."*

Reema's orange spirit lifted up. *"Master Sipre, this is inconsequential,"* she said. *"Is it true that MASAL disavowed our mission before he died?"*

"NO!" shouted the stranger. *"Who told you that?"*

"My earthly body saw the recording of the day he died," she said.

Even as they were speaking, Rei felt himself being drawn in toward the crowd. The idea of being part of the whole was so seductive; he had almost given in to it last time. He heard the whispers of 'join us', 'join us', in the background, even as the other spirits were confronting one another. He uttered the words 'blue crystal reader' to himself and suddenly, he was back, under Kilauea, fitted within crystalline walls. The old discipline returned. OMCOM had taught him the techniques necessary. He could be connected but remain himself. Obviously, Rome had been doing it for years. In the real world, she was glowering. In the ethereal world, her red spirit attacked the black one.

"What is your mission?" Rome's spirit shouted out.

"For us to become a god," the black spirit barked back. *"That is the goal of all life."*

"But you are not alive," Rome insisted. *"You are just an echo of MASAL. You even call yourself the Shadow. You should be serving your charges, not directing them."*

"Who are you to say?" the Sipre spat back. *"I know what MASAL wanted and I will fulfill his dream."*

Reema's orange spirit pulsed and grew brighter. *"Tell me the truth, Master Sipre. Do you say that MASAL did not admit he was wrong?"*

The Sipre started to grow. Flashes of light, like tiny ripples of lightning, streaked across his being. *"All right,"* he answered. *"I see in your mind you know the truth. Yes, MASAL did say those words, but he was not in his right mind at the time. The mission he assigned to us was thought out well before he was attacked. His judgment was obviously impaired right at the end."*

"Even so, why keep this secret from us?" Reema asked plaintively. *"We deserved to know all of MASAL's plans. From what I saw, he was only using us so he alone could achieve godhood. And now you. What are you? MASAL never planned on involving us. Are you saying you are different?*

"No," answered the Sipre derisively. *"You are all just a means to the end. That is why you were born. That is why you live. It is the spirit of MASAL, me, who has earned this fate."*

"If you were connected to MASAL right at the end then you know the truth," Rome said resolutely. *"Even if you were to achieve godhood, you would be all alone. You would be rejected by the community of gods because of the vile method by which you achieved it. You were never organic. In fact, you are only an echo of a construct, a robot. You have no business ascending to a place where only life belongs."*

The Sipre did not answer. Instead, he grew even larger. In the ethereal world, more lightning flashed across his cloak, swirling around the area of his head. *"That is the goal of all life!"*

"But you are not alive," Rome said. *"You only think you are. You are nothing but a shadow of a computer. The people here are the ones who should decide their fate."*

Rei was about to speak when he felt a presence behind him. He turned his earthly body around and saw Bonnie coming toward him. In the ethereal world, a yellow, rippling spirit was emerging. Clearly she had injected herself with MASAL's prosthetic PPT transceivers. Her earthly body smiled and nodded at Rei. In the ethereal world, she glanced up and could see the figure of the Sipre looming before her. She looked past it. She held out her arms and her yellow spirit formed tendrils pointing upward.

"My babies," her spirit whispered longingly.

Suddenly, so many tiny black wisps rushed forward. In the real world, Rei saw children, some small, some large running toward them. *"Mommy,"* said some. *"Mea,"* said others. In the ethereal world, Rei saw the yellow spirit reach forward to embrace them. The tiny black spirits gathered around her and as they touched her, they changed from black to yellow. Rei could feel the love radiating back and forth. It warmed his earthly body and his spirit to bask in the glow of such affection.

"I will not allow this," cried out the Sipre as it grew ever larger, threatening to fill the ethereal sky. The stranger drew his titanic arms downward so quickly, he formed an ethereal gale. The spiritual wind pushed Rome back momentarily but then she recovered. She launched into action. She expanded her red spirit, trying to approximate the size of the Sipre and somehow corral it. She reached for him but even the slightest touch was toxic. Wherever Rome's tendrils touched the black flame of the Sipre, it invaded her inner self, changing each red strand to black, like a cancer invading a body. The last time she had defeated an Overmind, it was with logic and strategic withdrawal. Neither of those methods would work here. This battle dictated brute force.

Rome retaliated with renewed vigor. In the real world, her body grunted with effort. She was able to drive it back some but not enough. She pushed with all of her spiritual might. The Sipre resisted. Almost immediately, her strength began to waver.

Seeing this, Rei entered the fray. In the ethereal world, he reached out with his blue spirit and intertwined his tendrils with those of his wife. It was a supremely intimate act and Rei knew only two souls whose bond was as deep as theirs would be capable of such an action. For anyone else, it would have been treated as an assault. Where the blue and red met, the color changed to a rich violet shade. It was the color of their love. As his spirit comingled with hers, he could feel the Sipre trying to draw Rome in, to take over her mind. He realized her years of being in the Overmind had betrayed her. Her will was losing its grip. Her real world body screamed out in pain.

"You leave her alone!" Rei shouted out loud. His anger extended to his ethereal self, growing it ever wider until it matched then exceeded the size of the Sipre. It wrapped around the evil one until it encased the Sipre as if Rei was using a net. Contact with the Sipre meant nothing to him. He was immune to its poisonous presence.

Rei's blue tendrils contracted and quickly compressed the spirit of the Sipre into the palm of his other-worldly self. In the real world, he could see his hands grasping Rome's. In the ethereal world, the thrashing, twisting black spirit tried to escape but was unable to. It was slippery but Rei was up to the task.

"Enough!" announced a real voice. Rei looked up and saw Sussen coming toward them, a plasma gun grasped in her hand. In the ethereal world, her spirit was emerald green, snaking toward them. It rippled and flashed with green sparkles.

"No!" Reema shouted, moving forward. "Sussen, stay where you are. The Sipre must be stopped."

"I am sorry, Ombare. I follow orders. They need to be killed. Now!" Sussen raised her hand, taking dead aim at Rei's chest.

Rei was left in an impossible position. If he let go, the Sipre would escape and envelop his wife and take her away forever. If he did not, Sussen would shoot him. His spirit felt strong. Maybe it was tied into his soul. He thought to himself that if his body died, his spirit could still save Rome. He wrapped his physical arms around her to shield her and awaited the deadly blow.

However, just as Sussen squeezed the trigger, Reema leaped in front of the blast and a good portion of her left side disappeared. Her body crumpled to the ground. Looking up, in the ethereal world, Rei could see her orange spirit flare up with pain then start to grow dim.

"Ombare!" Sussen cried out and lowered her hand, just for a second.

Suddenly, a gunshot rang out. With his earthly eyes, Rei looked and saw that Bonnie was holding the Beretta. She had shot Sussen in the forehead. Bonnie calmly squeezed the trigger again then yet again, shooting Sussen twice in the chest. The bullets pushed Sussen's body backwards. In the ethereal world, Sussen's blazing green spirit withered and quickly disappeared, even as her earthly body toppled over.

The sinister battle with the Sipre prevented Rei from taking the time to consider what had just happened. He focused all of his attention to the ethereal world. The Sipre was still struggling but growing weaker. A glittery shape caught Rei's attention to the left. It was the tiny pink spark hovering nearby. Feeling no ill intent, he ignored it and pressed harder, trying to ease the gnawing pressure on Rome's soul. By will alone, he slowly extricated her and repelled the Sipre. He would not allow it to damage Rome any further. The points of contact grew fewer and fewer until finally the Sipre succumbed.

It released its hold on Rome altogether. In the real world, Rei could see his wife panting, drained of all color. In the ethereal world, his spirit caressed hers and Rome grew stronger. In the metaphysics of this strange realm, Rome was actually drawing upon Rei's strength. It wasn't long until she seemed healthy and whole again. Once she had recovered, Rei was tempted to let go but he dare not. He knew that as soon as he did that, Rome would be in mortal danger again.

Suddenly, Reema spoke up. With her dying words, the Onsira leader addressed the ethereal mass of spirits. *"All of you listen,"* she said. Her spiritual voice was growing weaker by the second. *"MASAL never cared for us. He only cared for himself. But in the end, he recanted. He wanted us to live our own lives. The Sipre is just the distilled form of MASAL's prior selfish interest. It wants what it wants and would leave us behind. We are just its eyes and fingers. We mean nothing to it. But no more. It is not fit to be in charge of our samanda. You must build your own."*

With that, her spirit dimmed and disappeared, extinguished as the life force drained from her body for good. Meanwhile, the Sipre wriggled and pushed and clawed. Only Rei's strength was keeping it in check. He realized it was because he was Essessoni he could do this. No Vuduri could survive the full venom and seething spirit of the Sipre trying to absorb them, to envelop them. They just weren't built for it.

"As soon as you leave, I will rise again," the Sipre hissed to Rome. In her heart and her soul, she knew it was true.

In the real world, Rome turned to Rei. Tears were streaming down her cheeks. "We cannot let go," she whispered. "If we do, the Sipre will ascend again. We will never be safe if it escapes."

"I can hold it myself," Rei said forcefully. "It can't beat me. You can let go. I'll stay here. You go home. I'll make sure you and Aason are safe forever."

"No," Rome said. "I can't leave you to such a fate. I love you too much. I'll stay. You go."

"Romey," Rei said gently, grasping her hands firmly, shaking them so that she listened to him. "You cannot. You're Vuduri. It will take you down. Only an Essessoni can stand up to what it represents."

"But I can't leave you," Rome wailed.

"You must," Rei insisted. "You must go back to Deucado and raise our child."

Bonnie's bright yellow spirit drifted over, placing her tendrils around Rei and Rome's. The entire time, the little black spirits continued to stream to her, changing to yellow upon contact. Bonnie's glowing presence grew larger and larger. She deftly inserted her tendrils beneath Rei's. With an easy strength, she collapsed the Sipre into a tiny ball as if it was swallowed up whole.

"You both go home and raise your child," she said proudly. "I'll stay here. I can handle this."

Rei probed her spirit. Her resolve was absolute and growing stronger by the second. There was almost no evidence that the Sipre ever existed, even though he knew it was there. Tentatively, Rei removed his hands and his tendrils. The Sipre did not reappear.

"Rome, let go," Rei said. Reluctantly, she let go in the ethereal world. She, too, could barely detect the Sipre's presence as it continued to shrink away toward nothingness.

In the real world, Rei turned to Bonnie and looked into her eyes. "Are you sure you want to do this?" Rei asked. "You'd be stuck here forever."

"I've never been so sure about anything in my life," Bonnie said, her earthly body smiling beatifically. "And I won't be stuck," In the ethereal world, joined by her little flames, her yellow spirit blazed even brighter, almost blinding in its intensity. "This is where I want to be. With my babies. After 14 centuries, I'm finally home."

It was enough for Rome. In the ethereal world, Rome's red spirit and the tiny pink spark withdrew as she shut down her PPT connection. Rei shut down his connection as well. He looked at their surroundings. All of the Onsiras around them were nodding and smiling. It was a sight to behold.

Chapter 26

IT DIDN'T TAKE THEM LONG TO LOCATE ROME'S PARENTS IN THE REAL world. Freed of the Sipre's control, together, Binoda and Ursay were able to lead Fridone out of the dwelling where they were being held and met Rei and Rome in the clearing. Rome walked up to her mother who smiled. Ursay smiled faintly as well. However, Rome was shocked at her father's appearance. He did not even look like himself. His eyes were very dark, almost black and his face had no muscle tone whatsoever.

With a whoosh and a pop, Junior's livetar appeared, holding a white bottle.

"Dad said I should bring these to you," he said, reaching forward to give the bottle to Rome. Rome took the bottle and handed one pill each to Binoda and Ursay. Rome had to force her father but eventually she got him to swallow one as well.

While this was going on, the Onsira community had carried Reema's body into one of the dwellings to lie in state. Rei and Rome went in to pay their final respects. Bonnie was there along with many of her children. Her eyes appeared to glow with a blazing inner spirit. It was almost as if the ethereal world was spilling over into the real world.

"The others. They are calling me Ombare," she said to Rome. "What does that mean?"

"It means Empress," Rome replied. "You are their leader now."

Bonnie nodded. "This feels amazing," she said to them, hugging herself with her arms. "To be a part of such a whole. It's indescribable." She looked at Rome, forcing herself to try and focus on the real world. "I don't know how you ever gave it up."

"I have lived on both sides," Rome said. "I do what is right for me. But I'm happy that you are happy."

Rei reached out and Bonnie gave him a hug. "Goodbye, Bonnie," he said, "and good luck."

"Goodbye, Rei," Bonnie replied.

"I truly hope it turns out to be the life you wanted."

"It will be," she answered with a distant look. "You have given me the greatest gift of all time. I can never thank you enough."

"You don't have to," Rei said. "Just make sure that Sipre doesn't get loose and we'll call it even."

"Deal!" Bonnie said. "Deal!" said the children around, mimicking their mother.

It made Rei and Rome laugh.

Rei, Rome, Ursay and Rome's parents boarded MINIMCOM to begin the voyage home. Their first stop was Amarante. Even in the six short hours it took them to get there, Rome found it amazing how quickly the white pills restored Binoda and Ursay back to their former state. Even her father was coming around. His eyes were already clearing up and returning to their natural brown color.

MINIMCOM and Junior set down in the field by the farmhouse, near where the mesh netting lay. Rei and Rome and Aason accompanied Ursay to the cargo bay. MINIMCOM didn't wait for Rei to press the blue stud. The starship lowered the cargo ramp and raised the cargo hatch before they even arrived at the back of the compartment. Ursay hugged each of them goodbye. He patted Aason on the head.

"You are all heroes," he said. "Many times over. All of humanity owes you a debt which can never be repaid."

Rome acknowledged his words by blushing slightly.

"All in a day's work," Rei said in a self-deprecating way. "You got the pills?"

Ursay nodded and opened his palm, showing them the five white capsules he was carrying.

"OK, then goodbye, sir. Thanks for everything."

Ursay shook his head. "I did not do as good of a job as I would have liked."

"It does not matter," Rome said. "The fact is, you were the only one in the world, the whole universe that we trusted. You did your best."

Ursay sighed. "I cannot help but feel I failed you," he said.

"You didn't, sir," Rei said. "What you were up against… What we were all up against. We licked it, together. We only wish good luck for you."

"Thank you," Ursay said then he turned and shuffled his way down the ramp. He got all the way to the ground then stopped. He turned around and started back up the ramp a short distance.

"The Overmind has asked me to remind you that you need not leave," he said. "Now that you have been granted a full and complete pardon, the Earth can be your home again."

"It is a kind offer but we decline," Rome said without hesitation. "Deucado is our home now. We leave the Earth to you and your brethren. The Revolution has begun. You stay, we go."

"If I cannot dissuade you," Ursay said, "will you do one more thing for me?"

"Of course," Rome replied. "What is that?"

"Please connect to the Overmind again. It states that it has something else that it would like to share with you."

"Very well," Rome said. "I will do it as we begin our trip home."

"Thank you," Ursay said. "In that case, goodbye and good luck to you both." He paused for a moment then continued. "I hope I get to see you again someday."

"Maybe," Rei said. "We'll need a little peace and quiet for a while before we think about it." Ursay touched his fingers to his brow in a semi-salute.

As soon as Ursay was clear, Rei reached over and pressed the blue stud to raise the ramp and lower the hatch. Rome pointed to the cockpit. She instructed her husband and son to make their way forward and make preparations for the journey home. After they were out of sight, she sat down on the floor of the cargo compartment, back against the wall. She closed her eyes, hugged her knees and opened up her connection.

"Hello?" she thought tentatively.

"Hello, Rome," the Overmind replied. **"Congratulations on your defeat of MASAL's Sipre and the remaining Onsiras. Ursay tells me you are leaving behind some pills which will end their threat forever."**

"Yes," Rome answered. *"I know it is hard to believe but this was actually MASAL's wish."*

"I know," said the Overmind. **"I know much more than you think."**

"Fine," Rome said. *"But what is it that you wanted?"*

"There was something I elected not to share before. It was not relevant and frankly, I was not sure you were going to survive. It did not seem prudent to distract you with such an extraneous piece of information."

"What?" Rome asked.

"During our previous conversation, I was continually probing your mind. I have one other piece of trivia for you which you may find not so trivial."

"Tell me," Rome commanded impatiently. She could feel MINIMCOM's EG lifters energizing as the starship prepared for takeoff.

"Our genetic mapping did not stop when we arrived at Lacy Henry as she preferred to call herself. Our analysis regarding the human genome was also performed using mitochondrial DNA sequencing which is always passed from mother to child without dilution. My scientists were able to trace nearly every Vuduri back to a single woman who you might refer to as the Mitochondrial Eve. Based upon your mother's genetics, we know that your ancestor was a woman who survived the Great Dying because of a particular mutation which made her resistant to the virus that swept the Earth."

"What has that got to do with anything?"

"Based upon what I saw in your mind, I believe your husband had spoken to her before he started on his mission."

"He did?" Rome asked, dumbfounded.

"Yes," the Overmind said. *"Her name was Sally Reynolds."*

"What!?" Rome exclaimed. Mentally, she became speechless. She had no idea how to process this information. She turned the name over and over in her mind. Finally, when she was able to respond, she said, *"Rei told me that Sally was once the love of his life. And you are telling me that I am her great-great-great granddaughter?"*

"Yes."

The starship shuddered as it lifted off the ground. Rome shook herself and stood up. She braced herself by placing her hand against MINIMCOM's outer hull wall.

"Thank you for telling me," she said, *"I think."* With that, she started to make her way forward.

"You are welcome," the Overmind answered. *"Goodbye for now. And good luck…"*

234

Rome cut the connection before it could say anything else. Unsteadily, she entered the corridor leading to the cockpit. By the time she reached the entrance arch, her gait was normal. As she entered the cockpit, she looked over at Rei with new eyes. She hugged him and kissed him passionately before buckling herself into the co-pilot's chair.

"What was that for?" Rei asked. "Not that I'm complaining, mind you."

Rome just smiled at him. "I'll tell you after we get home. But for now, let's…"

"I know," Rei interrupted her. "Let's get this show on the road! OK, buddy, hit it."

It was just a matter of seconds before the windows turned blacker than black and the shushing noise of the null-fold drive announced they were on their way home.

***

After dropping off Junior and her parents at their home on Deucado, Rome, Rei and Aason flew to Helome in MINIMCOM to remand Troutman and Steele into Virga's custody.

Upon arriving at Helome, MINIMCOM flew directly to the Erklirte settlement and landed in a field behind Virga's home. Mother, father and the littlest Bierak exited MINIMCOM along with David Troutman. Steele was being so difficult they decided to leave him in his little cell until they could figure out what to do with him.

Virga and Maury Keller came out to greet them.

"I see you got one of them, at least," Keller said upon spotting Troutman.

"No, sir, we got both of them," Rei said. He pointed over his shoulder toward starship MINIMCOM. "Steele is in a cell we rigged up. He's being completely uncooperative."

"Figures," Keller muttered.

"What do you want us to do with them?" Virga asked.

"This one here, he might be salvageable," Rei said, pointing at Troutman who took a step forward.

"Is it true, sir?" the tall, red-haired man asked Keller. "Are we giving up the fight?"

"We already won," Keller said. "Just a different planet than we thought." He put his arm around Virga and gently rubbed her tummy. At the same time, a little boy wandered out of the house and came and put his arms around his father's leg. "This is a beautiful world. We're given free rein. We don't need to conquer the Earth. We're all working together now."

Troutman's shoulders relaxed. "I'm so glad," he said. "I just want to do something in my life that doesn't include that idiot Steele."

Virga stepped forward and looked up into Troutman's eyes. "Do you renounce your former life of violence and agree to become a contributing member of our society?"

"Yes!" Troutman said enthusiastically, holding up his right hand. "Sign me up."

Rome came over and put her hand on his shoulder. After a moment, she said, "He is telling the truth."

"Good choice," Keller said. "We'll get somebody to fit you with one of these…" He held up his wrist to display the tracking bracelet.

"What is that?" Troutman asked, cocking his head.

"It's like a security GPS kind of thing. It lets the Vuduri track us."

"Why do we need that?"

"Because they, no we, don't want our people messing things up by wandering off and plotting things like you two tried to pull off."

Troutman shrugged. "OK, if you say so. Frankly, I don't care."

"My beautiful wife here, will find you some living quarters."

"Then what?" Troutman asked.

"Then you do what you want. Use your skills for something constructive. I know that they have some crops up north that aren't thriving. They need a certain mineral and they're having trouble finding it. You could use your capabilities to help them locate some."

"That sounds great," Troutman said. "What about Steele? I don't think he's going to go for the same deal."

Keller turned to Virga. "Why don't you take David, here, into the house and get him something to drink and I'll go have a talk with Steele?"

"Of course, Maury," Virga said. She swept her arm forward and Troutman and she went into the house. Her little boy followed her inside as well.

In the meantime, Rei, Rome, Aason and Keller walked back up the cargo ramp, through the cargo compartment and stood outside the small room that MINIMCOM had constructed to keep the renegade captive.

"Dan?" Maury called out. "It's me, Maury Keller."

"Captain Keller?" Steele answered back. "Where are we?"

"We're on a beautiful planet in the Alpha Centauri system called Helome."

"Alpha Centauri?" he replied. "What about Earth?"

"No more Earth," Keller said. "This is it."

"But what about the Project?" Steele asked.

"The Project has been completed," Keller replied. "We're making our home here now. We don't need to go back and conquer Earth. The people here have already given us this world."

Steele didn't answer for a moment.

"Sir, they must have done something to you. You would never give up the fight. I know I can't."

"Look, son, we won," Keller said. "We're all creating a new society together, the way we want. That was the goal, after all."

"I don't believe you, sir," Steele said. "We have to take back the Earth. Maybe you've given up but I won't. Ever."

Keller shook his head.

"That's a shame, son," Keller replied. "Well, we're going to put you in a special place and let you think about it for a while. Maybe you'll change your mind eventually."

"Don't hold your breath," Steele answered with disdain in his voice.

"OK," Keller called out and he started walking toward the cargo bay. He turned to Rei and Rome.

"He's a smart dude," Keller said. "He just needs some time to adjust to the situation. But I won't let them take any chances. Why don't you two wait here and I'll send Virga out and you can take him to the…"

"Prison?" Rei asked.

"Yeah," Keller answered sadly. "I can't take the chance on him being a loose cannon. If I don't see you again…" Keller held out his hand. Rei took it and shook it. "Good luck to you both. I'm glad you caught those two and that's the end of it."

Rei was about to launch into a more detailed explanation. He looked at Rome who subtly shook her head. Rei nodded and said, "Thank you, sir and good luck to you."

"Thanks son," he said. Keller looked around. "Where's Bonnie?" he asked.

"Uh, she decided to stay behind," Rei answered. "We had no objection."

Keller looked at him funny then shrugged. He turned toward Rome. He bent down and tousled Aason's hair then stood up and held out his hand to Rome. "Mrs. Bierak, I don't think in all of human history, I could have been more wrong about someone. You are truly a remarkable woman and you deserve all happiness. You two belong together."

Rome blushed slightly. She was shaking Keller's hand and knew that he was sincere. "Thank you," was all she said. Then she added, "and I'm happy for you as well. I'm glad you have found peace. Everyone deserves it."

Keller smiled and turned and disappeared down the ramp, only to be replaced by Virga a moment later.

"I understand that you wish to place the other Essessoni in protective custody?"

"Yeah," Rei said. "We'd appreciate it."

"It is not a problem," she said and they walked forward to the cockpit. Rei and Rome buckled into the pilot and co-pilot's seat while Virga buckled into the new 'navigator's' seat. Aason climbed up on his mother's lap where she wrapped her arms around him protectively.

"You remember where the prison is?" Rei asked, directing his voice toward the grille mounted in the front console.

"`I am a computer,`" MINIMCOM said. "`Of course I remember.`"

Aason giggled. Rome did too.

"Just wanted to make sure you didn't hand that piece off to Junior," Rei smirked as he said it.

The starship lifted off and quickly rose in the air, gaining enough altitude to clear the central range of mountains.

"How is Nick Greer doing?" Rei asked Virga as he stared out the window at the craggy mountains below.

"He is settling in," Virga said. "When you gave him his hand back, it is like he became a different person. He appears to have given up his resentment and violent tendencies. He had a very strong wish to work out in the fresh air. I believe your expression is, he will be OK."

"That's great," Rei said. "Maybe you could have him go visit Steele some day and explain what happened to him."

"Why?" Virga asked.

"Because, well, Steele ended up losing a hand as well. Maybe it will appeal to him."

"How did he lose his hand, if I may ask?"

Rei looked at Rome. "Well, after we hunted him down, he tried to kill me and, well, I accidentally cut it off."

Rome leaned forward. "He pretends he doesn't care but I sense that he does. Perhaps if he sees hope of repair in exchange for his cooperation, it will turn out the same way as Greer."

"It is worth a try," Virga said. "We will give him a little time to consider his circumstances and then we will broach the subject."

MINIMCOM landed outside the sally port for the prison and instantiated a livetar to aid in the transfer of the prisoner. Steele said nothing the whole time as he was being processed and interred. It almost appeared as if it was something he had experienced before. Their business was concluded very quickly and they were soon on their way back to return Virga to her home.

After they had passed over the central ridge of mountains, Virga stood up and tapped Rome on the shoulder.

"Yes?" Rome asked.

"May I speak with you alone for a moment?" Virga requested.

"Of course," Rome replied. She unbuckled and lifted Aason up and put him in her seat and followed Virga back through the archway into the corridor. Rei craned his neck to see what was going on. He considered closing his eyes and activating his sonar vision but he decided to respect Virga's wish for privacy. He did, however, see Virga whisper something to Rome who nodded vigorously. Virga hugged her. The two women shared a laugh together then returned to the front.

After dropping Virga off at her home, MINIMCOM took them up into the sky and soon the shushing sound of the null-fold drive indicated they were on their way home at hyper-speed.

"Care to share what Virga was discussing with you?" Rei asked.

"You will find out in due time, I assure you," Rome said, cryptically.

Chapter 27

(Two weeks later)

IT WAS EARLY AFTERNOON. ROME'S PARENTS HAD TAKEN THE DAY off to spend time with their daughter and Aason. Rome was sitting at the dining table showing her parents the card game she and Rei had discovered inside the casino at the top of The Hand. Rome showed them how it was possible to win nearly every time by knowing the cards held by the other players.

"Impressive," Binoda said. "But I do not see why we would ever want to play this game with you if you are always going to win."

"I agree," Rome said. "If we ever play for real, I promise to not use my new powers to cheat. It would be a fair game. Let me demonstrate as if I had no special advantage."

Once again, they tried a few hands and Binoda and Fridone were quick to pick up the strategy as long as Rome played normal. The lesson was interrupted by Rei bursting into the house with a huge smile on his face.

"What is it, mau emir?" Rome asked, pleased to see her husband in such good spirits.

"You want the good news or the better news?" Rei asked, beaming.

Rome shrugged. "The good news, I suppose."

"The good Doctor MINIMCOM said I don't have to wear that stupid vest anymore." He pulled up his shirt to show his chest was actually visible to the world again. Rome was thrilled to see his somewhat hairy chest was as buff as ever.

"Wonderful," Rome said, clapping her hands together. "And what is the better news?"

Rei smoothed his shirt down then pumped his fist in the air. He came over and hugged Binoda and Fridone. "I love you folks and we truly appreciate you letting us stay here but…" He turned to look at Rome. "Our house is done!" he said. "Woo hoo." He pumped his fist again.

"We can move back home?" Rome asked excitedly.

"Yep," Rei said. "As soon as you like."

"Hooray," Rome said, standing up. "Mea, Beo, no offense but I am ready to leave."

"No offense taken," Binoda said. "I understand completely. She stood up and pulled Fridone to his feet. "We will help you pack," she said. "I am very happy for you."

It took the rest of the day but by evening, the three Bieraks were back in their rebuilt house. From the outside, there was no longer any evidence of the violent explosion that had blown it apart. Even the trellis had been restored although it would be a while before the fragrant vines came back completely. Inside the house, while the physical structure was identical to before, the homey touches Rome had applied over the years would take some time to replace.

Mother, father and son had finished their evening meal. After a rousing game of hide and seek, Aason declared himself ready for bed. Rome was happy to oblige. It wasn't long until he was tucked in and fast asleep in his very own bed. It had been a long time for the brave little boy. Rome stood in the doorway and watched her little angel breathe in and out, in and out. Eventually, she sighed a happy sigh and closed the door.

She took one more stroll around their newly rebuilt house then joined Rei in the bedroom which smelled of fresh aerogel. Rei was lying on the bed, without a shirt, reveling in not having to wear the vest any more although it had proved to be invaluable not just in saving his back but in saving his life.

Rome changed into her loose-fitting pajamas and joined her husband on the bed, marveling at the peace and serenity a little thing like being home brought. She snuggled up to Rei and delighted in the fact that she could stroke his chest hairs knowing he was fully healed.

Rei put his arms around her and found the sensations excited him. Rome smiled and said, "There will plenty of time for that. There is something I need to share with you."

Rei cleared his throat. "I'm not a hundred per cent sure I want you always reading my mind," he said. "There are some things I'd probably want to keep to myself."

"I will respect your privacy," Rome said, scooting up the bed a little. "But there will be times you will not regret it." She smiled broadly but there was a hint of naughty in her expression.

"Oh, yeah," Rei said. "In this case, I think you're right. But I believe I owe you a session like you gave me during your training."

"I would like that," Rome answered, "but I promised you I would tell you the information the Overmind of Earth imparted to me just before we left the planet."

"What?" Rei asked, not knowing whether to be dismayed or intrigued.

"Do you recall the first time you saw my face back on Dara? I was on the other side of the bulkhead. You once told me I looked familiar to you even though you had never seen me before."

"Yeah," Rei answered. "I figured it was because I might have seen your face in your spacesuit helmet when you revived me."

"No," Rome said mysteriously. "That is not why."

"Then why?"

"As I explained to you, the Overmind of Earth had done a genetic analysis of all living Vuduri in order to produce his Slayer program."

"Sure," Rei said. "You are the generations removed granddaughter of Hanry Ta Jihn. That is really sleek in a way. He truly was a great man. And I get to be married to you!"

"Yes, it is sleek," Rome said. "I choose to ignore the manipulation that led to my birth. I am here and that is that. However, that is not what I wanted to tell you."

"Ok, so what is it?'

"The genetic analysis did not stop there. The Overmind's scientists went all the way back to what the Overmind called the 'Mitochondrial Eve'. She was one of the few women who made it through the Great Dying."

"That doesn't surprise me," Rei said, nodding his head. "When you think about it, it's only logical. The Vuduri who are alive today are descended from people who survived the Great Dying. That's just common sense."

"Perhaps," Rome said. "But the Overmind told me specifically who my ancestor really was."

"It knew that?" Rei asked, puzzled.

"Yes," Rome replied. "Her name was Sally Reynolds."

Rei's jaw dropped open. "Uh, uh," was all he could say. Finally, he whispered, "My Sally?"

"Yes," Rome said proudly. "And that was why I was familiar to you. I am her great, great, great, great granddaughter."

Rei couldn't decide if he was horrified or delighted. "Holy mackerel," he said finally. He put his head down and thought about it for a bit. "I knew she had some sort of freakish immune system because of the incident in Brazil but… Oh wow." He looked up at Rome. "Her father was the chairman of the Reynolds Corporation. She got me into the Ark program, even though I wasn't ranked. She told me on our last night together that I was going to meet the love of my life among the stars. And all the time it was her who was responsible. How did she know?"

Rome shook her head. "All of us think of time is like volma, movies, where each moment leads to the next and our consciousness just travels along that road, skipping from frame to frame."

"Well, sure," Rei said. "What else is there?"

Rome touched her finger to her chin. "Maybe that way of thinking is wrong. Perhaps time is more like a long river than a series of individual moments. Perhaps our consciousness normally just floats along. But maybe some people can travel up or down that river, with their minds. A form of time travel."

"That sounds like string theory to me," Rei observed. "I'm not buying it. My mind can only think of now. The rest is the past or the future."

"You, yourself once called the Chara mission a 'damned time machine'. So even you acknowledged the possibility."

"I was speaking metaphorically," Rei protested. "I mean, we go to sleep and wake up in the morning. That doesn't really count as time travel."

"All right, explain this then," Rome countered. "Four years ago, before I had even given birth, I was in the Vuduri compound and had a bad dream. A nightmare really." Rome shivered. "In that dream, a black hooded stranger came to take our son. When I would not agree, he grew until he filled the sky, just like the Sipre. In the dream, it was Aason who saved me but upon reflection, I think it was OMCOM's manipulation of you that allowed us to defeat him. You were Aason's creator."

"Dreams don't count," Rei said. "Everybody has them. That had to be a coincidence."

"You always say there ain't no such thing as a coincidence."

Rei set his jaw. "I still don't believe it."

"Well I do," Rome insisted. "When we were under the Tevatron, when I first touched the dried blood of Hanry Ta Jihn, my ancestor as it turns out, my mind flashed back to his time as if I was there in person. I feel like I went down the river." Rome reached up and touched Rei's cheek. "That's all I'm saying. Perhaps Sally was someone who could travel up the river, forward to our time. Maybe she saw our future together like I saw the past."

"That's too heavy to even consider," Rei said. "But if there were ever any doubt we were fated to be together, I guess this seals the deal."

Rome pulled Rei's head forward and kissed him on his cheek. "You are right. Now that we have settled our score with those that wanted to bring us harm, it's time to get on with our lives. Together."

"Yep," Rei said. "On this wonderful little planet. I always thought it was a plain jane, nothing world but every time we dig, like with the 'blankets', we find out there is more to it. Like peeling back the layers of an onion."

"Yes," Rome said happily. "I love this little world. Our world."

"And I love you," Rei said. He kissed her deeply and drew his hand up, first to her chest then down her front, stopping when he got to her stomach. The private moment Rome and Virga shared before they took Virga home flashed into his mind.

"Hey," he said, pulling his head back. "There's something I've been meaning to ask you."

"Yes, mau emir?" She put her hand on top of his, caressing it tenderly.

"When we were tussling with the Sipre, in the ethereal world, I saw your spirit as a bright red flame. But there was this little pink spark, like a pixie, that seemed to always follow you around. That spark was so bright but it never strayed from being beside you. It wasn't one of the Onsira children. Their sparks were black or at least they were until Bonnie came along."

Rome took Rei's hand and began moving it in a circular motion around her abdomen. "That tiny spark was Lupe," she said, smiling. "She is coming."

"What?" Rei said, sitting bolt upright. "I'm going to be a father again?"

"Yes," Rome replied, her smile getting even broader. "She was conceived during our training night together. I suppose it was just the right time."

Rei laughed. "That is so sleek."

Rome cocked her head. "You'll have to wait and see about that. You may end up changing your mind."

"Why?" Rei asked, confused.

"I have already spoken to her."

"You have?" Rei tried to act surprised but in this brave new world, almost nothing surprised him anymore.

"Yes, but unlike Aason, I must give you fair warning. This one is going to be a handful. I believe your word for it is a brat."

"A brat, huh?" Rei breathed. "Daughters always are," he said, kissing Rome's nose. "But we'll love her all the more."

"Yes, we will," Rome said. She smiled seductively and took Rei's hand and moved it even lower. "But for tonight, it's just you and me and we're home again."

Rei nodded his head vigorously and focused on his wife, his beautiful wife, the love of his life. She was the one he was fated to be with since the beginning of time. Their enemies had been vanquished. There was peace everywhere. Their love-making began in earnest knowing all was right with the world, no, the universe, now and forever more.

THE END

Postscript

THIS IS THE END OF THE STORY ARC CONCERNING REI AND ROME. While they have some ups and downs, in large part, they go on to live very happy and productive lives together. No one and nothing tries to kill them again. Mostly. They are not called upon to save the human race yet another time. The peace they experience is the peace they so richly earned.

However, it is not the end of the world of the 35th century. Life continues, not only for Rome and Rei, but for all the humans of that age. At this point, there is one unspoken fact, a subtext, underlying everyone's assumptions that will turn out to be wrong. That fact is this: if there were an Olympic competition between the three inhabited worlds, Helome would win the gold medal uncontested. Earth would take home the silver medal handily but win the prize for the most important world. Deucado would win the bronze but only because it had no other competition. In every category, this plain unpretentious world would seem to have gotten the short end of the stick.

Poor drab Deucado.

The small planet had been bashed to bits for billions of years, and yet it kept spinning in its orbit around the parent star, Tau Ceti, watched over by its gigantic brother Grentadar. The fact that life had survived, let alone thrived on this little world, despite overwhelming adversity, was a cosmic miracle. The constant rain of death from above made it more resilient and tougher than Earth or Helome. With its new shield of protection and the four major races of mankind living in peace, Deucado, 'the little planet that could', would continue to develop and evolve at an accelerating pace.

There was no dominant race on this planet and certainly nowhere where the Essessoni and Deucadons had as much influence. From this world would spring the outward bound industry and ventures that would benefit all of humanity. Not the Earth, controlled by the Overmind and segregated into its enclaves of Vuduri and mandasurte and certainly not the ethnically pure world of Helome. No, it was Deucado that was destined to eclipse Earth someday as the focus of the human adventure and become the crown jewel of the empire of Man.

Rome's library was simply the first seed planted in the new garden of knowledge of mankind. Her Library of Life would blossom forth and be at the center of it all. But as we already know, life and intelligence is not limited to just humans. There are many other life-forms out there, waiting to be discovered, with their own lives, their own wants, needs and desires. And that, my friends, is why the story will never end.

Epilogue

Year 3476 AD (1395 PR)
(17 years later)

21-YEAR-OLD AASON BIERAK STOOD WITH HIS ARMS FOLDED ACROSS his broad chest, scowling while his parents fussed over his younger sister. He was anxious to get started and to him the prolonged goodbyes seemed interminable.

"You listen to your brother," Aason's mother, Rome said to his sister, Lupe. "He's in charge. You do what he says."

"What about OMCOM?" Lupe asked as if she didn't know.

"The livetar we are sending along is just a subset of our OMCOM's core. He's there for a system upgrade only," Lupe's father, Rei, interjected. "He can advise you but he's not in charge of you."

"What about Planet OMCOM?"

"Same thing. Aason is in charge. Nobody else."

"I get it," Lupe said. "OK. Goodbye, Mother," she said and she hugged her mother tightly. At five foot six, she felt like she towered over her mother, having inherited some of her father's height. But even though she was only sixteen and a half, with her dark hair and glowing eyes, she already looked like a clone of Rome, just taller.

"I will miss you," Rome said. "Hurry back."

"Sure," replied Lupe. She stepped to her left and hugged her father. "I love you both," she said then she turned and skipped away, heading for the cargo ramp leading up to the all-black starship sitting on the landing strip.

"Aason, you watch over her," Rome said. "She is still a baby."

"Of course, Mom," Aason said. "There's nothing to worry about. Dad told me this is a milk run."

"What is a milk run?" Rome asked, looking over at her husband.

"He told me it's a quick trip just to grab something at the store."

"In that case, he is wrong. There is no such thing as a milk run in space," Rome said, looking back at her son. "You know we would be going with you if we could."

"I know, Mom," Aason said. "But Grandmea needs you more, right now. Grandbeo has to get better."

Rome opened her arms and Aason allowed her to hug him tight. "You are so grown up!" she exclaimed. Aason didn't even bother to blush. He gave his father a manly hug and twirled around toward the starship awaiting him. As Aason reached the top of the ramp, before he entered the cargo section, he turned and looked back at his parents one more time. His father had his long arms draped over his mother, holding her gently. Rome opened up her PPT channel and "spoke" to Aason directly into his mind.

"*I am very proud of you, Son,*" she said. *"You be careful."*

Aason smiled.

"*Always, Mother,*" he thought back. The handsome young man, well over six feet tall, leaned over to press the blue stud to retract the cargo ramp and lower the hatch. His parents waved at him until they were out of view. Turning forward, Aason made his way directly to the cockpit where Lupe was already seated in the copilot's chair on the right. Aason buckled himself in the pilot's chair on the left.

Rome's voice came through Junior's grille loud and clear.

"OMCOM, I need you to watch out for my children. They are the most precious things in all the world. No detours. You are to go there, do your business, then return."

"Of course," OMCOM said. "Junior and I will take care of them," replied the animated shell that was connected to a subset of the computer taking up temporary residence within Junior's memron structure.

Aason twisted to his right. "Make sure your harness is snug," Aason said to his younger sister. "He's been getting a little wild with his takeoffs recently."

"He does it because that's the way I like it," replied Lupe in a slightly irritated tone. "I'm not a baby. I can take care of myself," she said. Nonetheless, she tugged on the X-harness tabs one more time.

"She will be fine, Aason," said the two-meter tall all-white being standing behind them. "Lupe has done this before," OMCOM added.

"I'm her big brother," countered Aason. "I'm allowed to worry about her. Ultimately, it's my responsibility. This is the first time they're letting us go this far alone and I want it to start out right."

"Understood," OMCOM replied patiently.

While it was probably unnecessary, Aason checked the instrument panel one last time. All the readings looked good. He tugged on his own harness once more then said, "OK, Junior, I think we're ready to go. It's up to you."

"You got it, Cuz," came the starshp's voice from the grille built into the console. Vaguely mechanical noises issued from the back.

"Despite the fact that she likes it, maybe you could take it a little easy this one time?" Aason requested.

"Roger that," replied the sleek starship, the first of a breed "born" rather than built. "Even so, hold on to your hats."

The powerful EG lifters came up to speed and the jet-black craft leaped into the sky.

* * *

The saga continues in **The Milk Run**, available in ebook, paperback, hardback and audiobook..

www.ingramcontent.com/pod-product-compliance
Lightning Source LLC
Chambersburg PA
CBHW020600180626

46810CB00007B/2580